MISCALCULATED RISKS

LAW SCHOOL HERETIC SERIES

MISCALCULATED RISKS

MARIA R. RIEGGER

MISCALCULATED RISKS

It was the beginning of my third year of law school, but not my last. I was halfway done. I was studying in the evening program at a large university in Washington, DC, and also working full-time. The program took four years instead of the usual three.

The DC area had effectively been my home since I was born. However, it was more complicated than that. I had been born here, but had spent several summers in Spain, visiting my father's family in Barcelona and Madrid. After completing my undergraduate degree, I worked in Barcelona for a few years, then in Paris for a year, and eventually became disenchanted with the lack of upwardly mobile positions available to women in both Spain and France.

Despite being fluent in Spanish, Catalan and French, I was still treated like a foreigner, even in Spain. I had the distinct impression that the "natives" resented foreigners who took jobs away from them. Even though my father was Spanish and I had Spanish nationality, it didn't matter. I had lived most of my life in the U.S., and the Spanish people I had worked with seemed to feel resentment toward me for that. Why, I didn't really know. I felt that part of it was jealousy. I hadn't really ever lacked anything in my life. Even after my father died, my mother spent all her energy making sure that my sisters and I had everything that we needed. Although I certainly had complaints about my mother, I loved her for that.

I thought it ironic that my Spanish coworkers were jealous of me for my "easy" life in the U.S. In Spain, they had nationalized health care, so that in theory everyone had access to treatment. However, as I experienced when I lived there, that meant long lines, inefficient service, and rude medical providers. Doctors didn't want to treat you. And when a young person went to the doctor with a complaint, they treated you with disdain, like you were wasting their time. Also, instead of private insurers making decisions about what medications, treatments, and procedures to cover, you had some bureaucrat making those decisions for you. Just like insurers, the bureaucrats were guided by cost savings, so that concern certainly was not erased with nationalized health care.

I remember one time when my family was visiting my father's relatives in Barcelona and my little sister got really sick with some virus. We didn't know what she had; she was vomiting and her face was green. My father and I took her to the doctor there. After standing in line to check in with the receptionist, we were told to wait outside the doctor's door, where he would call us in and spend a few minutes diagnosing what my sister had.

We waited for a couple of hours, and my father got sick of waiting and went to inquire at the front desk why it was taking so long. We were then informed that the doctor had left a long time ago, and, despite that, no one had told us anything. Oh, and also, by the way, the receptionist had "forgotten" to check us in on the computer. My father raised holy hell, yelling and screaming, tossing papers in front of the receptionist and kicking the receptionist's desk. He demanded that a doctor see his sick child. Eventually they found a doctor to see my sister, but the experience marked me. This is how they treat sick children here? I thought.

And when I lived there later as an adult my experience was no better. In fact, when I needed medical treatment I ended up paying to see a private doctor in a private clinic. So what was the point of "free" medical service, then?

It seemed to me that I would much rather pay less money in taxes and keep more of my own money, and then arrange my life however I wanted. That way I would have money to spend on what I wanted. In any case, no national government that I could think of (certainly none of the governments where I had lived, including the U.S.) did an overall good job of managing taxpayer funds. And government agencies were bloated. It's so easy to spend other people's money, I had thought.

But I digress. I was talking about my family. I digress often. My sisters make fun of me for that. I love to argue, and I love to use logic.

That was why I went to law school.

Like I said, my father was Spanish. His father is Catalan, and his mother is from a small town near Albacete, the heart of Don Quixote's *La Mancha*. Hence my last name, *Vilanova*, which means "new town" in Catalan. My father was born in Barcelona, and grew up speaking Spanish and Catalan at home. But he was ambitious, and thought that Barcelona was a small pond. He was an engineer, but felt that his talents were greatly underappreciated in Spain, more so when Franco was in power. My father was also good with languages and was diligent about learning English.

At some point, my father made it to the U.S. and stayed with an uncle until he found work. He was never entirely clear on exactly how he had made it out of Spain at the time. His English skills and his hard work eventually paid off, and he found work. He had told his family that he didn't have much of a future in Barcelona, especially under Franco's regime. And he wanted to see more of the world.

His U.S. salary was eventually good enough to allow him to rent a modest house in a suburb of Washington. My mother's family lived next door to him. My mother was just starting college when they met. The way she told me, they immediately fell for each other. At that time, there weren't many Spanish-speakers living in northern Virginia, and they had that connection. My father had black, wavy hair, which must have come from his mother's side of the family. There must have been some Arab blood involved there.

My mother's journey to the Washington, DC area was just slightly more dramatic than my father's. She was born in Buenos Aires during the 1950s. Things in Argentina for my mother's family went all right, but not great. My grandfather found work but the economy was so touch-and-go that he couldn't expect a regular paycheck, so he made up for that by working odd jobs.

In the 1960s my grandfather, who was one of the most intelligent people I know, sensed that greater turmoil was coming. So he moved his family to the U.S., where some of his other relatives had already immigrated.

My grandfather was more right than he knew, because only a few years later came *la Guerra Sucia*, one of Argentina's darker periods. By then, my mother's family was installed in the U.S., in a suburb of Washington, DC, next to my future father.

My mother's personality is larger than life, and she is gregarious and outgoing. She was also extremely beautiful when she was younger, with light skin and thick, dark, almost-black straight hair. She speaks Argentine Spanish and cooks Argentine cuisine. She's hot-blooded and stubborn. She and both my sisters dance the tango very well.

My parents had three daughters in fairly rapid succession, only a few years apart. I am the oldest, Lara is next and lastly, Ariel. The running joke in my family was always that Lara's personality is exactly like our mother's, Ariel's is like our father's, and I'm a toss-up. I'm moody and brooding like our father, but there's a little bit of my mother in me too. I didn't always think so, but discovered throughout the story that I'm about to tell that this was the case, and that it wasn't all bad.

I was talking about law school. That's right. Once again, I digress. Today was the first day of my third year. Wait. I haven't told you how I got back to DC. That's right. There's so much to tell, and it's difficult to keep straight.

After working in Spain and then France, I was disenchanted with the work culture there. Most of the time, I had been working as a translator/linguist. It was what I had trained to do, but it was solitary work. I was lonely, desperately lonely, and missed my family. I never thought that I could be that lonely. My mother, at that time, was living in a small city about forty-five miles south of DC. I figured I knew DC, and with my languages, maybe I could get some government work. So I moved back. My mother was ecstatic. She must have missed me or something.

I got a job with a government contracting firm doing Spanish and French and, very occasionally, Catalan translations and language/linguistic consulting. I was a diligent worker (having nothing else to do), and after a couple of years was promoted to Senior Translator/Linguist, or some such title. I reviewed the other translators' work and did high-level document translation. The pay was pretty good and the benefits were fine. I had my own apartment. But I wasn't busy enough.

I had always thought that the law was a good match for my over-analytical, overly-wired, never-turned-off brain and, after reading a bunch of law-related stuff, I decided to enroll. And I had been right. I loved it. It kept me busy enough that I didn't have time to think that much about my life, or lack of a significant other, or my problems, or my father, and how I hadn't been able to prevent his death.

But, as usual, life was about to happen. You know what I mean. Life. As John Lennon said, it's what happens when you're busy making other plans.

FIRST WEEK: **MONDAY (AUGUST 2010)**

I left the metro station and was walking to the law school campus. It was a Monday, the first day of my third year of law school classes. The evening students like me worked full-time jobs and attended school at night. The program took four years instead of the usual three. I couldn't believe that I was already halfway done with school.

People referred to it as the part-time program, but my friend Melanie and I laughed at that. We instead referred to it as the "evening program," because the evening students only took one class less than the full-time students. The difference between the day program students and the evening students was, I thought, profound. Melanie and I overheard the full-time students plotting their nights out, their drinking festivities and general rowdiness. They had a lot more free time than we did. They also were able to do more extracurricular activities, such as law review, law clinics and clubs. I was lucky if I managed to do most of the class reading on the weekends and stay awake during class.

Each semester was fourteen weeks long. They always flew by like nobody's business. Before long, I would be feverishly studying and outlining for exams.

I had started law school in 2008. The problem was that, during that year, the economy began to tank, and law firms began laying off attorneys and deferring the start dates for entry-level law school grads. Less business was being done overall, and fewer transactions meant that there was a reduced need for corporate attorneys. Companies also began realizing just how much they paid outside counsels. CEOs were balking at attorneys' fees, and were looking for ways to cut legal expenses. This all translated into fewer job opportunities for law school grads.

When I started law school I had visions of getting all these great offers with firms due to my good grades, my professional experience and my foreign languages. Unfortunately, that was looking more and more far-fetched. I felt lucky that I had a full-time job and could pay my rent and my bills, but I was also confronting the prospect of graduating with six figures of law school debt and not making any more money than I was making before I started.

I was also thirty-four years old, and when I graduated in a year and a half I would be thirty-six. How many good years did I have left? I thought. Would I be able to get a law firm position and repay my debt on only one salary?

Despite the worrying, in my heart I was still happy to have gone to law school. Deep down I felt that I was born to be an attorney. I was over-analytical and detail-oriented and couldn't stop thinking. In fact, one of the main reasons I had gone to law school was to stay super busy so that I wouldn't dwell on things. Over the years, I had noted that when I didn't have enough things to do, I started overthinking and then started to feel down. I would think about my father, replaying the events surrounding his death twenty years before over and over in my head, and thinking about how I could have done things differently.

I would think about my former boyfriend Santi, who I had left in Madrid all those years ago. I would think about what I could have said differently to Santi so that we could have stayed together. Even though I was doing well and had generally had a successful life, there had been missed opportunities. It made me feel a little depressed sometimes.

However, law school had restored some of my happiness. I was busy, I was studying interesting things and had met intelligent people. I had never had many friends, but counted my newfound law school friends among my best friends other than my sisters. Unlike many of the students here, I *lived* law school.

I went to school with some people who worked on Capitol Hill, who had to go to law school in order to keep or advance in their jobs, but they hated law school and their hearts weren't in it. That wasn't me.

I also went to law school with people who had gone straight from un-dergrad, and who were in law school because they didn't know what else to do, or because their parents thought it was a good idea, or because they were putting off working in a real job. I had no patience for that crowd.

I was looking forward to this semester. On Mondays and Tuesdays I had Criminal Procedure from 6 p.m. to 8 p.m., which would cover in large part the Fourth Amendment and basic civil rights. I also had Property on Wednesdays and Thursdays from 6 p.m. to 8 p.m., which would be a bear. It was a dense, complex class, but necessary, being a mandatory requirement to graduate. And on Wednesdays and Thursdays I also had International Law right before Property, which I hoped would be interesting.

The law school campus was small; it was basically one building with a grassy "quad" in the center where students hung out when the weather was nice, maybe playing frisbee.

The university was well-known and I felt lucky to be there. But sometimes I kicked myself for not going to a much cheaper state school. I had set my sights high, banking on the fact that I would be able to repay my student loans with a law firm job, but now I was having doubts. Oh well. It was too late for regrets now.

I had come straight from work, still in my work clothes. I was wearing a patterned skirt, which was form-fitting and hugged my curves. I was also wearing tights and a loose, short-sleeved, black silk blouse. The loose-fitting blouse complemented the hip-hugging skirt. I had noticed some turned heads both at work and on the metro.

At 5'6", I was above-average height for an American woman. I had my mother's thick hair, very dark brown that looked almost black. Today I had blow-dried my hair straight, but it was naturally curly, and if I put gel in it and let it air dry, it would dry curly. Both my parents were of European stock, with fairly light skin, and my skin color was no different from theirs. I had also inherited my mother's large dark brown eyes.

I worked out like a fiend, partly to have something to do, partly to work off my excess angst and partly because I was addicted to the endorphin rush. I loved to run and lift weights. As a consequence of that, I was pretty athletic and my arms and shoulders were pretty developed. However, I could not change my curvy hip bones, and it was a challenge to find clothes that fit properly.

I had angst because of a lot of things. I had angst because I was still mad about my father dying. I had angst because I had screwed things up with Santi all those years ago. I had angst about getting a job that I wanted after graduating from law school. I had angst because I was living in a city where 99% of the people thought the same way, and had the same opinions, and I was different from them.

But I also had angst because of baser, more physiological things. I was thirty-four years old and unattached. And I was horny. I was like a twenty-something man, thinking about sex and looking at prospective partners, weighing their potential sex appeal. It was like my body was telling me that it was time to have children and I wasn't listening. I mean, I *was* listening because I occasionally indulged my physiological needs, but I wasn't procreating.

Since I hadn't found anyone since Santi who was fulfilling enough to be a true partner, and because I didn't want to be having random sex with countless men, I would wait until I was about to explode, and then pounce upon the opportunity when it presented itself, and I would indulge my needs. Not with a guy I didn't know, but usually with someone I knew a little bit, but not well. Like a friend of a friend or someone in one of my law school classes who I didn't hang out with regularly. Not that that made the sex any less random, of course.

The last time I had done that was about three or four months ago. That would have to hold me for a while. I was averaging about one or two encounters a semester.

As I entered the main law school doors, I mentally seized the thoughts floating ominously through my head and shoved them away. I would undoubtedly take them out later, when I was alone late at night, trying to get to sleep, or when I didn't have enough to do.

The first thing I noticed at school was the crush of students. Most of them appeared to be very young. Somewhat depressingly, the youngest of them, those who were starting their first year and who had just graduated from undergrad, were twelve years younger than me. Babies. Children of the Millennial generation who sought instant gratification and superficial fulfillment.

Yes, I'm generalizing, but my opinion is based on my experience. Did they really know how difficult life was? Well, at some point they will get a rude awakening; at least, I hoped so.

Technically, my sisters were part of the Millennial, or Generation Y, segment of the population. However, having lost our father when we were all young, we knew what it was like to have to work for everything. Our mother had to go back to work after our father died, so a lot of the time there was no one at home for us. There was just me. From the time I was fourteen years old, my "youth" had basically consisted of cooking for my sisters, driving them around, and generally making sure that they were safe and stayed out of trouble. I didn't go out with friends or have anything resembling a social life. But I hadn't really minded, either. I preferred to be alone with my thoughts than out with vacuous, superficial people who didn't appreciate what they had.

I was brought out of my reminiscing when I saw Eric, a friend of mine. He greeted me with a shoulder bump. One time he had tried to chest-bump me. Ah, I don't think so, Eric, I had told him.

After the shoulder bump, he greeted me with a kiss on each cheek. Eric had a Brazilian father and an American mother, but had grown up in Brazil and had adopted the Latin American way of greeting, which was familiar to me and was how I always greeted my family and Latin friends.

Eric was a couple of inches taller than me, and had an easy smile. He was always laughing. He was attractive with a shock of thick, dark brown hair and beautiful blue eyes. He was also about nine years younger than me. He had started the full-time law program when I was in my second year, so we would graduate the same year. Eric was also an amazing dancer, with easy, fluid moves that seemed totally natural.

"*¿¡Isabel, como estas?!*" Eric spoke Portuguese and Spanish. I would occasionally practice Portuguese with him, but we mostly spoke in Spanish and English, depending on who else we were speaking with at the time.

"*Estoy bien, lo mismo,*" I shrugged.

"What, do you have a hot date tonight?" he asked, looking me up and down. Eric also joked a ton, and liked to embarrass me. I usually just brushed him off. If he really pissed me off, I would give him the finger. For some reason, he thought it was hilarious that a well-put-together woman would flip him off, and he always laughed when I did it, even if I was angry. He was probably riling me up on purpose, but I almost always enjoyed our exchanges.

I think that Eric gravitated toward Josh, another Latin friend, and me because he had come to DC straight from Brazil and didn't really know anyone. He spoke English very well, though, since he had always spoken it with his mother. He was friendly with everyone but mostly hung out with Josh and me. Eric and I were going to be in Criminal Procedure class together.

"Josh and I are sitting over there, if you want to join us," Eric said, pointing to a small table in what the students referred to as the "lounge" area. I went to join Josh.

Josh and Melanie were my best friends at law school. The three of us had started the evening program together. Josh was the same age as me, and worked full-time for a law firm doing patent work. He had a Ph.D. in Biomedical Engineering. Despite that fact, he also had a great sense of humor. Josh had a Venezuelan father and a blonde American mother. He and I spoke sometimes in Spanish, and sometimes in English.

When he saw me, Josh stood up and greeted me with two kisses, just like Eric. I had trained both of them to greet me with two kisses, which was the proper greeting in Spain. The first time Josh greeted me, it was with only one kiss on the cheek, and he embarrassingly left me hanging, with my face in the air waiting for the other kiss. *"¡En España son dos!"* I had said. From then on, he had tried to remember.

"How's it going?" Josh asked then.

"All right," I told him. I sat down and took out my Criminal Procedure book.

Josh was taller than me, about 5'10", with dark blond hair that was quite wavy, and brown eyes. He wasn't as skinny as Eric; he practiced martial arts, and was in shape. I had always thought Josh was handsome. And he was a real gentleman, which was rare enough these days. He opened doors for me and even offered to give up his seat on the metro.

Since I had met him, I thought it strange that he didn't have a girlfriend. He said there weren't that many eligible women where he worked, and, in any case, he didn't think it too prudent to date anyone where he worked. He was probably right about that.

Even though Josh was great, I wasn't interested in him romantically. He and I had political differences, and argued about them constantly. I said he wasn't being logical, and he said I didn't know what I was talking about. Eric always tried to veer us away from these arguments.

Josh was like a brother to me and, like I had told my mother countless times when she asked about my love life, I couldn't picture being in a romantic relationship with him. My mother thought I should be more open-minded, that I should go out and meet people and just have fun.

Fun. What the hell does that mean? If "fun" means "sex," then that was no problem because I could pretty much get all the sex I wanted.

But sex for me at this point was only the fulfillment of a physiological need. Well, sometimes it was "fun." It wasn't really romantic, but I didn't think that I needed romance, anyway.

Fun for me was arguing in law school class and pulling an A+ on an exam. Well, "fun" was also occasionally going out dancing with Josh and Eric, and occasionally laughing at jokes that they made. So I do occasionally have "fun" as my mother would describe it. I almost smiled. Maybe I wasn't totally a lost cause.

"Did you do the reading?" I asked Josh.

"No," he smiled.

Of course he didn't. Josh rarely did all of the reading, but he was smart enough to do decently on the exams.

Just then a small blonde girl came over to talk to Josh. She gave me a deep scowl. I smirked at her in derision.

Why Josh tolerated this girl, I would never know. Josh was nice to everyone. That was his best quality and also his main character flaw, in my opinion.

This girl was Sorority Girl. Her name was Ashley, or Adriana, or Alyssa, or something with an A or an R. I didn't remember because I didn't care to. In fact, I wish that I could erase every trace of memory about this girl from my brain, because I couldn't even stand to think about her.

I called her Sorority Girl, or SG for short. She had started in the evening program, and she had transferred to the full-time program. So she would graduate this coming May, and I wouldn't have to see her ever again, hopefully.

Sorority Girl represented all that I hated about the law school crowd that was in law school only because they didn't know what the hell to do with themselves, and Mommy and Daddy were paying for their tuition and their posh condos.

She was short, bottle-blonde and super skinny. Her parents had graced her with a trendy name so that people would automatically adore her.

She also wasn't very smart. She had been in all of my first-year classes and had hardly ever spoken. However, when she did speak in class, her comments made absolutely no sense. My friend Dinesh especially couldn't stand her or her comments. When she spoke, Dinesh put his hands over his ears and shook his head. I totally tuned her out.

She felt so entitled. She hung around with a bunch of guys who fawned over her and her blondeness. Dinesh and I couldn't stand how she talked about her weekend conquests. She hated me because I totally laid her out a bunch of times in class. She also hated me because she had heard the rumor that I had a 4.0, and she wanted to get better grades than me, of course. Don't know how the hell she expected to do that, anyway.

The rumor was true, I was happy to admit, although I never officially talked about my grades with anyone.

As soon as Sorority Girl saw me now, she said something quickly to Josh, and then left. She hated being anywhere near me. Well, the feeling is entirely mutual.

Melanie joined us then.

"Hey!" she greeted me animatedly. I stood up and gave her a huge hug. Melanie and I went way back. "I missed you," I told her.

"I missed you too!" she said. Melanie was beautiful; she was about my height, lean with light caramel-colored skin and huge, bright brown eyes. She had short, dark hair that framed her gorgeous face. God, her skin is perfect; not one flaw. I looked in the mirror and all I saw were dark circles under my eyes and lines at the outer points when I smiled. I tried not to smile too often.

Melanie was in the evening program too. She worked as a paralegal in a law firm in the city. Like me, she was dressed professionally, having come straight from work. She preferred sundresses over business attire, though. I always knew when she hadn't gone to work because she would come to class in a sundress and strappy sandals.

"Oh my God, you look great!" she told me then, elongating the words in her Texas drawl. "Turn around!"

I obliged her as she adjusted her dark-rimmed eyeglasses. Sometimes she also slightly embarrassed me. She didn't mean to. I just didn't like having attention drawn to myself.

"You look incredible in that skirt!"

Thank you, I thought, for drawing everyone's attention to my ass.

"Thanks," I said.

Melanie was, like Josh, a true friend. I would trust her with almost anything. That was another reason I was happy to have gone to law school. I had more friends than I had had before.

Melanie asked how my sisters were. I was telling her that Ariel had moved in with her boyfriend about three or four months ago, and they were happy.

I envied my sisters their happy relationships. I always told my mother that I didn't need a man, and that was (partly) true. I needed occasional physical contact but I didn't need a man around all the time. I could do everything myself.

"It's better to be alone than to be with someone who is not a good partner for you," I had told my mother.

"Yes, I agree," she had responded, "but I don't believe that in a city as big as Washington, DC, there is no man that could be a good partner for you."

She was wrong about that, I knew. First, in this town, there were many more eligible women than men. Second, the eligible men in DC were all jerks. You only had to listen to one of Melanie's dating stories to know that.

"Men don't really ask women on dates anymore," Melanie had said. "It's sad. They text to ask you what you're up to that night, and you know that at the same time they're texting like twenty other women, and that their end goal is just to hook up."

Melanie had stories about meeting men to go out, men who had asked her out and then who stuck her with the bill, who left her to go dance with other girls, and other such abominations.

My way was easier. Just sex and no strings attached. No relationships. No dinners out. No paying for anyone. I'm gone before the morning and no phone calls afterward.

But then I would go home alone and would feel empty. I would go to sleep alone and wake up alone. It didn't matter. I didn't want a relationship anyway.

"You have to *live*," my mother had told me once, before law school, when all I was doing was working. "If you live, I mean, really live your life, good things will happen to you."

"I *have* been living my life," I had told her. Besides, what my Mom said wasn't true. We were living our lives and then Dad died. But I hadn't said that to her.

"No, you haven't," she had corrected me. "You go through the motions. And you're looking for something. When you're constantly looking for something, you won't find it. You have to *live*."

What the hell is she talking about? I had thought. More profound words of wisdom from the overly dramatic Argentine oracle.

I hadn't known how right she was, but I was about to find out.

It was about 5:40 p.m.. I got up to walk upstairs to Crim Pro. Melanie, unfortunately, wasn't in our Crim Pro class, but we would have Property together on Wednesday, so we said goodbye until then.

"Let's go," I said to Josh and Eric. "I want to get a seat up front."

Josh was talking to some girl I didn't know. He was always talking to some girl.

"Of course you do. I'll be right there," Josh said. "Save me a seat."

"I'll try."

I grabbed my bag and my purse and headed upstairs. Eric came with me.

The classroom for Crim Pro was one of the largest lecture halls on campus, stadium-style. It could probably accommodate about 200 students. At the front was a desk, a podium and a microphone for the professor. In front of the seats were long tables, shared by the students. There were three sets of these tables and chairs, one set in the middle and two on the sides.

The room was already full of students, and it was loud. Everyone was chatting excitedly, and the energy in the room was palpable. I smiled to myself sardonically. In about twelve weeks, the animation in this room would turn to tension, and another week after that it would turn to sheer terror as final exams rounded the corner.

I walked toward the front of the room. My theory was that the further to the front I sat, the better my final grade would be. I theorized that that was because I paid more attention, since the professor was looking right at me and I couldn't start to daydream. I also had the idea that the people who sat far in the back were called on more frequently. So sitting in the front would also give me a bit of a respite. At least, that was my theory.

I sat in the center section of chairs, in the second seat from the right, if you were the professor looking at the classroom. I saved the seat on the end for Josh.

Eric sat behind me. "The second row is too far up front," he told me. "But I'll compromise and sit in the third row."

I put my Crim Pro book on the table to my left, in front of the seat I had saved for Josh. Then I took out a protein bar and started munching. I wouldn't eat dinner for another three and a half hours. After working out at lunchtime, I never knew how hungry I would be later.

Dinesh walked in then. He was Indian, but had obtained his Ph.D. in the U.S. Since then he had been working for a law firm in DC doing patent work. He and Josh had a lot in common, and the three of us hung out pretty frequently. Our first year, we had had a standing Thursday night drink date. Our second year had been busier, and we had gone out less frequently. Josh and Dinesh both had jobs that were higher-pressure than mine. They often had to go back to work after class, but I always headed home. As patent agents working for firms, they had billable hours to meet.

I had deadlines at work, but fortunately I didn't have to bill a minimum number of hours.

Dinesh sat to my right. The seats were filling up quickly.

"What's going on?!" I asked him animatedly. Dinesh was very friendly and was always laughing about something. He was a good guy.

He smiled. "Not much. How have you been?"

"All right. No complaints." That is, no complaints other than my usual ones about politics, the Millennials, the fate of the world, my own mortality, my mother, etc.

"Have you already done all the reading for the first three weeks?" Dinesh asked me then, on the verge of laughing.

"Of course! I have a reputation to maintain." I smiled.

Dinesh laughed.

"No, dude, seriously, I've only done the first week's reading," I told him truthfully.

"Where's Josh?" he asked.

"Downstairs, talking to some girl I don't know." I shrugged and gave Dinesh a half-annoyed look. "He told me to save him a seat but if he doesn't get here soon he'll be SOL." I had already given three people dirty looks, in effect telling them not to sit there.

"Excuse me, is this seat taken?" a deep voice said to my left.

I whipped my head around to say "yes" but my words instantly left me.

I was staring at possibly the sexiest man I had ever seen.

He wasn't very tall, a few inches taller than me. He was lean, and most definitely Arab, with light brown skin and piercing, dark eyes. His eyes were alive and alert. His hair was jet black, thick and curly. He must put some product in it, otherwise it would be frizzy.

He also had a carefully trimmed beard and goatee. It wasn't a full beard; it was barely enough to cover his jaw. It looked like he had just trimmed it. Of course. A day program student who had probably woken up at like 3 p.m.

I had never seen him before. I would definitely have noticed him. He must have transferred here or something.

I finally found my voice. I don't know what possessed me to say it, but instead of my usual gravelly, intense stare, and words of dismissal, I said something else.

"It was but—I don't think he's coming so—go ahead," I said without smiling. I took my book away from the spot I had been saving for Josh.

"Thank you," he said, smiling. His smile was gorgeous and it lit up his eyes.

I hadn't been particularly friendly. He looked younger than me. He was clearly a Millennial, and I couldn't stand most of them. I had also had enough of foreign men at work. He probably has aspirations to work on the Hill, maybe to work for some pro-Arab lobbying group. He was probably one of those people who thought that the U.S. was a horrible country that must atone for all the wrong it did in the world. DC law schools were populated with people like that.

Well, he was eye candy, anyway. I didn't mind looking at him, but I wouldn't talk to him.

I flipped open my laptop and turned it on. I began scanning the first case for that night, which I had already read, and looked over the sections I had highlighted. I logged into my personal email account to check if I had any messages from my sisters. I was admiring my nail polish, dark burgundy, almost black, when an instant message popped up from Eric.

> Josh will be mad that you gave his seat to that Arab guy you think is hot.

I wrote back.

> I don't think he's hot.

> That's a lie, Isabel. He is totally your type.

> How would you know what my type is?

> You like dark men. Remember that guy you hooked up with last year?

I did not want to be reminded of that right now. I changed the subject.

> Well, Josh isn't here. It's his own fault for not coming on time. I'm not his damn mother.

Josh came in then and sat next to Eric, giving me a look that I didn't entirely comprehend. His brows were drawn together and his lips were pursed. It wasn't annoyance. It was more like curiosity.

I opened up my document with the notes on the cases that I had typed up. I was reviewing them when Eric wrote back.

> BTW, that Arab dude has been checking you out since he walked in.

Liar, I wrote back. Then I closed my email account. I didn't need constant interruptions from Eric during class.

Then I somehow felt like I was being watched. I tried to surreptitiously shift my eyes to the left without turning my face. Then I saw him looking at me.

Does he think I'm attractive?

I turned my face toward him and looked right into his eyes. My face was pure annoyance. He looked at me, smiled, a little embarrassed, and looked at his laptop screen.

Damn right you should be embarrassed. The nerve to stare at me! I thought I heard Josh, or someone, giggle behind me. I ignored it.

That's all I need right now. Another freaking man to hassle me, and Josh and Eric cracking jokes about it.

Class started then and I paid attention.

When class was over I immediately stood up and began packing up my stuff.

"Are you going to the metro directly?" I asked Josh and Eric.

They both were, and so was Dinesh. I had been waiting for that Arab guy to get out of my way so I could exit my row, but he was taking his time. If he thought I was going to talk to him, he was sadly mistaken.

I had had enough of waiting. I scooted past him to leave the row. As I did, I said "Excuse me." I could be a real jackass but my mother raised me to be polite when need be.

He smiled and half-looked at me but his eyes didn't meet mine.

The four of us left campus and trekked to the metro. We walked more slowly than I liked because Josh, despite his long legs, was like molasses. We were all lugging our books and laptops, anyway, and even I was enjoying the respite from a rushed day.

"So, that's the guy you gave up my seat to?" Josh asked nonchalantly.

Eric and Dinesh laughed.

"Yeah, he's going to be her next conquest!" Eric laughed out loud.

"You think you're so funny, you jackass," I said.

"He was totally checking her out too," Eric said to Josh and Dinesh.

"He was not!" I protested.

"Yes, he was," Josh parried, his brown eyes twinkling. "I saw him too."

"Shouldn't you guys have been paying attention in class instead of looking at other men?" I was starting to get pissed off.

"Josh is looking for a date," Dinesh said, laughing at his own joke.

"He's right behind us too," Josh said then.

"Who?" I asked.

"That guy we're talking about."

Aw, Goddammit. I sneaked a look behind me. The Arab guy was about 100 feet behind us.

"Walk faster!" I told them. "He probably heard. I can't believe you people!"

I prodded them and they eventually walked more quickly.

With my herding our group like cattle, we eventually got on the metro. I hadn't noticed that Arab guy and I hoped he wasn't on our train.

There must have been some event happening that night in the city because it was standing room only on the metro. The four of us shifted our bags around and tried not to be in other people's way.

"Dude, your bag is on my foot!" I told Eric.

"God, Isabel, chill. You *so* need to get laid."

"Say that a little louder, why don't you?" I told him.

"Well, you *do*!"

"God, how old are you, Eric?!"

Josh and Dinesh laughed, Dinesh almost doubling over with laughter.

"I don't believe you people," I complained.

"You people?" Josh said. "What did *I* do?"

"You're laughing too!" I whispered vehemently.

The thing was, Eric was right. He had said that to get a rise out of me, but it was true. My last sexual encounter had been a couple of months ago and I was already getting wound tightly again. How did guys handle it? Maybe I didn't want to know.

The train car was overly crowded. As the three guys continued joking, I gazed around. I didn't see that Arab guy on the train, thank God. All I needed was for him to hear that I needed to get laid. I tried to think about something else.

The train stopped at the next station. It was Pentagon City, and a bunch of people exited, leaving us more room. I felt a little less claustrophobic.

I watched the people on the platform. Then I saw him. That Arab guy. He must have been on another train car. He was walking quickly, and he looked pensive.

Then he looked up and our eyes met. I quickly averted mine.

But I looked back. He was still looking at me as he walked. He smiled. I turned my face away.

"What are you glaring at?" Josh asked me then.

"Nothing," I answered. "No one."

I exited at Franconia, the end of the blue line. I was always alone on the metro for the last couple of stops. Eric lived at Crystal City, and Josh got off the metro at King Street in Old Town Alexandria, where he lived. Josh usually drove Dinesh home, so he left at King Street too.

Then I was alone with my thoughts. I suddenly remembered Hannah Arendt. *There are not dangerous thoughts. Thinking itself is dangerous.* That was certainly true.

I couldn't believe that I still remembered my undergraduate Philosophy class. I guess it's because I have no life.

When the train arrived at the Franconia metro station, I exited and then walked outside the metro station, onto the sidewalk. I was renting an apartment in a building across the street from the metro. I almost always walked home. It only took a few minutes.

The worst part was that you had to walk under a small overpass, which wasn't well lit. But there was always heavy traffic, so I never considered it a big deal.

My Mom probably wouldn't like it if she knew that I walked home alone, but I was a big girl now, I figured. Once I turned thirty years old I refused to take any more of her mothering crap. I also refused to park at the garage and pay the daily $4.75 parking fee on top of the metro fees I paid, especially considering that I was paying a rent premium for living next to the metro station.

I finally arrived at my building. You had to use a key fob to open the main door. I took a look around to make sure no shady characters were milling about (you never knew, living so close to the metro). Once I was certain, I swiped the key fob and entered, making sure that the door was shut behind me.

I walked upstairs to the second floor. I never bothered with the elevator unless I was carrying furniture or something heavy. Taking the stairs was faster than taking the elevator anyway, and I liked the extra exercise.

As I walked upstairs I took out my keys. I didn't pass anyone as I walked down my hallway.

My apartment had only one bedroom. When you walked in, the kitchen was directly on the left and the living room was in front of the kitchen. Further down the living room, I had a dining table, in front of a large window, which had a view of the outside parking lot. At least the large window afforded a good amount of sunlight. Across from the living room was a hallway, off of which were a bedroom and a bathroom.

In the living room, on the right wall, was a large console with my flat screen TV and several family photos, including some of my father.

I didn't have a proper den, so I usually studied at the dining table or sitting on the sofa opposite the TV. The sofa was pushed flush against the left-hand wall and there was a small coffee table directly in front of it.

I dropped my backpack on the ground and opened the fridge. I took out some leftover quesadillas I had made the day before and reheated them in the microwave. Cooking was fairly easy if you lived by yourself. When I cooked, I made a lot of food and ate leftovers all week. That way I didn't have to worry about what I was going to eat when I got home after class. It was impossible for me *not* to cook a lot of food. That was another thing I had inherited from my mother. I couldn't cook in small quantities.

I took my plate to the sofa and sat down. I wouldn't study any more. At this hour, the law of diminishing returns had set in and, even if I tried to read, my mind was too tired to mentally register anything.

I started thinking about my mother then. I should call her. She knew this week was the first week of class and would want to know how it went. I should probably visit her sometime soon too. She lived alone.

I always wondered why she never got remarried. She had been young when my father had died, like around thirty-eight years old, not much older than me. She currently had a long-term boyfriend, but he didn't live with her. I wondered how she had coped with her sex drive, or even if she had one at that time. If she had been anything like I was now, she would have been crazy horny. I had always believed that my amped up sex drive was because of my age, the whole biological clock and all.

Ugh! I didn't like to think about sex and my parents in the same thought. But thinking about sex made me think about that Arab guy. I did think he was hot, even though I had told Eric otherwise. Maybe he would be my next "conquest," to use Eric's term.

Geez, I was so horny that I was starting to think even Eric was sexy. Eric was attractive, but I had never considered sleeping with him. For one thing, he was nine years younger than me. Second, he was a good friend of mine, and I couldn't do friends with benefits. That would ruin the friendship and I would have one less friend. And I already had so few friends that losing one would be horrible.

When I was done eating, I lay my head back on the sofa. Only five minutes, I told myself. More than that and I would fall asleep here.

I looked around my apartment. This was my life. Work and law school and occasionally, hanging out with my sister and my law school buddies. I could vent with my sister and with my friends, but it wasn't the same as having a partner. A partner who was also a lover.

I had friends, I had a family who loved me, I had occasional sex, I had intellectual stimulation at work and at school and I had sufficient money. But I didn't have someone to come home to.

Most days, I told myself that that was a good thing. I had total control over my entire life, and I told myself that I liked that. There were certainly elements of that that I liked. I liked coming home to my apartment the exact way I had left it. I liked doing whatever I wanted, whenever I wanted. I liked never having to check with anyone about what I did. I liked not having to put up with someone else's family. Mine was enough work as it was.

But there were also days when I was honest enough with myself to admit that not having a partner bothered me. I would never, ever admit that to my mother, or even my friends. During moments of weakness, I would occasionally admit that to my sisters, but I knew that they would never share that information with anyone.

I realized that it bothered me now. I would graduate in a year and a half. Then maybe I would meet some guy at the law firm where I ended up working or something. At least, that was what I had told myself. Based on my interviewing experiences and the current economy, however, the law firm thing was seeming more and more like wishful thinking.

"Why would you want to work for a law firm?" my mother had asked me. "You'll be working sixty to eighty hours a week."

"What the hell else do I have to do?" I had responded.

"Don't curse," she had said. "It's not ladylike."

"I don't give a shit what's ladylike, and I'm thirty-four years old. I do what I want."

"Yes, I know, Isabel. You've always done what you've wanted," she had said with exasperation in her voice.

"Law firm experience is necessary for what I want to do," I told her.

"And what is that?" she had asked.

"You're on a need-to-know basis, and I don't see how you would need to know that right now, seeing as how I am paying my own way."

That had shut her down. My philosophy was, *quien paga, manda.* Whoever paid was in charge. I had been financially independent for a long time, and I would be damned if I was going to take her unsolicited, unlawyerly advice.

I was tired. I got up and prepared my lunch for the next day and the coffee maker for the next morning. Then I got ready for bed. I checked that my front door was locked with the deadbolt set. I went to the far side of my bed and knelt down. I opened my gun safe underneath the bed and made sure my guns were there, just in case.

As I got into bed, I again thought about how I liked having control over my life. But that was a bit of a lie. I had never considered myself a romantic, in any sense of the word. But I would readily trade a little bit of control over my life for someone who made me feel—something—something more than a short-lived orgasm.

I closed my eyes. It took a little while but, eventually, sleep found me.

I stepped out of my apartment building to go to work and walked over to the metro station. When the weather was nice, it was great to be outside, if only for a few minutes.

Since my metro stop was at the end of the line, I almost always got a seat in the morning. I was constantly lugging tons of stuff, including my purse, lunch bag and backpack for school. On Mondays I also carried my gym bag, which I left at work all week and took home on Friday. Luckily, I didn't have class on Friday, so I didn't have to lug my school stuff to work and then home.

The DC metro was a riot. It was fairly clean, that was true. In fact, it was one of the cleaner metros I had ever been on. However, it was incredibly expensive. It cost about $4–$6 per trip, so about $10 a day. During rush hour, the prices were more expensive. That was simple supply and demand. During rush hour you have a captive market.

For me, the good thing about living so close to the metro was not having to pay the $4.75 daily parking fee. I also got a transit subsidy from the company I worked for. My company was a government contractor, and they tried to generally match what the government would pay its employees. Government employees received a transit subsidy, so employees at my company got one too.

I wasn't sure it actually helped, though. I had the idea that that fact only pushed the metro prices up even higher, since the DC transportation agency figured that government workers had their commute paid for, and thus wouldn't care how much it cost.

But it costs the taxpayers more money. And for the amount of people I saw constantly crammed into the metro trains every day, I couldn't believe that the prices had to be that high in order for the DC transportation agency to make money. Something was up.

That was only one thing about the metro, however, and not the most entertaining.

I didn't consider DC residents "rude" by comparison with other people in other cities. However, there were almost always rude people on the metro. For one thing, the people who worked in DC, and who took the metro, were pretty intolerant of tourists. The tourists didn't know that if you wanted to stand, without moving, on the metro escalators, you were supposed to stand to the right and, if you wanted to walk up or down the escalators, you were supposed to walk on the left. These poor tourists were constantly being yelled at to get out of the way. I got that. I liked to walk too and, especially if I was in a hurry, that irked me. But the tourists also brought much-needed revenue to the city. Should you people really be driving them away with your rudeness?

Then there were the people who slammed their way onto the metro trains as soon as the doors opened at a metro station, without giving people on the train an opportunity to deboard. Many times I had to push and shove my way off the train, holding onto my bags.

Then you had the people who had their earbuds in, completely oblivious to everyone and everything around them. Don't get me wrong. I really enjoy listening to my music on the metro too. But you need to be aware of what is going on around you. That meant when you enter the train, you shouldn't stand there in the entrance, but you should move further inside the train to make room for others getting on. How many times had I had to shove past people to get on the train, some of whom elbowed me? Sardines in a can.

The other day I had been shopping at the mall at Pentagon City. I was walking in the food court, looking for something to eat and listening to my favorite reggaeton music. Then I passed a blind man tapping his walking stick, but not really making any progress. He stood in the same place, tapping around. I watched tons of people walk around him, teenagers, older people, etc. I took out my earbuds and approached him.

"Excuse me, Sir," I had said. "Can I help you find something?"

"Yes, the elevator." He had sounded so frustrated.

I wasn't sure at first whether he meant the metro elevator or the mall elevator, because he was actually located at the mall exit that led to the metro. So I asked him.

"Are you going up?"

"Well, that's what they're for."

OK, I get it. "You're really close," I had said, and had taken his arm, weaving him around the crush of people. I did a bad job of it but I got him to the elevator. He had thanked me.

Why didn't anyone notice him? That's part of the me, me, me mentality. It's all about me and what I need/want. Who gives a shit about other people, right? And why would you even consider thinking about what it was like standing in other people's shoes?

Don't even get me started, Melanie and I often said to each other. The other day, I had told her recently, I saw a heavily pregnant woman standing on the metro carrying two bags. No one offered her their seat. I had looked around, in shock. Men and women both were pretending not to see her, shoving their faces into their newspapers and their smart phones. So I had offered her my seat.

"What happened to all the gentlemen?" I had asked my brother-in-law Patrick recently. It seemed like when I moved back to the U.S. from Spain a few years ago, they had all disappeared.

"Men have been emasculated," Patrick had explained. "They feel resentful. I think that's why they refuse to give up their seats for women anymore."

I guess that's why I like Latin men. They treat you like a woman, make you feel that you're a woman.

Well, I certainly felt like a woman. And being a feminist, being empowered, doesn't mean that I can't enjoy when a man makes me feel like a woman.

I was thinking about all of this as I exited the metro at Crystal City. I got a few stares from men on the metro today. I was wearing a black suit and a sleeveless emerald green blouse. The suit was tailored. I was forever having to buy clothes that fit my hips, then having them taken in everywhere else.

I was usually overdressed for the office. There was no official dress code in the company, but I tended to dress up. Some people wore jeans, but most men wore dockers and either button-down shirts or polo shirts, and most women wore business casual skirts and pants.

Always dress for the job you want, not the job you have.

I was a realist and I didn't really expect to be running this shop some day. However, if I had to stay here after law school, I hoped to at least have a chance at snagging a manager job.

The possibility of staying here was also looking more and more likely every day.

I wore my hair straight today, partially held out of my face with a clip. My hair was getting a bit too long.

The Crystal City area had an underground shopping center with restaurants, coffee shops and stores. Many people who worked in that area could get to their jobs using the underground walkway, not ever having to go outside. That was terrific during the winter. DC was hot and humid in the summer, but could also get really cold during the wintertime.

I took the underground walkway now to avoid the humidity. There was nothing worse than arriving to work already sweaty. And I would have to wear these clothes until at least 9:30 p.m. when I got home after class.

After leaving the underground tunnel, I walked through an above-ground, glass-encased walkway. I was hurrying a little, at the end of my walk, half-walking and half-dancing salsa (still listening to my music) and was about to turn left to take the elevator up to my office, when I ran face-to-face into who I referred to as The Turkish Guy.

"Hi!" he said. I didn't really know him, I just knew who he was. He worked for another company in the building. I don't remember what he did exactly. I also didn't remember his name, although he had told me at some point. I had been running into him occasionally for the past couple of months. He kept trying to ask me out, but I kept making excuses/ignoring him/pretending that I had somewhere urgent to be, etc. The bad news was that he knew where I worked. The good news was that I had been doing a pretty good job of avoiding him, until now, apparently.

I half-smiled, because I really had no other choice but to acknowledge him. I slowed down my stride a bit but didn't stop walking.

"How are you?" he asked me, smiling a broad smile.

"Well. I—uh, have to get to work. See you later." I got to the elevators. He followed me there.

"I haven't seen you in a while," he said.

Yes, that's on purpose, I thought, but didn't say anything. I only left my office at lunch to rush to the gym, and I acted like I had blinders on.

"Are you busy this weekend?" he asked as I pushed the up button to call the elevator, any elevator.

"Yes," I told him. That was not really a lie. I did have plans. I planned to see my sister on Sunday and to study for the rest of the weekend.

The elevator opened a few seconds later. He still had time to say, "Maybe coffee after work?"

"I have class every day after work," I told him, getting into the elevator. I half-expected him to follow me inside. I was relieved when he didn't.

"See you later," I told him as the elevator doors closed. I had no intention of seeing him later, but I said something to talk over whatever else he may have said before I could get away from him.

I exhaled. That had been close. Would I have to come right out and tell him that I wasn't interested in dating him? It may be harsh but he was always so direct. I wasn't sure what else to do.

My life was a bit depressing, I realized. Despite what my mother thought, I really did not know anyone currently that I would consider dating. I started thinking about the men I knew. If Eric were ten years older and a little more mature, I might consider dating him. I wasn't interested in dating Josh. Dinesh had a girlfriend, but we were buddies. It was difficult to imagine dating him.

There was no one else.

Then I suddenly thought of that Arab guy who had sat next to me in class last night. Oh, who the hell was I kidding? He was eye candy, nothing more. I was 100 percent certain he and I would have nothing in common. Maybe it would work out if we never spoke. I smiled. What a "relationship" that would be. Well, for some guys that's probably their dream relationship, having sex and never having to say anything.

That sounded like most of my hook-ups.

I exited the elevator and walked to my office. I swiped my card on the sensor and opened the door.

I walked past the receptionist's desk to my cube, saying hi to the receptionist on the way.

The office was a cube environment. I had a larger cube than most of the other translators, because I was a Senior Translator, and had to review others' work. Management liked me because I did high-quality work that was timely. Consequently, I was in high demand and sought after by the clients my company worked for. But most of the other translators didn't like me because I was highly detailed-oriented and critical of their work.

I tried being nice, because I really wanted the opportunity to advance in the company if I stayed there. To do that, I needed to be diplomatic. However, frequently the other translators pushed me too far and I ended up having to be firm, sounding like a borderline jerk. If I told them what I really thought, then I would sound like a downright jackass.

Foreign-language translation is a highly subjective job. There were usually many different ways to convey the same meanings in the text. I spent an inordinate amount of time arguing with the other translators about syntax, diction and semantic ranges. Most people would think it was an absolute snorefest, but I was a total nerd about linguistics.

I got to my cube and dropped my backpack under my desk. I took out some snacks and left them on my desk. I took my lunch and went to the kitchen to put it in the fridge.

In the kitchen I ran into Abdul, one of the many foreign men I worked with. I didn't work directly with him, since I didn't translate Arabic, but we frequently engaged in small talk.

"Hi, Isabel," Abdul said. I couldn't help but notice that he was staring at me. In fact, he moved his eyes from my feet all the way up to my face. "You look very nice today."

"Thank you." Abdul was nice, but he was always sneaking looks at me, like he knew that he shouldn't. Other men in the office were more blatant. In fact, sometimes I thought that the entire office was one complaint away from having to deal with a sexual harrassment charge.

Looking is free, I guess. I checked men out too, but not so much at work. In my opinion, there weren't any men at work worth checking out, anyway.

I went back to my desk, logged on and checked my emails. I had an employment contract to finish for today, from Spanish to English. It had to be done by the end of today but I had made good progress, so I wasn't too worried.

I also had an email from Tim, a new translator. He had worked as a missionary or volunteer or something in South America before coming to work for the company, and his spoken and written Spanish was good. I had doubts about his skills as a translator, though. He wanted to talk to me about my revisions to his work.

That's not a good sign. He's going to argue with me.

I emailed him back.

> I have a project to finish this morning but we can meet this afternoon, say around 2:30 p.m. in my cube. Thanks, Isabel.

I wasn't looking forward to it but it wouldn't be the first time.

I liked my job, but I didn't always like dealing with the people here. In fact, one of the things I really liked about being a translator was that it was a solitary job. It didn't require a whole lot of teamwork. In high school, I had absolutely hated doing group projects, since that meant that I ended up doing all of the work because I didn't want to get a bad grade.

Undergraduate was different, since most of the people there were over-achievers. Law school was like that too, but thankfully didn't require much group work. I could be my own solitary self and I loved that.

That morning I finished the contract translation, double-checking and then triple-checking it. As I was writing an email to send it to my boss, Miguel, another translator, passed by my desk.

Miguel was from Mexico. He was nice enough, but a little intense.

I looked up and met his eye, not really meaning to. I half-smiled in ac-knowledgement. I didn't like him or dislike him, but I considered it rude to fail to acknowledge someone's presence. That's how I was raised.

"Hi, Isabel," Miguel said as he stopped and leaned against the outside of my cubicle. Miguel was one of the younger guys (by younger I meant about my age), and he was single. It was a disastrous combination in my mind be-cause that meant he saw me as potentially someone to date. He was actually pretty good-looking, but he wasn't my type and, in any case, I didn't want to date or hook up with anyone I worked with. The last thing I needed was to have a reputation at work as the promiscuous Spanish girl.

Great. Now he's going to chat. Wait, did he just look at my cleavage?

Most of the people here knew that I didn't chat much. I didn't have any real friends here, except for one, another Spanish translator from Murcia, Spain.

"Hi," I said back.

"How are you doing?"

"Well," I said.

"What are you working on?"

"Why?"

"Just wondering."

Yeah, I bet you are. I had the feeling that half the guys in here wanted to sleep with me, and the other half saw me as competition for promotions. He probably thought both things.

"Nothing interesting, the usual stuff."

"Sooo," he started.

Oh, God, don't ask me out, you fool. He had never asked me out before, but I guess there was a first time for everything.

"Some of us are going to dinner on Friday."

I said nothing, since he had not asked a question. I never went to dinner or happy hour or anything else with my coworkers. I didn't see the point, really. I was never happy enough for "happy hour," anyway. And I certainly didn't want to be around a bunch of my drunk male coworkers.

"Are you interested in coming?" he asked me.

"Thanks, but I have plans," I lied. I had no plans Friday night, other than possibly painting my nails, going to the shooting range and/or watching old Westerns.

"What are you doing?" he asked then. Nosy, I thought.

"I'm having dinner with friends from law school."

"Well, then you can bring them!"

God, he was persistent. "I don't think I can. We have a reservation, I think." I needed to shut this down. "Thank you, though." I turned back to my computer screen. "Sorry, I have to send this project. I'll talk to you later."

He left and I relaxed a little bit. I planned on keeping my head down for the rest of the day.

At 12:00 I grabbed my bag and walked over to the gym, which was next door to my office. My midday workouts were sacred. I never ate lunch out with people because I didn't want to miss them. It was a chance to disconnect and it also energized me for my nighttime classes.

I got on the treadmill and walked for a couple of minutes. Then I cranked it up and started running. Techno music blared in my ears. I imagined I was on a long, straight path and gunned it. It felt great.

Showered, hair washed and blowdried, I was back in the office. I left my gym bag at my desk.

I walked into the kitchen to get my lunch out of the fridge and nuke it.

The kitchen had two refrigerators, two microwaves and two round tables, and several people ate their lunch in there every day. I never did.

I could hear my coworkers before I even got to the kitchen. Some were chatting in English and others in rapid Arabic.

When I walked into the kitchen, the chatter stopped immediately. I had the cold realization that they had been talking about me. I wouldn't have known if they hadn't stopped talking since I didn't speak Arabic, and I hadn't been paying attention to what the English speakers were talking about.

I didn't look at them or greet them, and got my lunch out of the fridge.

I hated having to nuke my lunch with them there, because I had to stand there, waiting, for about two minutes, counting down until I could leave.

"Well, hello to you too," one of them said, obviously annoyed that I hadn't greeted them when I walked in.

I turned around, with a smile plastered on my face. "Hi," I said. The more I talked, the more they would talk to me and ask me questions I didn't care to answer.

"So, do you have a boyfriend yet?"

Like that question.

I didn't like to lie, mostly because the ruse would be difficult to maintain, but I also didn't like to discuss my personal life with them.

"Why do you ask?"

The guy who had asked me smiled. His eyes twinkled a little.

"Just wondering. How can a girl like you not have a boyfriend?"

"Yeah, so it's really not—"

"Isabel!!!!! Where have you been?! *No te he visto en todo el dia.*"

Thank God! It was Peter, my only true friend here. He had walked in with a flourish. Of course, it was about time for his afternoon coffee.

Peter McBride was Spanish, but you certainly wouldn't know that by his name. He had an American father, of Irish descent and former U.S. military, and a Spanish mother. He had been born in the U.S., but his family moved back to Spain when he was a toddler. He spoke English with a Murcian accent; I loved that. The Castilian accent made me feel so nostalgic.

Peter was about forty-five years old. He was married to a Spanish woman, and they had a gaggle of kids. I had been over to their house to watch soccer games. He was a Madrid fan and I was a Barcelona fan, but there was no ill will between us.

He wasn't super-tall, about 5'10". His hair was curly and almost all gray. He looked good with gray hair. Of course, men with gray hair were distinguished and mature. Women with gray hair were old. What a double standard.

Peter and I had started at the company the same week. When he introduced himself in English, I couldn't reconcile his name with his accent. It was a mystery to me. I didn't speak English with a Spanish accent, so he hadn't made the connection that I was Spanish, despite my name.

Later that day, I had been talking to someone else in Spanish. Afterward, Peter had stopped by my desk.

"Where in Spain are you from?" he had asked me.

"How do you know I'm from Spain?" I had retorted.

"Just for the couple of words I heard you say," he had answered in his heavy accent, smiling broadly.

"*Pues soy de Barcelona.*" It wasn't a complete truth.

"*Uuuuyyy, catalana,*" he had mused.

Then we had exchanged family histories.

Peter was a really good guy. He was like a beacon of light to me at the moment.

As he stepped near the counter to prepare his coffee, I moved closer to him.

"*Tio, me has salvado la vida ahora mismo.*" Then, lowering my voice, "I owe you for getting me out of that conversation."

"*Porque?* Are these people bothering you again?" he asked in a teasing manner.

"No, just asking me the same stuff they always do." I paused. "Not to mention, they shut up as soon as I walked in the room," I whispered.

"Ah," he answered.

"I think I'm going to learn Spanish," someone was saying to the others at the table. I ignored him.

Go ahead. Make my day, punk.

Peter and I continued chatting.

"*Como estas?*" he asked me.

"*Bien,*" I answered without enthusiasm.

"*Y como van las clases?*"

"Class just started," I told him. "*Pero de momento, bien.*"

My food was ready. I said goodbye to Peter and left, ignoring the others.

2:30 finally came around and I had to meet with Tim. As I had expected, it didn't go that well.

He was at my cube right on time.

"Have a seat," I told him as politely as I could. I motioned to the extra chair in my cube.

Tim got right to the point.

"Isabel, I don't agree with some of your comments."

This does not bode well, I groaned inwardly.

"OK." I paused to collect my thoughts. I had printed out his contract translation and my revisions and I looked at the paper in front of me. "Which ones do you have questions about?"

"Well, first, you marked this wrong and it's not wrong." He pointed to his version and I looked at mine.

"Everyday," I read. "Yes, it should be two words, like I said. 'Every day.' Here it's a noun."

"But it's spelled as one word in the dictionary."

"Yes, as an adjective. As in, everyday objects. As an adjective, it's one word. As a noun, it's two words."

"But it's in the dictionary," Tim insisted.

You're not listening, I thought. Why was I surprised? This is how many people his age converse. They wait nervously until you shut your mouth, then start spouting off, without even registering what you said. I was starting to lose my patience but I kept calm. I took my English-language dictionary from my desk and opened it.

"Here," I pointed. "Everyday, A-D-J. Adjective. It cannot be one word when it's used as a noun."

He huffed. Oh my God, he still doesn't get it.

Then he went on.

"Here," he said, pointing.

I looked again. "Provision of Service Agreement. OK, what's your question?"

"You said it's wrong."

"OK, what's your question?" I repeated.

"It's not wrong."

"OK." I paused again. "It may be technically correct, but have you ever seen the title 'Provision of Service Agreement' in an English contract?"

He was silent.

"Have you?" I pressed.

He was uncertain.

"I don't know," he finally said.

"The correct translation is 'Service Contract' or maybe 'Service Agreement.' That's what this is, a service agreement. 'Provision of Service Agreement' is too wordy and unclear. This is a contract for services. You can't translate these terms literally. You have to think about how to render this in English, keeping the meaning in the source text but writing it in a way in which it is normally expressed in English. Here, your use of 'provision' is superfluous."

"But it's correct then?"

"No, it's not correct."

"I don't agree."

Again, you're not listening. I refused to repeat myself.

"Well, what did Martin say?" I asked. Martin was our boss.

"He agreed with you, but I don't agree with him."

OK, so Tim was pissed off.

"Well, I'm sorry, then. But take this as a learning exercise. Before you turn a project in, read it several times in the target text and ask yourself whether it is meaningful in English and whether it is expressed naturally in English."

Then we talked about several other phrases that he had not translated in accurate U.S. legal jargon. He had used "responsible" instead of "liable," for example. And he had used "conserves the right" instead of "reserves the right" because, again, he had translated literally.

By the end of our conversation, he wasn't happy with me.

"OK, well, I'm not in law school like you are. I would not have known that."

"I understand, but you don't have to be in law school to be a good legal translator. Look, legal translators take classes and get certifications in how to translate legal documents." I know, since I had done such classes right after starting this job. "You can do that to improve."

"I don't need that," he said then. "And I didn't do my undergrad at UVA just to have to do this menial work."

"Then find another job." I was seething but I wasn't going to waste my energy on him.

He continued. "And if you make all these corrections to my work every time, then I won't be able to get my raise."

"Look, I'm sorry, but I have a job to do." So that was what this was about. He wanted me to be lenient, but I couldn't do that.

"Can't you give me a break, Isabel?"

"What?" I was incredulous. "Like I said, I have to do my job. Now, if Martin doesn't agree with me, that's one thing."

But Martin almost always agreed with me; that was apparently Tim's problem. Martin was an excellent translator and a decent manager. He liked me because I paid attention to the details. Everyone also knew that I was his go-to translator for Spanish and French. Consequently, I was usually busier than other people.

Martin had also hinted at a possible promotion and/or raise when I finished law school. I knew he couldn't promise anything at this point, but it would be nice in case I ended up staying at the company. But I wasn't going to bet on a raise, not in this economy.

"I knew you'd say that," Tim said then. He rose from the chair.

I was starting to get angry. I rose as well.

"You know, Tim," I said as he turned to leave, "You want to get ahead? Learn from your mistakes and work hard, accept constructive feedback and be the best at what you do. Mediocrity gets you nowhere."

I sat back down. We were done. He left in a huff.

Later that day I stopped by Peter's cube and we chatted for a few minutes while I drank my coffee. We were discreet and there was no one around. Peter knew about what had happened with Tim earlier because, apparently, Tim had gossiped to everyone. Not professional.

Peter agreed with me that most of the younger translators had that same attitude. We both speculated that Tim wouldn't last that long at the company. It didn't seem fair that there were other people who would probably work harder and be more appreciative of the job.

One of the reasons that I liked Peter was that he was an eternal optimist. I was a pessimist through and through. I always expected the worst; that way, I wasn't easily disappointed.

Sometimes Peter asked me why I wore black so often.

"I'm in mourning for my country," I had told him. For the lack of civility, for the men and their lack of backbone, for the women who are becoming more superficial and insecure.

Peter would smile and say that everything would work out.

"Peter is like your work husband," Ariel had told me.

"My what?" I had asked. "I don't have those feelings for him."

"No, I mean, there doesn't have to be any sexual tension to have a work spouse," Ariel had explained. "It's like someone who supports you at work, someone you can talk to, who's a good friend."

I guess Peter and I were work spouses.

When I got back to my desk, I took a deep breath. Yes, this is my life. This and law school and the occasional hookup.

Of the three, law school gave me the most satisfaction. But I only had two more years. After that, I didn't know what I was going to do.

I left work at 5:15 and rushed to the metro. I had changed my heels for flats before I left the office. I scarfed down a handful of almonds on the way, hoping I didn't choke in the process.

I only had a few stops on the metro. Luckily, I got a seat. By the next stop, which was Pentagon City, it was standing-room only.

At Pentagon City a bunch of people got on the train, including a young women with a toddler. The toddler was huge and the woman was about my height but really skinny. She was trying to hold on to the toddler and a big bag that probably carried her son's stuff in it. She put her son on the ground but he cried and fussed, wanting to be picked up. So she picked him up again. He looked tired. She had a hard time holding on to him and balancing while standing on a moving train.

I looked around. Again, nobody offered her a seat. Again, I lamented the current state of society.

I caught her eye, guarding my seat so that no one else would take it. I motioned to her. "Why don't you sit here?" I said.

"Oh, thank you so much!"

"It's no problem."

"Thank you!" she said again. She sat and put the toddler on her lap, where he was content.

We were arriving at Rosslyn, where a bunch of people got off. The stop for the university was the next one. I stood by the door.

One of my favorite Reggaeton dance songs started playing in my ears then.

I started to dance a little. It was impossible not to.

The song continued, the heavy bass beat in tune with my heartbeat. I was at about 45 percent capacity now, moving my feet and mouthing the words.

Then I had the hand motions going.

As the train started to slow down at the metro station, I had the urge to look up for some reason. I looked to my left, and I saw the Arab guy from class last night, standing further down the train in front of another door. He was looking right at me, and he was smiling.

Jesus. I had had enough of Arab guys for today.

When our eyes met, he didn't look away. Oh, so he thought it was freaking amusing that I was dancing?!

I continued to look at him with a hard stare. Then I looked right into his eyes.

God, his eyes were beautiful. And he had such long lashes. I could see them from all the way over here.

Wait, what am I thinking?!

The train stopped and the doors opened. I was paralyzed for a second, then I exited, running up the escalator so I wouldn't have to run into him.

I swiped my metro card to exit the station. I hurried to the upper escalator, the one leading outside. I ran up that one too, which was a workout with my backpack.

The air was still humid but it felt good to be outside. I shoved my sunglasses on my face and hurried across the street, hoping that the Arab guy wouldn't catch up with me.

Then I realized that I was a little turned on.

I was already in my seat in Crim Pro when the Arab guy showed up. I had my face buried in my book to the right side of my laptop so I couldn't see him. I didn't even acknowledge his presence, but I felt him. I felt electrified, like all systems were go.

Oh, this is *not* good.

I was being a jackass at not even saying hi, but I was afraid that my face would give me away. It felt hot, as if I were blushing furiously.

I heard Eric behind me.

"What's with the silent treatment, Isabel?" he asked.

"What?" I pretended that I had just noticed him when he said that.

I turned around to the right to look at Eric, so that the Arab guy wouldn't see my face. If Eric saw that my face was red, he didn't say anything.

"I was wondering why you're being so quiet. It's so—"

"Uncharacteristic. I know. I was reading the cases again."

"You know it's annoying when you do that, you know?"

"What? When I reread cases?"

"No, when you finish people's sentences."

"Dude, I always know what people are going to say. They're so predictable."

"But it's annoying," Eric said. "And, by the way, I resent the fact that you think *I'm* predictable."

"Well, Eric, you know I don't give a shit what people think about me."

Josh and Dinesh were there by now. Right after they sat down, class started, thank goodness.

When I got home that night, I was way too wired to sleep. I took a cold shower and read Property to fall asleep.

I did fall asleep, but I'd be damned if I didn't have a sexy dream starring that Arab dude in my Crim Pro class.

I woke up thinking, oh this is *so* not good.

Wednesdays and Thursdays were a pain because I had two classes. I had International Law from 3:50 p.m. until 5:50 p.m. and then I had Property right after that, and didn't leave campus until 8 p.m. That also meant that I had to lug my backpack with my laptop, my International Law book and my Property book. My backpack was heavy, so I carried my Property book in my arms, along with my purse. Inside my backpack I also had plenty of snacks. It was going to be a long afternoon/evening.

None of my friends were in my International Law class. This was both good and bad. It was good because I didn't have to worry about Eric embarrassing me. It was good because I wouldn't be interrupted constantly by them asking me, "What page are we on?" or "What did the professor say about X case?"

But it was also bad because my friends kind of reeled me in so that I wouldn't make any outbursts in class. I had no patience for Millennials, and even less for lameness. Invariably, there were always at least one or two lame students who made comments in class that were either completely inane, completely irrelevant, or both. When Eric, Josh, Dinesh or Melanie were around, I would somehow be less likely to speak out when someone was making a meaningless point. They tempered me a little bit. My sisters did, too. But when I was by myself, sometimes all hell broke loose.

I took a deep breath. Tonight would be okay because it was the first day of class. We wouldn't talk about anything of substance.

I lugged all my stuff up the stairs of the law school's main entrance. As I reached the door, a couple of young guys were walking inside. I was pretty sure that they saw me with my backpack and my purse and my Property book. But they let the doors fall closed on me.

Nice, I lamented, rolling my eyes.

I managed to open the front door without too much difficulty. My International Law class was on the fourth floor, so I decided to be easy on myself and take the elevator. I walked over and found it was open, with a bunch of people standing inside. As I moved deliberately toward the open doors, they began to close. I looked at the faces of the people in the elevator, some young students and a couple of more mature people, maybe older students or professors. They let the doors close, even though they clearly saw that I was obviously walking toward the elevator. As the doors closed in front of my face, I said sarcastically, "Thanks so much!"

I don't know why I was surprised. Stuff like that happened all the time in this damn town. People were so rude.

I whirled around. Great. I haven't even gotten to class yet and I'm already pissed off.

As I turned around, I came face-to-face with that Arab guy. I had no choice but to look right at him.

"That was rude," he told me. "I'm sorry." His brows were furrowed and he was half-frowning.

He really does think they were rude. He's not just saying that. Years of semi-self-imposed solitude had led me to constantly observe people. I was fairly adept at reading expressions. His confused and unnerved expression was genuine.

"Not your fault," I said neutrally. I didn't care to talk to this guy, but the truth was that he didn't have to apologize for other people's lack of manners.

"Do you need any help?" he said. "I—I can help to carry your books if you want."

The "to" isn't grammatically correct, was my first thought. I couldn't stand incorrect grammar. But I didn't correct him. For some reason, it would have made me feel like a jerk, not that I cared what this guy thought about me.

Yes, I thought. I would really appreciate that. But I didn't say that.

"No." I shook my head. "No thank you."

I walked past him gingerly.

I felt like I should say something. "I have to get to class," I muttered.

I wondered why he offered to help me. No one ever did. That's not true, I reconsidered. If Josh or Eric were here, they would help me with my books. They were very gentlemanly like that.

It's because they're Latin. Well, Eric is half Brazilian, and I guess that's technically not "Latin," but the cultures were similar enough.

Does this guy have ulterior motives? Did he hear that I was easy?

That wasn't true. I wasn't easy. Well, maybe I was kind of easy if you caught me at the right time. In any case, I decided that he could not have heard that because he was new here, and I hadn't seen him hanging out with anyone, and so he probably would not have heard any gossip about me. Unless he had asked around.

I could imagine the conversation. Hey, you know that girl Isabel? The one who wears hip-hugging skirts and who has cut arms? The one who mouths off all the time and who hangs around guys? Yeah, her. Does she give it away? If not, what do I have to do to talk her into my bed?

The answer was simple. Wait until she is so horny she can't stand it, then be in the right place at the right time. Oh, and she likes really dark men, so you're in luck, whatever-your-name-is.

I smiled to myself. That was about right.

Since I always thought the worst of people, I figured that he just wanted a hook-up. I was a Class A pessimist, as my sisters liked to say.

Instead of waiting for the notoriously slow elevator to work its way back down to the first floor, and have to stand there awkwardly with that Arab dude eyeing me, I hauled all my stuff up four flights of stairs.

I finally got to the classroom. As I approached, I saw a girl struggling to open the heavy door. She looked really young, and wore the traditional hijab. I had seen her before, around the law school. I didn't think that we had ever had any classes together. Maybe one of the larger classes. She had a gorgeous face and flawlessly smooth skin. I was so jealous. She was doing the same thing as me, lugging a heavy backpack and a big law school textbook in her hands. She was also carrying a water bottle.

I grabbed the door. "I'll get it," I told her. I held it open for her. Again, where are the guys to hold the door for her? No one saw that she was struggling?

"Thank you," she said, smiling shyly. God, she can't be older than twenty-five. I am officially old.

After she went inside I started to maneuver my book to my other hand to be able to hold the door open while I walked inside. I was again starting to lament the loss of civilization as we knew it. Poor grammar and men who were lame jocks. This is the future of our country. I shook my head.

"I'll get it." I heard a now-familiar voice.

The Arab guy held the door for me.

I was shocked. I don't know why, the way this week had been going so far.

"Are you in this class?" I asked him. Then I wondered why I was talking to him.

"Yes," he nodded

"*Madre de Dios.*" I felt my eyes go upward.

"Sorry?"

"Nothing." I started to walk inside. Then I remembered my manners. "Thanks," I said over my shoulder.

The classroom was one of the smaller rooms. It probably couldn't seat more than thirty or forty people at the most. Long tables and chairs were divided into two sections. I sat in the section on the right, if you were looking from the front of the classroom, in the second row, in the leftmost seat at the end of the row. The Muslim girl I had held the door open for was sitting directly behind me.

As the Arab guy approached, I silently pleaded, don't sit next to me. I don't know why I cared.

But apparently he couldn't hear my thoughts, or God had a sense of humor, because he sat right next to me (again).

As he walked past, he said, "Do you mind if I sit here?" At first I thought he was talking to someone else.

Then I came back to reality and looked up. He was looking at me. And, for the first time, I noticed his accent. He spoke with a faint, French-tinged lilt.

"Um, I'm not the boss here so . . ." I made a gesture with my hands, indicating that I guessed he could sit there if he wanted to. If I *were* the boss at this school things would be *so* different.

He sat down, then greeted the girl behind me in Arabic.

Dude, if he knows her then why didn't he sit next to *her*?!

Then I thought, of course he knows her. All the Arabic speakers at the school seemed to hang out together.

I put in my earbuds and turned on my music to drown out the chatter so that I could review my notes for the cases tonight. My smooth Reggaeton came on.

The music made me want to get up and dance. Instead, I settled for bobbing my head and moving my shoulders to the music.

My left shoulder itched where my bra strap was. It was still hot outside and I was a little bit sweaty, especially on my back where I had carried my backpack. I took my jacket off and draped it on the back of my chair.

I put my left hand lazily on the my left shoulder and moved my bra strap about a centimeter to the side, and scratched a little bit, not like a man-scratch, but slowly. I was aware that my bra strap was probably showing, but I didn't care.

Then I felt a strange sensation. I couldn't explain it. I suddenly had the urge to look to my left. I did so, and the Arab guy was looking at me out of the corner of his eye. I gave him a cold stare. He saw me and looked away quickly.

I shook my head. Looking is free, anyway. That's all you'll ever get to do, look.

But I wasn't so sure that was right. A part of me believed that maybe he wasn't as bad as I thought, that maybe he didn't have ulterior motives or that maybe he really was just polite.

No, he's like any other Millennial and any other foreign man I've ever met. They're never any different. Jesus, Isabel, get a grip.

Class started. I turned my music off and took my earbuds out.

I left International Law class in a rush since I only had ten minutes until my next class began. I couldn't believe that the Arab guy was in that class too, and that he had had the audacity to sit next to me.

On the whole, I didn't really have a problem with it since he was eye candy, at least for me. I suddenly thought of my sister Lara then. She didn't like goatees, but she wasn't the one that had to look at him four days a week, so that was all right.

But his presence next to me was distracting. I found myself not wanting to make a fool out of myself for some reason. What the hell do I care what he thinks about me?

I don't care what anyone thinks about me.

I walked to my Property class, which started at six p.m. Josh, Dinesh, Eric and Melanie were all in that class too. The gang would be all there, and I was looking forward to it. However, it would be impossible to save all of them seats, so I figured I wouldn't save any.

I entered the classroom, which was a bit smaller than our Crim Pro class, but still stadium-style with three sections.

I sat in the center section, again in the second row, in the last seat on the right if you were the professor looking at the class. Melanie was already sitting in the seat behind me and Eric was next to her. The three of us greeted each other. I again hung my jacket on the back of my chair.

I took out my textbook and opened my laptop, switching it on. The property cases were dense, and I had read over them twice in preparation for class. I scanned my notes and the sections I had highlighted.

Suddenly, someone said, "Excuse me" and gingerly pushed past me.

Annoyed, I pulled myself further into the table to let whoever it was pass. Then I realized that that lilt sounded familiar.

I looked up a little to the right. Holy shit, that Arab dude. He sat to my right. Jesus Christ.

I looked away quickly, but not before sneaking a look at Melanie behind me. She was raising her eyebrows and gesturing toward me and, not so inconspicuously, toward him. OK, so apparently Eric wasn't the only one who thought that this dude was my type.

The Arab guy started to set up his laptop and I saw him sneak a look at me out of the corner of my eye. I decided not to acknowledge his presence. He had deigned to talk to me earlier in the other class, but I had the impression that here he was a little intimidated because I had my posse with me.

OK, I figured. It's not such a big deal that we have the same classes. If he had transferred here, he would have to take Property. The other two classes were coincidental, since they were electives.

The truth was, I was kind of a fatalist. My sister Ariel had told me that meant that I was a romantic to some degree, but I didn't agree with her.

"It's not the same thing," I had said.

She had ignored me. "It is. But Isabel, you can't mean that you don't have control over your own destiny."

"Oh, I believe that you do," I had corrected her.

"Then you're not a fatalist."

"I believe that there are things beyond your control, and how you deal with them is up to you."

"OK, so you're like a fatalist 'light,'" she had said, smiling.

I guess I was. Some things were fate, and some things were your own making.

I was abruptly brought out of my reminiscing.

"Hey, Isabel," Eric said then, and I could hear the laughter in his voice. Shit, he was about to embarrass me.

"Got any hot dates or hookups planned this weekend?"

Ugh, I had been right.

"Screw you, jackass," was my reply. I didn't even look back at him.

Then I heard Josh's voice. He had sat next to that Arab guy. Great. Now Josh and I would have to converse across this guy all semester. That was going to be awkward.

"She probably has a long line of men waiting. She makes them take numbers," he told Eric.

Ugh. *De Guatemala a Guatapeor.* From bad to worse.

"Leave her alone, you guys," Melanie said, the only one who came to my defense.

Dinesh had come in and had sat behind Josh, next to Eric.

"What's this about having a hot date, Isabel?"

That was it. I would stop this before they got to talking about my hookup habits.

I whirled around, so fast that I saw the surprised look on Dinesh's face.

"That's it!" I was pissed off, but embarrassed as well. I didn't want the whole school to know about what I did on my "time off," so to speak.

"The three of you, shut up right now! Or—" I was staring them down, pointing my finger.

They were all looking at me. I saw the Arab guy trying to sneak a look at me out of the corner of his eye, but he didn't dare look directly at me.

"Or what?" Eric said, laughing.

I had an epiphany then. "Or none of you will get any of my notes for the rest of the semester. No! For the rest of the year! I don't care what the reason is. I don't care if you broke a nail, or if you got the swine flu, I don't care!"

"Jesus, Isabel, OK," Eric said, and his smile immediately disappeared. He, most of all, couldn't risk me not sending him any notes. Otherwise, Eric would actually have to pay attention in class and do the reading without relying on me to help him. The three of them all knew that my notes were excellent, too. Josh and Dinesh wouldn't be able to survive without me sending them notes when they had to miss class to work late.

But I wasn't done.

I continued in an angry half-whisper. "And don't talk *about* me or *to* me for the rest of this class or I will seriously reconsider my relationship with you three. In fact, I'm already wondering what the hell I get in return for giving you my notes when you don't bother to show up."

I turned around to face my laptop screen and Eric had written me a message. "Do you mean for the rest of this class today or the rest of class this semester?"

"Shut up!" I said out loud, glaring at Eric. A guy sitting in front of me jumped out of his seat.

"But I didn't say anything!"

"That goes for electronic and phone communication, too."

Dinesh was holding in a laugh. I turned around and faced my screen. Then I heard something. I swiveled my head slightly to the right.

The Arab guy was laughing a little, very softly, trying not to draw attention to himself.

I softened a bit. I suppose that if I had been an outsider during that exchange, I would have laughed, too.

I couldn't help smiling. It actually was funny how I had put the three of them in their place so quickly.

"If you think that's funny, you should see us on the weekends," I said in a low, neutral tone of voice, without looking away from my screen.

The Arab guy looked at me then, turning his head a little to the left. He still didn't dare look at me directly. I got the feeling that he wasn't sure whether I was talking to him or not.

I smiled and continued reviewing my notes.

Then he spoke. "Is that an invitation?" he asked, almost under his breath, in his soft French accent.

Still looking at my computer screen, I put an incredulous, what-the-hell look on my face.

"No," I said carefully, not moving at all.

"Who is she talking to?" I heard Dinesh ask Eric.

"I don't think she's talking to us," Eric replied.

Class had ended. I had a meeting that night for one of the few extracurricular groups I was involved in, not that I was that involved in them. But at least at the beginning of the semester I felt obliged to attend the meetings. There would also be free pizza there, and that would take care of dinner.

I had tried to persuade Josh to attend.

"No thanks," he had said with a mischievous grin, "I'm really not that interested in the Federalist Society."

"Well, we probably wouldn't want you there anyway," I had told him.

I didn't bother asking Eric. Eric wasn't serious about much, except for Law Review. I couldn't believe he had made Law Review. I had to admit, though, that he was intelligent. But he also liked to party. Work hard, play hard, that was his motto.

Dinesh didn't do any extracurriculars either. He was swamped with work as it was and his firm was paying his law school tuition, so of course he felt obliged to exceed his billable hours.

Melanie was in a rush to get home that night.

So there was only me.

I grabbed my stuff and said goodbye to my friends, ignoring the Arab guy. I literally ran out of the classroom and found the room where the meeting was going to be held. People were already helping themselves to pizza.

The Federalist Society is a national organization that has law school chapters for law students. It's a group of conservatives and libertarians who are interested in protecting the Constitution. Now that I think about it, you don't need to be conservative or libertarian to respect the Constitution, but what do I know?

The group is founded on the principles that the state exists to preserve freedom, that the separation of governmental powers is central to the United States Constitution, and that it is the province and duty of the judiciary to say what the law is, not what it should be. I certainly agreed with the group's ideas that there were too many activist judges, who wanted to craft the law as they thought it should be instead of deferring to the law as written. It made me depressed to think about how some "progressives" in this town wanted to bypass the Constitution.

I was busy enough without doing the extracurricular stuff, but I wanted to be involved and do something before the very principles on which this country was founded were eroded.

I dropped my stuff at the end of one of the long tables and grabbed some pizza. Not my ideal dinner, but it would do.

I sat down and started munching. I didn't eat daintily after eight p.m. I ate like a ravenous horse. By this time, I was usually starving. If my mother could see me now, shoving food down my throat like a frat brother.

"You should be more ladylike," she would say.

I wanted something to do because I really didn't know anyone here that well, so I took out my Crim Pro book and started looking at next week's cases. I was able to tune out most noise. At work, I had to translate almost all day in a cube environment, with other people talking around me. I was used to tuning them out.

I continued shoving pizza in my face until the meeting was called to order. At that point, I wiped my mouth, swallowed the last bit of food and took a sip from my water bottle. Then I looked up.

I'd be damned if that Arab guy wasn't sitting in the row in front of me, two seats to the right. He was looking to the left a little bit and when our eyes met, he smiled briefly. I quickly whipped my head away and looked to the front, to focus on the speaker.

An Arab dude in the Federalist Society? This had to be a first.

Maybe he was doing opposition research. He wouldn't be the first person to do that, I was sure.

My cousins in Spain had this saying that two coincidences were just that, coincidences, but three "coincidences" were not coincidences at all. Well, this guy was in all three of my classes and was here too. Maybe this wasn't a coincidence at all. Was I a fatalist or way too paranoid? I didn't know.

I got home late that night, but was still a little wired. I put water to boil to make herbal tea and turned on my laptop.

After deliberating for a couple of minutes, I said out loud, "Screw it."

I went to the university's law school homepage, and logged into my account. Fortunately, you could search by your registered classes and get a list of the students in that particular class.

I brought up the list of students in my International Law class, since that class was smaller and, hence, the list would be more manageable. The students were listed in alphabetical order with their photos and full names.

I saw the photo of the Muslim girl who sat behind me. Her name was Zara. A beautiful name.

Then I found who I was looking for. The Arab dude.

His name was Tarek Cordiez. His last name immediately piqued my interest. I had thought that his French accent when he spoke English was because he was from a Middle Eastern country that was a former French colony and, therefore, would still have French-system schools. I had assumed that he had learned Arabic and French simultaneously and, subsequently, English, and that that explained why he spoke English with a bit of a French accent.

However, his last name was French. At first glance, some people may think it was Spanish, pronouncing it "Cor-dee-es" or, in peninsular Castilian, "Cor-dee-eth."

In all earnestness, it was difficult to definitively ascertain the exact origin of the name Cordiez. However, first, it was decidedly not Arabic. Second, while it was possible that, linguistically, it did not derive from French, I had encountered the name as a last name of French people.

This bit of knowledge was actually informative. It told me that this guy's father's family was most likely French. In fact, maybe even his father himself was French. That would also explain why his skin tone was a bit lighter than that of the other Arabs at the university.

It would also explain why this guy seemed to be more approachable than the other Arabs I knew, both at work and on campus. There was an intensity about him, but there was also a kind of openness. He certainly wasn't going out of his way to avoid *me*. In fact, now that I considered it, there was something decidedly French about his mannerisms, about the way he held himself and his expressions, and also the way he held (or tried to hold) my gaze when our eyes met. It was almost like a playfulness, with his eyes alive and twinkling. That was typical of French men. When I lived in Paris, I had actually found it quite attractive.

Okay, so he grew up in France, or at least lived there for a while. Or, alternatively, he had a French father, from whom he picked up those mannerisms.

I was very interested now. Maybe he wasn't doing opposition research at the Federalist Society meeting after all. Maybe he, like me, an immigrant or the child of immigrants, had embraced the opportunities and the civil liberties that our families were denied in their home countries.

Don't get ahead of yourself. For all you know, this guy is just after a good lay. Well, weren't we all?

Except that this "guy" had a name now. Tarek. I immediately regretted looking up his name. Now he was a person instead of some lame law-school non-entity. A person with an actual name was much harder to ignore than a nameless, faceless, vapid, verbal diarrhea-spouting law school student.

Tarek. It was an aesthetic-sounding name. Well, Tarek, it looks like it's going to be quite a long semester.

I had no idea how right I was.

Our International Law professor was nice and very young. It was a depressing thought that my professor was younger than me. He was counsel at a prestigious law firm, and had clerked at the International Court of Justice.

I had briefly entertained the idea of working in public international law, but had come to the conclusion that that type of law was too aspirational, too pie-in-the-sky. The ICJ decisions had no enforcement mechanisms which, sometimes, was a good thing. The bottom line was that it seemed to be to be a complete waste of time.

Yesterday, the first day of class, the professor had talked about how the ICJ decisions were educational and instructive. It was a different way of looking at the law.

I preferred contracts, transactions, things I could sink my teeth into. I liked to get lost in the little details. Interpreting legal language was, on some level, not unlike my day job translating foreign-language documents.

Class had started. The Arab guy, uh, I mean, Tarek, was next to me, as usual. He was wearing a long-sleeve button-down shirt with the sleeves rolled up to the elbows, and jeans. God, he looked good. I didn't dare look too closely. I didn't want him to catch me looking at him. I took a breath and directed my attention to the professor at the front of the class.

About halfway into the class, I was beginning to lose my patience. The professor had been talking about, theoretically, whether or not the Supreme Court should formally consider ICJ decisions and international law and treaties in its decisions. Some lame punk was commenting that the Supreme Court should, in fact, do so. That made no sense, in my mind.

I could feel the situation degenerating quickly. The student was some girl I didn't know. She was saying, "All countries should respect international law. The U.S. shouldn't think that it can bully other countries."

I couldn't take it anymore, and Eric, Josh and Dinesh weren't here to keep me under control.

I finally spoke, without raising my hand, and all eyes turned on me.

"It's really a simple concept," I began, a bit sarcastically. "Let me explain. Foreign law has no place in a Supreme Court decision because it is not U.S. law. If Congress has implemented legislation adopting a treaty, then under the Constitution that treaty is the law of the land, and the Supreme Court can consider it. However, if the law in question is not part of U.S. law, that is, has not been adopted under the Constitution of the U.S., then the Supreme Court is wrong to even consider it. Could you imagine a situation where the highest Venezuelan court considers some random U.S. law? It would never happen. Why should the U.S. Supreme Court be any different?"

Several people were looking at me, but it didn't phase me. If anything, it fed me like oxygen fed a fire. This was how I rolled. My mother didn't call me Fire-breather for nothing.

I continued without pause. "Further, treaties are entered into by the executive branch and ratified by Congress. Therefore, if the Court considers and is persuaded by foreign law that has not been adopted in the U.S., it is unconstitutionally usurping power that, per the Constitution, has been delegated to the executive and legislative branches. Not to mention, just because a law is followed in other countries does not mean it is constitutional under U.S. law or should even be considered persuasive."

The professor then asked me, "What about international law and international custom? Should the Supreme Court consider that?"

"The answer is still no," I continued. "Unless the law has been adopted as U.S. law under the Constitution, i.e. by Congress and/or through a treaty under the constitutional process, the Supreme Court should not consider it."

The professor continued with his questions. "But what about the idea that all nations should respect this form of international order?"

"Practically, it will never happen," I said, self-confidently. "All nations act, and should act, based on their own national interests. As an American citizen, I want the U.S. government to act in American interests, not in the interests of foreign governments at my expense. And I certainly don't want the U.S. government to make American interests subservient to some international order that may not benefit me. Do you think the Mexican or Syrian governments care about U.S. interests or the interests of some international world order? In any case, it's predictable that all national governments act in their own interests. So we know what to expect. It's called being a rational actor, for those of you who don't remember your torts class."

Some other lame student in the first row spoke up then. "Well, the U.S. has more resources and should help other nations because it's lucky to have more resources and more money."

"Really?" I asked, incredulous. I was getting more worked up. "If the U.S. merely gives handouts to other nations, they won't be motivated to improve their situations. Anyway, do you think the people in African countries get any of the money and food the U.S. sends them? It all goes to the dictatorial governments. Throwing money at these countries does not improve the economic situation of those people."

Then I delivered the coup de grace. "And if we're going to use finances and resources as criteria for assisting other nations, the Arab nations have the most money due to the oil industry, so why don't they 'assist,'" using my air quotes, "as you said?"

There were a couple other Arab students in the class besides Tarek and Zara. They turned to look at me now. I also felt Zara's eyes bore into the back of my head.

A bunch of students were also looking at me with a look that said, "What the hell are you doing in this class if you think that way?"

I didn't care. To his credit, the professor was respectful and nodded. He went on to a different subject and my tension subsided. I started twirling my pen in my right hand; it was kind of a nervous habit. I was sort of a nervous person and was always moving, shifting my legs or moving my hands in some way.

Jesus. If this is the best this country has to offer, we are totally and royally screwed.

After International Law, I made it to Property on time. I struggled out of my backpack and sat down in a huff. Then I immediately stood up, since I would have to let Tarek pass by me to his seat anyway. I put my Property book down on the table and took out my laptop, plugged it in and turned it on.

Tarek arrived then and walked past me to his seat. He looked at me and nodded in acknowledgement. I glared at him. Dude, we're not friends, I thought. Then I realized that we had never properly introduced ourselves. As far as I was concerned, that certainly meant that I didn't have to acknowledge his presence if I didn't want to.

For once Eric, who was already sitting in his seat, didn't say anything. Thank God! I didn't think I could take much more of his crap.

Class had started and the professor was going over one of the cases that dealt with possession and property rights. I was still somewhat worked up from International Law class, and at the same time found it unbelievable that those students were all about reining in U.S. interests. Why? That made no sense. If you think the U.S. is so bad, then why aren't you criticizing other nations for their human rights abuses and treatment of women?

I tried to concentrate on Property now. It was difficult but I reviewed the portions of the case under discussion that I had highlighted while reading the day before.

The case we were talking about now was about a landowner who had contracted with another party for the latter party to have rights to drill on the land. That party had found some valuable minerals on the land, and the main issue was whether the landowner or the other party had rights to the minerals.

The professor called on Sorority Girl.

"Well," the girl began, "isn't this an unconscionable contract?"

"Oh my God," I said, exasperated. Apparently, I had said that loudly enough for everyone around me to hear, because Tarek, Eric, Josh, Dinesh and the guy sitting in front of me all turned around and looked at me.

"Isabeeeellll," Eric said softly, trying to calm me down.

I was not going to be able to hold my tongue. Especially since the girl speaking was SG, and she was a total waste of space.

"What do you mean?" the professor asked SG politely.

Geez, he is being way too polite. I clenched my left hand into a fist so hard that my nails were digging into my palm.

"Well, I mean," SG continued, "isn't it unconscionable that the second party made the landowner sign this contract that makes him give up any rights to minerals or oil or anything else found on his land?"

I couldn't hold it in any longer. "That question is completely irrelevant," I exclaimed, with disdain in my voice.

Both SG and the professor turned their heads toward me.

I continued. "You asked a contract formation question in a property class. For purposes of this course, and the exam, your question is completely irrelevant. First, the property exam is not going to include any questions on contract formation. We covered that in another class, maybe you don't remember. Of course, when you're a practicing lawyer in real life, you will have to recognize all of these issues but for purposes of this course, your question is a waste of time."

Take that, Tarek. If you didn't think I was a jackass before, you certainly think so now.

SG huffed but was silent. The professor seemed kind of dumbstruck, so I continued.

"But if you want to talk about contract formation, then by all means, let's talk about it. First, it's a quid pro quo situation, so, unless we have other information, which we don't here, both parties mutually agreed to a bargained-for exchange and the landowner got money for selling the rights. It's not like he gave them away. So we have no reason to think, based on the facts we have, that this is an unconscionable contract. Are you satisfied now?"

The professor finally found his voice. "Thank you," he said to me, in a way that closed the issue. Then he turned to SG. "Yes, we really have no indication that this was an unconscionable contract."

Toma, I mouthed silently.

The discussion wasn't over, however, because as soon as class ended SG came over to my desk. I had tried to whizz out of there but she caught me, backpack and purse in hand, walking away from my desk.

"You're a jerk!" she told me, as though that would have an effect on me.

I looked at her full in the face. I was a good three to four inches taller than she. "Tell me something I don't know."

"Why did you say all that?" There was venom in her voice. I noticed out of the corner of my eye that Tarek and my friends were all looking at us.

"Because someone has to keep everything on track. This is a top-tier law school and you're asking completely irrelevant questions. Jesus, how did you even get in here?!"

"You think you're always right!" she spat.

"No, I don't *think* I'm always right. I *am* always right." I was going to leave but I had one more thing to say.

"You don't realize it, but my existence and the way I do things, while unfathomable and reprehensible to you, are necessary." I glared at her. "Maybe one day you'll get it, but I'm betting against it."

I grabbed my backpack and headed out the door. Josh came with me and Eric and Dinesh were waiting for us.

"Isabel!"

I turned around, dumbstruck. It was Tarek.

I looked at him. "Yes?" I said, half-annoyed.

"You forgot your jacket."

He was still at his desk. He took my jacket off my chair and held it out to me as I walked toward him.

I was bothered at being so close to him. It was bad enough having to sit next to him in three classes fantasizing about kissing him.

I took my jacket from him, making a point of not touching his hand when I took it.

"Thank you." I managed a half-smile.

"Sure," he said.

I left then with my friends.

"Dude, harsh," Eric said.

"What? I thanked him!"

"No, not him! You were so harsh to Alyssa."

"Yeah, well, you know that's how I operate," I told him.

"I wouldn't expect anything less of you, Isabel," he said then.

What did *that* mean?

At home that night, I thought about Tarek again. I didn't want to like him. And I didn't want to be attracted to him. But he was making those two things exceedingly difficult for me.

FIRST WEEK: **SUNDAY**

It was finally Sunday. I had studied all day Saturday and a little Sunday morning. I was ready for a break.

I drove to Lara's apartment building and got there at around 11 a.m. Lara and her husband Patrick lived in old town Alexandria, quite a posh area with red-brick homes and downtown condos. There were also tons of restaurants. They both worked downtown, so that area was a good pick for them.

Lara and Patrick lived in an apartment in an upscale building. I found a parking space right outside.

Lara met me downstairs, at the main door of her building. We always greeted each other the same way, enthusiastically, as if we hadn't seen each other in a long time.

I hugged her tightly. She was the only thing keeping me grounded in this town.

Lara and I really didn't look a lot like each other. Lara was gorgeous, with our mother's beautiful face. She had blue-gray eyes, courtesy of Mom's Austrian father, and light brown/dark blonde hair. Her hair was thick and very curly. She often put lighter highlights in, and it looked incredible. She had an easy smile and her eyes danced all the time. She was a joy to be around. My mood always lightened instantly whenever I saw her.

"How are you doing?" she asked me. "How are classes going?"

"So far, so good," I told her, except for this hot guy who is sitting next to me in all of my classes. I had no doubt that by the end of the day, I would be telling her all about him.

"You look great!" I told her. "You highlighted your hair again. It looks awesome!"

"Thanks!"

We walked inside the building.

"So how does it feel to have a day off today?" I asked her.

"Oh my gosh, it feels great! I have to tell you about everything!"

Being with Lara instantly lifted my spirits.

We took the elevator to her apartment and Patrick opened the door for us.

I adored her husband. They had met in undergrad; Lara studied Microbiology and Patrick studied Computer Science.

Patrick's family was German, and he spoke German fluently. I kept telling him that I could get him translation work if he was interested. But he had enough to do with his full-time job in software and making sure my sister didn't go crazy during her residency.

Lara was doing her internal medicine residency, specializing in infectious diseases. She was great dealing with people. I was an introvert and she was a total extrovert, just like our mother. She thrived on being around people. I usually found being around people tiresome and energy-sapping, although even I had to admit that I felt good around my law school friends.

"That's because they know you, and they're on your intellectual level," Lara had told me.

Patrick was an introvert too, and he and I got along fabulously. Sometimes I wished that he had a single brother my age.

Patrick was pretty tall, about six feet, with dark brown hair and blue eyes. Typical German, I always said to him. He also had what I called the German walk. His walk was ramrod straight, like he was doing a march. I could pick him out from a crowd a mile away because of the way he walked. We laughed about it all the time. Despite his German roots, he was a good sport.

I greeted him now with a big bear hug.

"So are we going to the pool or what?" he said.

"Let's do it!" Lara said.

We had planned to sit outside by the condo pool since it was such a nice day. It was September and soon the weather would turn cool, at least, I hoped so.

We changed and grabbed towels and snacks. Lara lent me some girly magazine, the kind that I only read when I was at the pool or the beach with her. I noticed an article with the title, "How to Make a Man Fall in

Love with You" or some similar bullshit. I'm going to read this, I thought, for the hell of it.

We settled down by the pool, lying back in our chairs. The pool usually wasn't too crowded. I got the impression that this apartment building was populated by mostly old, retired people.

"Oh man, this is the life," I said. I was starting to totally relax.

"I talked to Mom today," Lara said then.

I knew what was coming. There goes my good mood.

"How is she doing?" I asked. I hadn't spoken to my mother in at least two weeks. She would want to know how law school was going. I also hadn't been to her house in at least three months. She only lived an hour away but the traffic on Interstate 95 was legendary, and sometimes it took me two hours to get to her house and two hours to get back. And that was unacceptable because I had designated the weekends as study time. I had no time during the week to read and outline, like the lame full-time students did.

I still felt bad about not going to see her more often. I loved her, but I couldn't stand the look she always gave me. She looked at me with sadness. I was sure that she was remembering my father, and why he had to die so young. And I was sure that she blamed me for it. I could see it in her face, in her eyes.

"She's doing all right," Lara told me. Then she leaned toward me conspiratorially. "Mark apparently talked to her about moving in together, or getting married."

"Are you serious?!" Mark was my mother's boyfriend. My mother never mentioned these things to me. Lara and Ariel were more her confidantes than I was. I had been very close to my father, and when he died I felt like part of my heart was torn out, the part that gave a shit about something. I figured that any world that could take him away from me was horrible. Given the general state of society, Millennials and all, I was right about how the world was. I was convinced that the only reason I was still here was to make sure that my mother and my sisters were okay. Everything else was gravy.

And I couldn't believe that Mark was talking to my mother about marriage. "What did she say?"

Lara smiled. "She's thinking about it."

"I can't believe it." I liked the idea of them being married. Mark was really good for her. He worried about her and was nice to her. And he loved her, I could tell. At first when he started hanging around, I told my Mom that he liked her. I knew then. A lifetime of nothing to do but observe people had made me pretty good at reading them.

"I know," Lara agreed.

"I think your Mom likes the idea of being independent more than anything," Patrick said then. "But I also think that she really loves him."

"Well, that would be awesome," I said. Everyone would be married except for me. Lara was married. Ariel was living with her boyfriend and, eventually, they would get married. Oh well, I had the feeling that that was how it was supposed to be. I guess I would have to be content with being the crazy aunt.

We talked for a while about Mom.

"And she said that she's a little worried about you," Lara said then, with an apologetic look on her face for bringing up the subject.

I sighed a long sigh. "What's new?" I asked sarcastically. "I should go out more, I should date, I should have more friends, I should study less, I should stop scowling, I should stop cursing, I should join a singles' group, I should have more fun, etc., etc."

Lara laughed. "Oh my God, I love you, Isabel."

I sighed again. "Honestly, Lara, what does she want to hear from me?"

"That you're happy."

"I *am* happy . . . sometimes," I hedged. Well, I thought, I'm happy in law school class, I'm happy when I'm dancing, and I'm happy very briefly when I fulfill a certain physical need once in a while.

"You know what she means," Lara said.

"Yeah, she means I would be happier with a man."

"It's not just a man, it's someone who cares about you, who is a partner for you," she paused, lowering her voice, "who gives you regular sex." She smiled.

"Oh geez," Patrick appeared a little embarrassed. "I'm going for a dip in the pool." He put his magazine down on the chair and walked toward the pool.

"I get regular sex," I told her.

"Please," Lara said, "how often does 'regular' mean?" She used my air quotes, and I couldn't help giggling.

"At least once or twice a semester," I said. Lara knew this; I didn't know why she was asking, probably to prove a point.

"And with random guys."

"Yeah, well—" I had nothing to add. She was right. It wasn't completely fulfilling. I had never said that it was. It just satisfied a primal need.

Then I thought of something. "It's better to be alone than with someone who is not a good fit for you."

"I agree," Lara said. "Mom's point is only that you don't try to meet people."

"Yeah, and she thought I would meet someone in law school, and now two years have gone by and I haven't met anyone. The reason is because there is no one worth dating in my class."

"I know. Maybe after school is done, you can join some social group, like Meet-up or something."

Melanie and I had talked about that. I liked hanging around Melanie, so maybe we could do that together. That was assuming that we both stayed in DC. Melanie planned to stay here. She wanted to work on the Hill. I was open to going anywhere. I had even thought about going back to Spain after law school, but the employment situation was so bad there that it probably wasn't a real possibility.

"Maybe you could meet someone you liked," Lara continued.

"I don't like anyone."

Lara smiled. "You like Josh and Eric."

"That's different. They're my friends, and I'm not interested in them romantically."

"I wonder why Josh is single," Lara said then.

I wondered too. "I think he hasn't met the right girl." He had dated a couple of girls since I had known him, but not seriously. "Plus," I added, "We don't really have time to date, those of us with jobs and in the evening program."

"Isabel, I really don't mean to give you a hard time. I know it's tough."

"Yeah, I know." I smiled at her. "Besides, I'm not looking, anyway," I added quickly.

"You know," Lara began. Oh no, I thought, she's up to something. I can see it on her face. "I think there's this guy in my residency class that you would really like."

"Not the blind date, Lara," I pleaded.

"No, no, I mean, we could all go out in a group or something."

"Maybe," I said. I was intrigued, though. "What does he look like?"

"He's attractive, I think he's like thirty or thirty-one—"

"Is he Latin?" I asked, a little bit hopefully.

"I knew you would ask that. No, but he's dark, dark hair, dark eyes. He's really smart."

"Is he doing infectious diseases like you are?"

"No, he's doing rheumatology."

"Interesting. Did he ask you to set him up or anything?"

"No, no, but I think he'd be open to dating."

Open to dating. I scoffed inwardly. I refused to scoff openly at my sister. I loved her and I knew she was trying to help. For some reason, coming from her it was okay. Coming from our mother, it was annoying.

"I promise that I will think about it," I told her.

She smiled broadly. Whenever she smiled like that, it lit up her entire face. Her eyes sparkled and grew huge.

Patrick came back then. "The water's great, you guys should totally go in." He wrapped a towel around himself and sat down.

"We will in a minute," Lara told him. Then she turned back to me. "So tell me about your classes so far."

I exhaled. I had been waiting for an opening. "Actually," I began, "I kind of—met this new guy."

Lara and Patrick both leaned toward me at the same time.

"New guy?" Patrick said, interested.

"I don't mean new to me—I mean—I don't mean that I'm interested in him or anything—I mean, new to the school."

"He's a first-year?" Lara asked.

"No, he must have transferred here. I've never seen him before. But he's in all of my classes. And he sits next to me in all of my classes. We've talked—I mean, we've exchanged words, really, only a couple of times. He knows my name."

"So he's piqued your interest?" Patrick asked me.

"Yes, a little," I admitted. "But we haven't formally met." Then I proceeded to tell both of them about everything that had taken place between Tarek and me since I had first seen him.

Lara was smiling, interested.

"Isabel, I think this guy is into you," Patrick told me.

I shook my head. "I don't know. I'm not sure."

"Are you interested in him?" Lara asked me point-blank. That was her style. She was logical, like me, and it was all about getting down to the bottom line.

Patrick leaned in a bit. "Yeah, has your type changed from the hot-blooded Latino to the hot-blooded Arab?"

I laughed. Patrick always made me laugh. I could see why my sister had fallen for him. "He seems nice," I admitted. I was still confused about seeing him at the Federalist Society meeting. There was something I couldn't quite put my finger on.

I had been telling myself that Tarek was just another annoying Millennial. But I was totally truthful with my sister; I always was. "I'm not sure."

Lara smiled, another broad smile.

"Well," she said, raising her eyebrows, "I haven't seen that expression in a long time."

I was confused. "What do you mean, that expression?"

"You're discombobulated."

I smiled. She was right.

SECOND WEEK: **MONDAY**

I was feverishly reading for my Criminal Procedure class. I had read the last two cases rather quickly the day before, and I was going over them again, highlighting and typing up notes. I tapped my pen on the book as I read, admiring the contrast with my dark grey nail polish. I didn't usually do frou-frou things like paint my nails, but I liked them dark. It had been a decent study break last night. After spending time with Lara and Patrick, I had studied a little more after dinner.

Lara had given me another huge hug when I had left her house the day before. I could tell that she wanted to spend more time with me, that she was worried about me, but her schedule was so crazy that we could only see each other once in a while.

I don't know why everyone is so worried about me. I've been able to manage for thirty-four years. Jesus. Sometimes my mother treated me like I was six years old. Why did she call Lara to complain about me? If she has something to say to me, then she can freaking call me and say it to me directly!

I sighed and pushed all thoughts of my mother from my head. I needed to concentrate. I didn't have time to be pissed off about her right now. There was plenty of time to be pissed off later.

Today I was wearing all black. I decided that I was mourning the decay of civilization as I knew it. I had on black skinny jeans and a black silk, sleeveless blouse with black flats. We didn't really have a dress code at work, and wearing jeans was acceptable. However, I usually tried to dress at least business casual. Today I had woken up late and had been in a rush. I hadn't slept that great the night before.

I was rather successfully tuning out all the chatter around me, people making plans for the upcoming weekend, showing each other Internet videos and engaging in vapid conversations. I heard a female voice say, "Are my breasts too big?"

No, breasts can never be too big, not if you're asking a guy.

"Hey, John!" some guy said into his phone, "Where are you at? We're waiting for you!"

Where are you *at*?! I died a little inside. The *at* is totally unnecessary. Oh my God, strike me down right here with a bolt of lightning or something.

Then suddenly a soft voice cut through all the chatter.

"Hey, Isabel."

I whipped my head up, looking over my open laptop.

It was Tarek.

Jesus. I hadn't even heard him approach.

I decided to take in the entire sight of him. Since he had addressed me directly, I finally had an excuse to take a good look at him. I decided afterward that it was kind of a mistake. Taking in his entire body, I could feel my nipples become instantly tender. Oh my God.

He was wearing a black T-shirt with dark jeans. His T-shirt hugged his chest, which, like his entire body, was lean and muscular. His short beard and goatee were neatly trimmed. He was certainly dark enough to be what Lara and Eric called "my type," although I usually went for Latin men. I guessed his age to be about 28, but his eyes held an experience that made him seem more mature.

He wasn't super-tall. I guessed that he was between 5 feet, 9 inches and 5 feet 10 inches. I was 5'6" so I more or less did a quick comparison. His curly black hair hung in carefully groomed, tight tiny ringlets around his face and almost down to his shoulders. He was incredibly sexy. He probably had to spend a lot of time on his hair, moussing it up, and that if he let it go it would probably be frizzy. His curls reminded me of Lara and her unruly hair, although her ringlets were more tousled and larger, and always framed her beautiful face perfectly. She was forever straightening it, but I kept telling her it looked gorgeous in ringlets, like Tarek's curls did now. I felt myself softening a little at the thought of my sister, but I steeled my reserve and plastered a semi-scowl on my face. My scowl and general surly attitude were my defense mechanisms. After enough unpleasantness, people generally left me alone. I liked it that way. Eric, Josh and Dinesh were somehow building up a tolerance for it. It was starting to piss me off. Lately, everything was pissing me off.

I had to admit, however, that I was intrigued as well as annoyed. Few people had the nerve to come and talk to me like this, with no warning.

I decided not to say anything at first. I just stared and raised my eyebrows.

He waited a good three to four seconds before he spoke. The left corner of my mouth started to go up into a smirk. Invariably, there were only two reasons a guy like this, a semi-stranger no less, would deign to talk to me. If he was going to miss class and wanted to get my notes, he was shit outta luck. And if he wanted a booty call, well, I wasn't quite sure yet how I would handle that. Little did I know, he wasn't going to ask me either of those things.

"Hi," he began, a bit shyly, "I'm Tarek. I'm in class with you."

As if I didn't know that. He had a deep voice. I also listened more closely to his accent than I ever had before. It was French, but like French "light," not the heavy French accent of someone who had lived in France his entire life and learned English in a classroom. But there was a hint of another accent, too, that I hadn't really paid attention to before. That must be the Arabic accent. I was a translator and a linguist, and this piqued my interest a hair. Still, he wasn't the first foreign guy I had ever met.

"Do you honestly think I don't know who you are?" I asked without smiling. I was annoyed, at his brazenness at approaching me and at the fact that my nipples were so tender. God, I hope they're not standing at attention right now. I couldn't risk looking down at them because then he would notice.

He paused for a moment, as if he hadn't expected such a surly response.

He looked at my laptop, then back at my face.

"Do you mind if I—"

I kicked the chair opposite me out from the table before he even finished the sentence. He seemed surprised but didn't lose his composure. I was grudgingly impressed by that.

He sat down opposite me in one quick, fluid motion. I would soon learn that he always moved like that, like he breezed through life always in a hurry. We were alike in that way. But I would have sat down more clumsily, moving the chair around, scooting it into the table. Not him. It was a small table and we weren't that far away from each other.

I closed my laptop without taking my eyes off him.

"Are you reading for Crim?" he asked.

"Talk," I said. "What do you want?"

"It *is* Isabel, right?"

I didn't see the point in refusing to tell him my name. He could look at the law school's student directory, and look at the people in his classes, and figure it out.

I crossed my arms. "Isabel Vilanova." I said my last name properly, with a Spanish accent. I couldn't stand Anglicizing foreign names.

"Are you Spanish?"

"Yes." In my experience, in the U.S. when most people say "Spanish," they meant "Hispanic." Either way, in my case the answer was yes.

He continued looking at me. A less secure person would be unnerved by it. However, this was not my first rodeo with a Middle Eastern man. I knew how direct they could be.

His next question was audacious, and surprised even me.

"So what's with all the black?" He was trying not to smile.

I almost smiled, a little smile, but I caught myself in time.

"What do you mean?" I asked back.

"That's very lawyerly of you," he continued, "answering a question with a question."

"Well, I *am* studying to be a lawyer, so . . ." I let the sentence trail off.

He continued. "The dark clothes, dark nail polish, dark lipstick—"

"Look who's talking," I waved a hand at his black shirt, interrupting him.

"You even dye your hair," he continued, ignoring me.

"No, I don't. I've never dyed my hair." That wasn't entirely true. I occasionally had it highlighted, but hadn't done so in a long time.

"That's your natural color?" He was incredulous.

"Yes." Where the hell was he going with this?

"It's almost as dark as mine."

"Yes."

"Are you always this—"

"Peeved off, surly?" I interrupted him.

"I was going to say hard to reach, but you're those things too." I could tell by the look in his eyes that he was intrigued.

I realized then that I was enjoying this repartee. It made me afraid. If I continued to talk to him, then maybe we would become friends. And if we became friends, then maybe I would end up falling for him. And if I fell for him, well who knew what would happen then? I didn't want that. I would rather remain closed off. Besides, I figured the four friends that I had plus my sisters were enough.

I decided then that this small talk had gone far enough. There were only ten minutes until class and now there was no way I was going to finish my two cases in time. The thought made me beyond annoyed.

I leaned forward on the table, still crossing my arms, closer to him.

"Look," I said slowly, "If you're going to ask me out, why don't you just do it, so that I can say no?"

He laughed softly and shook his head. At this point, almost any man would turn and leave in a huff. The fact that he didn't, and that he didn't seem put off, intrigued me more than anything else so far.

"I wasn't going to ask you out."

"Really? I'm disappointed." My voice dripped with sarcasm. Then I changed my tone. "Out with it. What do you want?"

"I wanted to know if you wanted to study together."

Well, that was a surprise. I honestly had not been expecting that. Everyone here knew me, or didn't know me. They either knew I was a loner and studied on my own or didn't notice me, and therefore wouldn't ask me to study with them anyway.

"What, like a study group?"

"Yes."

"Just me and you?"

"Yes."

"No." I said it without thinking, on automatic pilot. If I started to think about it, I would say 'yes' only because I was horny.

"No what?"

"You're slow today," I said. "No thank you, I'm not interested." Why would he think I would be, anyway?

"I've noticed you in class," he said then.

Of course he had. Who hadn't? I was on top of my game. I *lived* law school. I loved to argue and craved the intellectual stimulation.

I continued to stare at him.

"You're really smart and I thought that—we could help each other."

You mean *I* could help *you*.

"Flattery will get you nowhere," I said icily. It was a half-lie, though. I responded fairly well to flattery.

"I just transferred here," he said then.

"I know," I said.

"How would you know that?" he asked, a bit confused.

"So you think I'm a fucking moron?"

"I didn't say that." He was surprised, either at my tone or at my cursing, I didn't know.

Now I felt like I had to explain how I knew. "This is my third year here. I've never seen you before. And I would have noticed you," I added the last part without thinking. Smooth, idiot, I said to myself. "But you're not taking first-year classes, which tells me you've already taken them. Add that all up, and it leads to the fact that you transferred here."

He nodded slowly. "Very good."

He's arrogant. What a novel concept, an arrogant Arab man.

Tarek continued. "Look, I'm a good student. I'm—" he was struggling for the correct word and I felt a little bad for him for a split second, "—studious."

"I don't know that. I don't know *you*." I got the feeling that he was a loner, though, like me.

His eyes twinkled a little bit. He was thinking about something. I had the feeling he was still trying to convince me. It wouldn't work.

"Would it bother your boyfriend to study with another man?"

Jesus, who did this guy think he was? I smiled. "I don't have a boyfriend."

"Would it bother your husband?"

"Don't have a husband." I sighed. What the hell? It was time to cut this off. "Look, I study better alone. Thanks but no thanks."

"Are you sure?" he smiled again, flashing white teeth. He had exceedingly long eyelashes, and dark eyes, and he knew how to use them to his advantage.

I got pissed off then. "Look," I said, tossing my pen on the table. "You think that just because you're gorgeous you can come over here and convince me to do whatever the hell you want? Nice try, but I wasn't born yesterday. You can flash your eyelashes at me all you want, but the answer's still no."

He looked genuinely surprised. "Wait, you think I'm—gorgeous?"

"Of course. Any woman who thinks otherwise is a fool, and I don't suffer fools. Not in law school, not anywhere."

He didn't say anything.

"Speaking of fools," that may be a little harsh, but I had let this conversation go on far too long, "I need to finish these cases. Look, sorry, but I don't have time to babysit Millennials. We're done here. I'll see you in class."

To his credit he didn't looked pissed off or angry. He looked . . . in-trigued, like he was trying to figure me out.

Good luck. You'll need it.

He rose from the chair then. "See you in class, Isabel." He smiled and left.

I watched him go. When he got back to his table, where he had been sit-ting alone, he caught me looking at him. As he had been standing there, I had been raking my eyes over his body, from his shoes, very slowly over his lean legs, his stomach, his chest, his neck and his face. As my eyes reached his face, I noticed that he was looking at me. He had been looking at me the entire time! He smiled a broad smile. I looked away quickly but it was no use. He had seen me eye him like a piece of meat.

Damn! Damn him and his black curls and sultry smile. I buried my head in my Criminal Procedure book.

I couldn't help thinking that he was indeed as smart as he tried to make me think he was. In a short time, he had discovered a good amount of in-formation about me, including that I was a loner, and that I wasn't married and didn't have a boyfriend. Well played.

I couldn't lie to myself. He frustrated me. But I was intrigued.

I was in Crim Pro class ten minutes later, still thinking about the conversa-tion I had just had with Tarek. My head was still a little fuzzy from it. Why had he been so insistent?

Oh well. I put it out of my mind.

In Crim Pro, we were still talking about the Fourth Amendment. The cases for tonight were about whether the government needs a warrant under the Constitution for searches and seizures in certain types of situa-tions. First up were the cases about beepers.

The professor was speaking. "In *U.S. v. Knotts*—"

Beepers. Who the hell uses a beeper anymore? Maybe doctors, that's it. Wait, did Tarek just look at me? I wasn't sure.

"Ms. Vilanova!"

My head snapped up. The professor had called on me. Holy shit. The room was silent. I could hear a pin drop. What had he asked? Oh yeah, *U.S. v. Knotts*.

"The holding in the case was that tracking the beeper was not a search, so a warrant was not necessary," I said with determination.

"Yes, but—"

Oh no. Was that wrong?

"But I asked what the facts of the case were, not the holding," the professor said.

Oh.

I didn't know it at the time, but the next few seconds began a stream of events that would be life-altering for me.

"Let's ask the gentleman next to you," the professor said then. Then he looked at the seating chart in front of him and when I saw that he was struggling with the last name, I knew he was about to call on Tarek.

"Mr.—"

Tarek pronounced his last name for the professor. Oh, this should be good.

It was, but not in the way that I was expecting.

Tarek answered the question with so much confidence that I wanted to slap him right there.

"The facts here were that the police were tracking a chloroform container with a beeper inside, and the police had obtained the consent of the company that sold the chloroform to place the beeper there before the defendant picked up the container. Then the police tracked the defendant using the beeper."

The professor continued. "Did the Supreme Court find that this was a search?"

Tarek again answered confidently. "The Court did not have the occasion to decide that, because it determined that the defendant did not have standing in the case."

"Why not?" the professor asked.

"Because the owner of the property, in this case, the company, gave consent to have the beeper placed, and generally when that happens a third party, here the defendant, does not have standing to complain about that. But the Court did state that visual surveillance would have revealed the same facts about the defendant's movements, so in that case the beeper was no different from visual surveillance, suggesting that it may have been a permissible search."

"Very good."

Jesus Christ. Maybe he *was* smart. Or maybe he had been lucky.

I looked straight ahead at my laptop screen. I wasn't going to let this phase me. He had gotten me all worked up with his long eyelashes and his gorgeous smile, confusing me. I wouldn't let it happen again.

The professor was asking about the *U.S. v. Karo* case now. I raised my hand confidently.

But I'd be damned if Tarek hadn't raised his hand a split second before I did. Since no one else had raised their hands, the professor called on him. *Dammit.* My hand made a fist under my chin.

He was explaining the facts of the case now. "Here the police tracked a beeper in an ether can. A DEA agent had informed the police that the defendant had ordered ether and would use it for drug purposes, and the police obtained a court order authorizing installation, but the order was found to be invalid. The police then followed the defendant to his house and used the beeper to determine that ether was still in the house."

The professor then asked him about the holding.

"The Court found that it wasn't a search because there was no reasonable expectation of privacy. Placing the beeper didn't violate the defendant's Fourth Amendment rights since the can the beeper was placed in belonged to the DEA, so the Fourth Amendment wasn't implicated by the fact that the defendant received a can that contained an electronic tracking device. Police can theoretically track the beeper wherever it goes without a warrant, although the Court did state that police could not track the beeper inside a private residence without a warrant."

"And why is that?" the professor asked.

"Because the house is not open to visual surveillance as, for example, the whereabouts of a car would be."

"Right."

I was going to kill him. I saw Tarek look at me out of the corner of his eye, but I continued typing my notes. The fact that he looked at me suggested that he was putting on this show for my benefit. *This won't win you any points, dude.*

When class was over, I grabbed my stuff and pushed past Tarek's seat. I wasn't even going to give him the chance to say anything to me. What would he say, anyway?

I was silent on the metro ride home, sitting with my eyes closed so that the others wouldn't talk to me. I was in no mood for chatter.

After Eric left, Josh sat down next to me and remarked, "Interesting, huh?"

"What's interesting?" I asked, although I knew what he meant.

"That guy that sits next to you in class, he seems pretty smart."

"Tarek," I told Josh.

"What?"

I looked at Josh. "His name is Tarek."

"How do you know his name?"

"You find it so strange that I know someone's name beside yours?" I said sarcastically. I sighed, then dropped the sarcasm. "He introduced himself to me today, before class." I didn't tell Josh that before that I had looked him up in the law school directory. Telling Josh that would mean that I had some interest in Tarek, and I wasn't ready to admit that.

"He talked to you?"

"Yeah." I shrugged.

"About what?"

"Nothing important." I wasn't ready to divulge that Tarek had asked me to study with him.

"Oh." Josh's brows were furrowed.

I was perplexed. "Why do you look so confused, Josh?"

"No one ever talks to you. I mean, besides us." By "us," I knew he meant himself, Eric, Dinesh and Melanie. And indeed, for the most part, that was true.

"Well, I don't know what to tell you." That was an accurate statement. I didn't know what to tell him because I wasn't quite sure what was going on myself.

I was seething by the time I got to campus for International Law class on Wednesday. Tuesday night in Crim Pro had been a repeat of Monday night. I had raised my hand multiple times, only to be outpaced by the jackass sitting next to me. The cases had been really interesting too. I was livid at the memory of it.

"In the *Dow Chemical* case, the Supreme Court held that using a special camera to enhance images while performing an aerial overflight of an industrial plant was not a search, so that no warrant was required, although the Court left open the possibility that it would consider satellite imaging differently."

"In *Florida v. Riley*, the Court found no expectation of privacy, and therefore no search, when police used a helicopter hovering 400 feet above the property, noting that a member of the public could gain access to the same information by using aerial surveillance, and that no law prohibited that."

"The Fourth Amendment applies only to government actors, but, by extension, also applies to private actors acting at the direction of public actors such as the police."

Those were Tarek's highlights during Crim Pro on Tuesday. At the last comment, I had laughed and said, "Oh my God." At that point almost everyone around me kind of looked at me, or tried to without attracting the professor's gaze.

At the end of class, I was packing up to leave and Tarek had asked me if I was going to the metro.

"Not with you," I had told him, smiling.

Freaking arrogant jerk.

On the metro, Josh had said to me, "You were so cold."

"What are you talking about?" I knew, though. I was playing dumb.

"Why were you so mean to Tarek?"

"Dude, haven't you noticed? I'm mean to everyone." I scoffed.

"He probably likes you and he's trying to get your attention."

"Damn good way of doing it, too," Eric had said then. "Probably the *only* way to get her attention."

I had opened my mouth to say something but then couldn't think of anything to say.

Today, arriving at campus, I had replayed Eric's words in my head. It didn't matter. Whatever Tarek did, I was determined that it wasn't going to get my attention. The only thing that mattered as far as classes were concerned were my grades on the final exams. Everything else was superfluous.

As I entered the main doors and walked along the main hallway to get to the stairs, I ended up face-to-face with Tarek, coming from the other direction.

"Hey," he said.

I considered ignoring him, but I had been raised by an Argentine woman, and that would have been anathema to her. Not that I cared what my mother thought of me.

"Hey," I said back, before ducking into the stairs and racing up them as fast as I could go.

I got to class with ten minutes to spare. I took out a bag of almonds and started munching.

When Tarek got there, I stood up to let him pass by me to his seat without looking at him. He greeted Zara and they were chatting in Arabic. I ignored them and began reviewing my notes.

Class started, and the professor was talking about an article that we had read on nuclear testing. Specifically, the Marshall Islands had made an objection to the U.S. about the U.S. doing nuclear testing in the sea near the Islands. It had happened a long time ago.

I was remembering the case. The Marshall Islands were an island nation in Micronesia, but they were freely associated with the U.S., meaning that people from the Islands could live and work in the U.S. I think they were termed "U.S. nationals" instead of "U.S. citizens." At the time of this case, the Islands were under a Trusteeship Agreement with the United Nations, meaning that they were considered a U.N. trust territory. The U.S. was also responsible for the defense of the Islands at the time.

Well, good luck with that objection.

"Isabel?"

Jesus, the professor had just called on me. He had taken to calling the students by their first names. Actually, I preferred it that way. I was sure that I was older than he was, anyway.

"Sorry," I began, "you asked about the objection from the Marshall Islands?"

"Yes, what was the objection centered on?"

Fortunately, I knew the answer to that question. "The Marshall Islands objected on the basis that the testing impeded their fishing and boating."

"Right, so what is the relevant law here?" the professor continued.

"Well," I was thinking, "the Islanders argued their right to use their own territorial waters as well as fish and boat in waters that were not necessarily their own territorial waters under the principle of the freedom of the high seas, generally."

"Yes, certainly. And what other laws apply here?"

What other laws? International laws. This could be anything. I was drawing a blank. Shit, shit, shit. I didn't remember.

"Umm—," I began, trying to buy time.

But my effort was worthless, because once again Tarek raised his hand and the professor called on him.

He again spoke confidently.

"The Trusteeship Agreement that administers this territory is also relevant here, since it sets forth the powers and restrictions on what the trustees can do. The Islanders asserted their rights under the Trusteeship Agreement, such as the protection of economic development and health of their inhabitants. However, Article 51 of the United Nations Charter is also relevant, since it provides that nations have the right of self-defense, and the U.S. argued that under this right it was able to do the nuclear testing. Also, at the time of these events the U.S. was responsible for protecting the European countries after World War II, so the American nuclear tests were for the defense of Europe as well as the U.S."

I couldn't resist sneaking a look at him. He was looking ahead and grinning. I was thinking that it was totally worth an assault and battery charge to slap that grin off his damn face. Then I reconsidered. It would be even more difficult to get my law license with that charge on my record, and with tons of witnessing law students to boot.

Man, that very fact saved him right there.

The professor went on, but he didn't call on me for the rest of the class. I was both relieved and angry about that. Was he not calling on me because I hadn't known the complete answer?

When class was over, I shoved my laptop into my backpack aggressively. Then I forced myself to calm down. Letting people see me worked up only meant that I cared about being shown up in class. When I didn't. Well, I actually *did* care, but I would be damned if I would let anyone know that.

I considered talking to Tarek for a second. I actually considered taking him up on his offer to study together. Then I shook my head.

What was I thinking?

I left and went to Property class.

Property class that Wednesday evening was a repeat of Crim Pro the day before. Tarek was called on and went out of his way to demonstrate his knowledge of the laws regarding finders and lost and abandoned property.

Show off, Eric had messaged me.

Yes, but he's doing this for a reason, I ruminated.

Then Tarek constantly raised his hand to answer questions.

Dude, Eric messaged me then, if he's going to be doing this all semester, we're going to need to grab drinks before class.

I couldn't help giggling at that. When I did, Tarek looked at me, undoubtedly thinking that I was giggling at him. Let him think that I was then.

"Ms. Vilanova."

Aw shit. The professor had said my name, but I had been half-listening and there had been no question with it.

"Yes, sir," I said respectfully.

"Did you have a comment?"

Oh, I get it, because I had giggled.

"No, sir," I said. Then I went back to taking notes. It galled me that I was writing what Tarek had said in class in my notes, but he had been spot on with the law.

Wait a second. *He had been spot on with the law.* He really did know this stuff. You couldn't fake it. You could fake stupid but you couldn't fake smart.

An idea was forming in my mind then. But I wouldn't see it out tonight. Tomorrow.

International Law class had been a repeat of the day before, with Tarek spouting his knowledge like some law-school oracle.

Since there weren't that many students in that class, it wasn't uncommon for almost everyone to have a chance to speak during a session. I didn't volunteer that day, and the professor only called on me once. Luckily, I had a sufficient answer.

However, Property class that day was almost excruciating.

The professor was talking about recording statutes. They applied when different people claimed the same piece of land. The courts applied them to figure out who had legal title to the land. Although I had read the text for class that night, my head was spinning.

"Ms. Vilanova," the professor had called on me. I had had my hands against my head and was staring at my laptop screen. Jesus. All of my professors must have gotten together and agreed to royally screw me this week. I had been called on in *every* class.

He continued. "What is the first-in-time rule?"

OK, I knew this. "As demonstrated in the *Tapscott* case," I began, "first-in-time is a common-law rule; it's basically first-in-writing, meaning that whoever the property was transferred to first, that person is the legal owner of the property, assuming that the person transferring the property had legal title to it at the time it was transferred.

"Right."

Phew.

But he wasn't done. "So, the recording acts—"

I didn't speak because he hadn't asked a question.

"What do the recording acts do?"

I knew that, too. "They are exceptions to the common-law first-in-time rule. Each jurisdiction could have its own recording act, and you would need to read it to see how to apply it."

"Right. So in a race jurisdiction—"

Oh God. Please don't ask me to explain the different types of recording acts.

"—what's the rule?"

I spoke slowly to give myself time. "The rule is—that the grantee, the person receiving the property, must be the first to record his interest. That is, whoever records the deed first with the local government gets title to the land, even if that person received the land after the land was transferred to someone else."

"Yes."

I exhaled to lower my pulse. This was so nervewracking.

"And so what does it mean when a jurisdiction is a pure notice jurisdiction?"

I got this, I told myself. I read from my notes. I would trip over my tongue if I tried to explain it in the abstract, so I used an example.

"For example, if A transfers land to B, and later A transfers the same land to C, the subsequent purchaser, here C, gets the land if he had no notice of conveyance to B, the first subgrantee."

"That's right," the professor said.

Toma, Eric had messaged me.

But my high at getting those answers right was short-lived.

"And what about a mixed race/notice jurisdiction?" the professor asked me then.

What about it? I thought.

"Umm—," I had struggled with this one. "When the subgrantee—"

I was taking too long. I would say who raised his hand now but by this point it's freaking obvious.

Much to my dismay, Tarek explained what a mixed race/notice jurisdiction was to perfection.

My head was spinning. To add insult to injury, upon further questioning by the professor, Tarek also explained what actual, constructive and inquiry notice meant; and also demonstrated his knowledge about the shelter rule, which applied in notice and race/notice jurisdictions.

What made me even angrier than Tarek showing me up in class was the fact that I was rapidly taking notes on what he was saying because everything that he was saying was right.

When class was over, everyone was getting up to leave. Tarek stood up and closed his laptop, putting things away in his bag.

He didn't look at me; he was looking down as he packed up, but I glared at him anyway. My expression was venom, bordering on loathing but with a touch of awe. I couldn't believe it. Who the hell did this guy think he was?! Did he want to get me into bed that desperately? Or did it make him feel superior to show any female that he was better than she was?

To their credit, Josh and Dinesh didn't say anything. I could see Josh looking at me out of the corner of his eye, half-smiling, or maybe half-smirking. But he kept quiet.

I stood up quickly, almost aggressively. As I did so, Tarek turned and looked at me. People, Dinesh included, wanted to leave the row, so I stepped out of the way and let them pass. I stood in front of Tarek, at the end of the long desk. I stepped closer to him, so that only he could hear. He was still looking at me intently.

I crossed my arms, tapping my dark nails on my bicep in my pent-up anger. "You're a typical Arab man, you know that?" was the first thing that came to mind.

"How's that?" He seemed wary.

"Freaking arrogant, like any other Arab man I've ever met. You think you're better than everybody else, don't you? Driving your fucking BMW and wearing your tailored shirts that you probably bought with your family money!" I kept my voice low but there was anger in it.

He seemed shocked. "*I* think I'm better than everyone else? Tell me, Isabel, why are you so intent on shutting everyone out?" He was calm, so calm that it made me practically rabid.

He knew me. I didn't know how, but he had figured out a little bit. I was going to shut this line of inquiry down and fast.

"So were you fucking serious about studying together or not?" I asked him, arms still crossed. The angrier I got, the faster the f-bombs dropped.

He looked like he wasn't sure what he should say. He also looked a little shocked every time that I cursed. "Yes," he said carefully.

"So do you still want to or not?"

"Yes."

"All right." I was going to call his bluff. What the hell? At worst, it would be a disaster and I would go back to studying by myself. At best, he would help me with the material, maybe do some outlining for me, and I would have a better chance of pulling another 4.0 this semester. Maybe if it didn't work out, I could still manage to get a good lay out of it.

"So," I continued, still angry but controlling my voice, "are you busy this weekend?"

"No," he said. I could tell that he was still wary of me.

"So let's meet downstairs, at the main entrance, at 10:00 on Sunday morning."

"10:00?"

I leaned my upper body toward him a little bit, arms still crossed. He seemed taken aback by the gesture, because he instinctively leaned backward a little.

"Yeah. Why? Is that too early for you? Will you still be recovering from your orgy on Saturday night?" My voice dripped with sarcasm, so much so that I was surprising even myself.

He laughed then. "No, that's fine. I'll be here."

"And that doesn't interfere with your religious observances?" I asked, still sarcastic.

He was still smiling. "No."

I held out my hand.

He looked at my hand, then looked at me.

"Give me your phone," I said icily.

He looked a bit suspicious, but he slowly handed me his phone. As he did so, our fingers touched. I scrolled through the options and got to the mailbox. I added my cell phone number and handed his phone back to him. "Here's my number. Call me if you can't make it."

"Do you want my number?" he asked me, and I saw his eyes light up a little.

I opened my mouth in a hurry to say no, but then reconsidered. I could always cancel if I had second thoughts.

"Yeah," I said nonchalantly, as if I didn't care either way. I took out my phone.

He told me his number and I recorded it.

I put my phone away. Josh was waiting for me near the door, chatting with someone.

I relaxed a little bit, then looked back at Tarek. "OK, well then, I'll see you Sunday. We'll do Crim, then Property. So read the cases for next week and we'll outline them. Then if we have time, we'll start outlining all the other cases we've read so far. Pay attention to the main rules and the facts. And remember, I don't suffer fools."

"OK," he smiled. "See you Sunday, Isabel."

I shook my head, unbelievingly, and left him there.

I joined Josh and we walked to the metro.

"What did you say to him?" Josh asked on the way.

I suddenly remembered that I hadn't told Josh about Tarek asking me to study with him a few days ago. I decided to give him the bottom line.

"We're going to get together this weekend to study."

Josh laughed.

I gave him a what-the-hell look.

"So you're into him?" he said incredulously.

"I didn't say that."

"You didn't answer my question."

I breathed out a long breath. "No." It was only a half-truth. I thought Tarek was amazingly sexy, and he had an energy about him, like in his head the lights were always turned on. Unlike so many of the jocks I saw around here. I was beginning to become very intrigued about him. But for now I was only going to pick his brain. I had no idea what I was actually getting myself into.

"We're only studying together," I told Josh.

"For now," Josh smiled.

For now, I thought.

For the rest of the week, I couldn't get Tarek out of my head.

SECOND WEEK: **SUNDAY**

It was 9:45 the following Sunday, and I was sitting on a sofa at the main entrance of the law school. The campus was deserted. I had known it would be. It was way too early in the semester to be outlining, or studying at all, really. I always started early, so I could cram as much as possible into my outline, and didn't have to scramble so much at the end. On an exam, if I could include a few more ideas, a little bit more analysis, or throw in a couple of extra, obscure cases, I could get some more points, and that might be the difference between an A- and an A. In essence, my studying strategy was an all-guns approach.

I was wearing dark boot-cut jeans today, with a form-fitting black V-neck T-shirt. I was also wearing ankle boots with a small heel. The best thing about these boots was that they had silver zippers on the side, and that made them look a little biker-chic. I wore light makeup and mascara, my absolute favorite facial accessory. I wore my hair down and straight, and my sunglasses were pushed back on my forehead; I liked to use them as a headband.

I had my laptop open and was sipping coffee from my thermos, reviewing the Crim Pro cases. I loved that class. I was flipping through the most recent case I had read when my phone rang. It was Tarek.

If he bails on me this late, I'll kill him! Freaking undependable, snotty, arrogant Arab!

"Yeah?" I answered half-pissed off already.

"Hey, Isabel. I'm at the Starbucks next door. Do you want anything?"

"Oh," my tone changed. I felt a little bit like a jerk. "No thanks, I'm good."

"OK, I'll see you in a few minutes."

"OK, bye." We hung up.

A few minutes later I saw him walk up the steps in front of the main entrance. I pretended not to notice him when he walked in the door. I kept my head buried in my book. I felt a momentary panic. What the hell was I doing? I didn't know this guy at all. This was totally unlike anything I would ever do. I kept my family and close friends close and everyone else miles away. What had possessed me to meet with him like this, just the two of us? It hadn't been logical at all. Oh my God, I am losing my mind.

Well, if I was in fact losing my mind, I reasoned, then I needed him to help me get good grades this year and the next. That made sense.

I looked up as he approached. He moved very quickly, and almost silently. It was unnerving. This guy had Type A written all over him. I would know. I'm a Type A person.

"Hey." I inclined my head without smiling.

"Hi," he smiled. He looked great in jeans and a grey T-shirt. His hair fell in messy curls around his face. He must have tried to tame it, but it hadn't really worked. He had also shaved this morning, I could tell, and his goatee was trimmed. I felt myself softening a little bit. Then I took a deep breath and steeled myself.

"How are you?" he asked, still smiling.

"I'm all right." I sipped my coffee. Then a musky scent reached my nostrils. His aftershave smelled really good. Under normal circumstances, I would have shrugged this off. But since the beginning of the semester, everything had seemed a little off. I opened my mouth.

"Are you wearing cologne?" I asked, almost accusingly.

"No," he said; he didn't seem bothered by my question. "Probably my aftershave." He looked at me. "Does it bother you?"

"No, it's just—" I felt like I should say something, like I needed to set the stage. I was trying to figure out how to word it.

"What?" he asked. He wasn't upset, or embarrassed; he seemed curious.

"I mean, you know this is just studying, right?" I paused, searching. "I can help you with your grades and you can help me with mine. This is a mutually beneficial thing. That is all it will be. You get it?"

The absolute last thing I needed was another Arab man coming on to me and badgering me. They were so direct and insistent. I had had enough of that at work and enough of it last year (it was a story I didn't care to repeat). The only reason I was even going to hang out with Tarek was because he seemed smart enough to help me keep up my 4.0.

He nodded and half-smiled. He seemed a little embarrassed at first, but he quickly regained his composure. "Yes, no problem." His expression was neutral, but for a split second I saw something in his eyes, something I didn't have time to fully register.

I relaxed a little. "OK, then," I said. "If it's all right with you, I thought we could stay down here, no one will be around."

"Sure, no problem," he said. His faint French lilt came through a little bit. He sat down on the other end of the sofa, put his tea on the table and took out his laptop. "No one studies this early in the semester. Josh said that you're pretty much the only person who does."

I raised an eyebrow, annoyed. "Josh told you that, huh?" I wondered what else Josh had told Tarek about me. "When did you talk to Josh about me?"

"I've seen him around several times."

Obviously he had seen Josh without me, to be able to grill him.

"He also said you had the best grades of anyone he knew," Tarek added.

"I don't see how he would know that. I never tell anyone about my grades." I made a mental note to kick Josh's ass.

Tarek shrugged. "Well, he seems to think that, anyway." He looked at me and smiled. Stop smiling! I thought.

Tarek continued speaking about non-law-school-related stuff, much to my annoyance. "He also said that Vilanova is a Catalan name, not Spanish, and that you speak Catalan." He looked really interested now. Did he even know where Catalan was spoken?

"Yes, that is true." I made another mental note to kick Josh's ass so hard he would forget he had other body parts.

"So you're from Barcelona?" Tarek asked. OK, so I guess he did know where Catalan was spoken.

I put my coffee down. "Not exactly," I answered cautiously.

"So where are you from?"

I hesitated, thinking how to answer. I didn't know.

"It's a loaded question."

"Sorry?" Tarek looked a bit confused, and his brows furrowed together.

"I don't know how to answer that," I told him, hoping it would close the discussion.

It didn't.

"Well, where were you born?" Oh my God, this guy didn't stop!

"Virginia," I answered honestly.

"Where are your parents from?" Tarek pressed gently.

I figured I would get this over with so we could get down to business, studying, that is.

I let out a long breath that I had realized I had been holding for several seconds. "My father was from Barcelona. He moved to the US as an adult."

"Was?" Tarek asked.

Damn him for noticing the verb tense.

"He died a long time ago." And I couldn't stop it. And I think about that fact every day of my life.

Tarek looked instantly concerned, and there was something else in his eyes that I didn't understand.

"Isabel, I'm so sorry."

"It's OK," I said honestly. "It was a long time ago." I was a jackass but even I wasn't enough of one to make him feel badly about that. I changed the subject quickly.

"My mother is from Argentina; she immigrated here with her family when she was a teenager. My parents met here."

He nodded, apparently interested in this family history. "So you speak Spanish and Catalan?"

"Yes, I spoke Spanish at home with my parents. But my paternal grandfather's family speaks Catalan and I speak Catalan with them. They all live in or near Barcelona." Then I added, without really knowing why, "I also speak French."

"Really?" Tarek smiled, and his entire face lit up. "I speak French."

"I know," I said without thinking.

"How did you know that?" he asked, curious.

"So you think I'm a moron?" I countered.

"I didn't say that." He looked confused again.

"I'm kidding," I assured him, but I had only been half-kidding. "It's your accent. You have a little bit of a French accent."

"No one ever picks up on that," he said, impressed.

It's because you look Arab, I thought, and most people don't associate French with that, although so much of the Arabic-speaking world was controlled by the French at some point, and French is still widely spoken in those areas. It's because no one thinks anymore; people stereotype constantly because it's easier. It's the same with me, people look at me and see light skin and think *gringa*, despite my almost-black hair and attitude.

"I just—," I was trying to figure out how to get back to the subject of studying for Crim Pro, "I have an ear for languages. I pick them up really easily." I paused, wondering how much to divulge. "My day job is a translator. *Je travaille comme traductrice, comme linguiste.*"

From then on, we spoke sometimes in English, sometimes in French, depending on who was around and what we wanted to say.

Tarek continued to appear really interested.

"So how did you learn French?" he asked. "You have a great accent."

"I started taking French lessons when I was really little, and I just continued them. My parents noticed early on that I loved languages. My mother had these French tapes that I would listen to. I've also traveled throughout France and I lived in Paris for a while."

"How often do you go to Barcelona?" He was too inquisitive.

"Once a year, or once every two years. I worked in Barcelona, too, for a few years." I paused for a second. "Look," I told him, "We should start with the cases, or else time will fly by." I was also thinking of my stomach, and how long I would last until lunch.

He smiled. "Don't you want to know where I'm from?" He was leaning on his side against the couch, a little playful, his eyes twinkling. That was a characteristic typical of Frenchmen, I noted. It was a clue that confirmed what I had been thinking about recently.

I looked directly at him. "I know where you're from."

He looked at me incredulously. "How would you know? Have you, what do you call it, cyberstalked me?" He was still smiling. Damn his attractive smile. It was more difficult to think about studying now. And damn the fact that I wouldn't get involved with him. I didn't need another Middle Eastern man hounding me. I would have to admire Tarek from afar.

"I figured that out without cyberstalking you, don't worry." That was a true statement, I noted. I had in fact cyberstalked him, but hadn't really found anything. I had been thinking about where he was from and had narrowed it down to a pretty educated guess.

"Your father is French and your mother is Lebanese," I began. His eyes widened and he looked impressed again.

He didn't say anything so I continued. "It's not that hard to figure out. Your last name is French. You are obviously," I made a waving gesture with my hand from top to bottom, "of Middle Eastern descent. You're about—," I took a wild guess, "Twenty-eight years old. You may have been born in Lebanon." I was thinking out loud now. "But I'm guessing your parents either met in France or met in Lebanon and then left at some point. You were born in France around 1980 or 1981, but you spoke Arabic at home, at least with your mother." His eyes widened further, and I felt that I had to explain. I was able to totally nerd out on him, linguistically, that is.

"You speak with a faint French accent, but speaking Arabic requires the production of several different sounds. Native Arabic speakers are usually able to pick up other languages with ease, without a really strong accent. Native French speakers, who don't speak other languages, unless they're really gifted, always speak foreign languages with a really heavy French accent." I paused, sizing up what he thought of my diatribe at this point. I wasn't sure. "So I'll say that you grew up in France, speaking French with your father and Arabic with your mother, but came to the US with your family when you were . . . about . . . thirteen years old."

"Fifteen," he corrected.

"Close enough." I smiled, a genuine smile. In fact, I felt that it was the first genuine smile I had ever given him.

He was still sizing me up. "That's impressive."

"I told you; I'm not a freaking moron." I smiled again. I tempered my cursing a little bit because I had the feeling that he didn't like it, not that I cared about what he liked.

"But how did you know that my mother was from Lebanon? She could have been from another Arabic-speaking country."

"That was just a good guess," I admitted. "Lebanon is the most liberal of the Middle Eastern countries. If your mother married a non-Arab, her family is probably Christian or very liberal Muslims, likely from Lebanon. Lebanon is also a former French colony. French is still taught there, even today. France sent their military over during the war, so it makes sense that your father met your mother there. Likewise, if your mother's family fled Lebanon before your mother met your father, it makes sense that they would go to France, where they spoke the language and could get visas. So which was it?"

"They met in Lebanon," he answered without missing a beat.

"So your father was French military?"

Tarek nodded.

"Very interesting," I said, meaning it. It was also incredibly romantic, how his parents met, I surprised myself by thinking.

"But you're wrong about one other thing," he said then.

"Oh?" I raised an eyebrow and crossed my arms. "What would that be?"

"I'm twenty-nine years old, not twenty-eight," he smiled.

"That's irrelevant." I paused, looking at him. I couldn't help smiling again, another genuine smile. He seemed to relax a little bit more.

"So are we done with introductions now and can we please start studying?"

"Sure." His grin was from ear to ear. "Since you said 'please.'"

My initial impression about him after our first conversation, when he had asked me to study with him, had been correct. He was intelligent, sharp and quick-witted. I found myself trying to stay two to three steps ahead of him in my analysis of the cases. He had actually done the reading, too, and had prepared notes. That was exactly how I studied. I said as much.

"Oh my God," I said, grinning in spite of myself and shaking my head.

"What?" Tarek asked.

"I think you study exactly like I do."

"Really?" He was smiling now too.

"Yeah, I—everyone thinks I'm crazy because I try to read the cases beforehand, and then take notes on the important stuff, the rules and how the cases are differentiated from other cases that apply the same rules, and then take notes in class, and then go over my class notes and my reading notes to make sure my outlines are as all-encompassing as possible."

Tarek nodded, seemingly impressed. But I wasn't sure if he really was impressed or if he was humoring me.

"I usually take notes when I read too," he said. "Not too detailed, just the main points, like you said." He paused. "You have time to do all that with a full-time job?"

I didn't bother asking him how he knew I had a full-time job. He saw me in class in my work clothes and must have seen my work placard hanging around my neck, that ubiquitous Washington, DC accessory. Besides, I had already told him that I worked as a translator.

"I try. I don't have much else to do, anyway." I smiled a little.

"So you're in the part-time program then?"

"Uh, yes, but that's a misnomer. My friend and I call it the 'evening program.' Because the 'part-time' students," using air quotes for 'part time,' "only take one less class than the full-time students."

"Wow, that's—impressive." He paused. "It's a lot."

I shrugged. "I like to be busy."

I was hungry and took out a bag of *frutos secos*. I offered some to Tarek and he took some, thanking me.

Frutos secos was an interesting term, I pondered for a moment. It was the Castilian Spanish term for "trail mix," but the Spanish always translated it as "dried fruits," which wasn't accurate, since it was made up of nuts, raisins and other varied snacks, which perhaps included, but not necessarily, some actual bits of dried fruit. But "dried fruits" was a poor translation. It was an illustration of how you couldn't translate everything literally.

"What are you thinking about?" Tarek asked me then.

"Nothing," I shrugged.

"Oh, you looked like you were thinking about something."

I shook my head, a little unnerved.

"Are you on a journal too?" Tarek asked me, shaking me out of my thoughts.

Ah, the law school journals and the associated hierarchy that came with them. Everyone, or almost everyone, aspired to be on "Law Review," the university's main law journal. Being on a journal meant that you spent most of your time checking citations and doing other similar tasks. It was a huge time suck. It did, however, mean that you got to write a "note," that is, an article, which was usually published. The publication was certainly a feather in your cap. A 'lesser' journal was good too. All law firm recruiters, and all recruiters in general, thought it a positive thing for a student to be on a journal.

"No." I smiled all of a sudden. "I'm too old for that shit. Checking citations and doing grunt work." I paused. "What about you? What journal are you on?"

"I'm not on one. I transferred so I can't be on one."

"Oh, yeah," I said. I couldn't tell if he was glad or disappointed that he wasn't on a journal. I figured that if he was half as ambitious as I was, he was somewhat disappointed that he wouldn't be able to put that on his resume.

"I think you should consider yourself lucky. Someone as intelligent as you should not waste your time with it."

He didn't say anything. I reconsidered what I had just said. "I'm not saying that people on journals aren't intelligent," I explained. "But it's mostly menial work, and I'm not sure how intellectually stimulating it is, other than writing the note. I mean—for people who went to law school right after undergrad and haven't really worked, it's a great thing to have on their resume." I didn't want to come off as snobby. Then I wondered why I cared about how I appeared to this man.

"Oh, I agree," he said then. "I was just surprised that you called me intelligent." He smiled, piercing me with his eyes.

My cheeks were suddenly hot. Oh my God, I *had* referred to him as intelligent. With my light skin, I knew my cheeks were probably really red by now.

But I played it down. I leaned back nonchalantly. "You know that."

"Know what?"

"You know that I think you're intelligent. Because I would never agree to study with someone who wasn't."

He smiled again.

I looked at my watch. It was 12:45.

"Can we do one more hour?" I asked him.

"Sure."

"Do you mind if we do Property?" I loved our Crim Pro class, but I needed more help with Property, not that I would ever tell him that.

"Whatever you want." He smiled.

Whatever I want. I smiled inwardly.

"Well, I want a lot of things." Wait, what? Why would I say that?

"Well, which of those things can I help you with?" He said immediately. His smile appeared flirtatious now.

OK, I would put an end to this.

"Right now, with adverse possession." I smiled outwardly now.

"OK," Tarek said.

I'd like to adversely possess *him*, I thought. Then I giggled at my own lame joke.

"What's so funny?" Tarek asked.

"Nothing," I said. "Like I said, adverse possession."

We were packing up to leave. "Did you drive here?" I asked Tarek.

"No, I took the metro."

I was surprised. "But there's always track work on the metro on the weekends. And this weekend there aren't any parades or roadblocks or anything. It's easier to drive."

"Yes, but my car is at the mechanic. Hopefully, I can pick it up tomorrow."

"Your BMW?"

"Yes, it's about twelve years old. My uncle bought a new car recently and he gave me that one so I would have a car when I came here."

I suddenly remembered my comment last Thursday about him owning a BMW. I felt bad.

We picked up our stuff and began to walk toward the main door.

"So where did you transfer from?"

"I was in Miami." He told me the name of the school.

"So why come to DC? I mean, that school is a really good one. And besides, you can't beat the weather down there."

"I wanted to be in DC. I thought I might want to do something involved with politics."

Oh, great. I thought. One of *those* people.

"I'm sorry to tell you, but you can't be president since you're a naturalized citizen."

"I know." He looked at me, and then realized that I was suppressing a smile. "Oh, you're joking."

"Well, yes, but that's also a true statement. It's in the Constitution. Maybe you haven't read it. I have a copy at home I can lend you."

"Ha ha," he mocked me. "I *have* read it."

"Well, sometimes I think a lot of the people in this country haven't."

"That may be true," he agreed, but I wasn't sure if he was saying that just to agree with me.

"But you would have read it because you're in the Federalist Society," I said a bit playfully.

"Yes, that's right." Then he added, "I was surprised to see you there."

"I was surprised to see *you* there," I countered.

We were outside. I made an executive decision. Whether it was a bad one or a good one, I couldn't say.

"Look, can I give you a ride home? I have my car here. It'll take you forever on the metro with the track work they're doing."

He looked at me and seemed to be weighing something in his mind.

"You don't mind?"

"No. Seriously, I don't mind."

"I would appreciate that."

"It's OK. My car's on this block." I had managed to find a prime parking space.

We walked to my car in silence. I drove a black compact car, easy for jetting around the city. In my true fashion, I had my vocal bumper stickers all over the back, including my NRA sticker and another that read "Proud

Conservative." The Millennials hated them. Most of the ones I knew were intolerant of anyone with views that diverged from their own.

I went directly to the trunk and opened it.

"Here," I told Tarek, "you can put your stuff in here."

"Thanks," he smiled.

We got in the car. "Pentagon City, right?" I asked as I started the car.

"How did you know where I live?"

"I saw you leaving the metro the other night, remember? I assume that's where you live."

"Oh, yeah." He smiled.

"Geez, you make me sound like I'm stalking you," I said. "Honestly, I have much better things to do with my time." Then I added, as if an afterthought, "And I have no trouble getting men anyway. I don't need to stalk them."

"Oh, really?" He seemed interested.

I shrugged. I pulled out from the parking space and got going.

I could feel electricity in the air; the silence seemed to underscore it.

Tarek touched the crucifix I had hanging from my rearview mirror. It was made of wood; I had bought it in Barcelona a while ago.

Lara had laughed at me about it. "You're so Latina," she had said. But I liked having it there.

"You're Catholic?" Tarek asked me.

"Well, I was raised Catholic. Both my parents are."

"So you go to church?"

"I go to church regularly." That was a true statement, but not entirely. I was suppressing a smile.

"If you ever want company, I'll go with you. I should go more often."

I was shocked. Was he asking me to go to church with him? What the hell? Sometimes I thought I had this guy figured out, but other times I felt that I was totally off base.

"You're Catholic?" I didn't believe him.

"Yes," he nodded.

Wait, that made some sense, I thought. His French father would most likely have been Catholic, although most French people didn't really practice as far as I knew.

"So your mother is Christian too?"

"Yes. Some people in her family are Christian, and some are technically

Muslim but they don't really practice." He looked at me and smiled. "Like you said."

We sat in silence for a moment or two. I was thinking.

"Well, thanks for the offer, but I only go to church twice a year," I told him.

"I thought you said you went regularly."

"I do. I go every Christmas and Easter, regularly."

I couldn't help laughing at my lame joke.

"Oh, my God," he said, looking out the window and shaking his head.

"But I should go more often. Besides, I haven't been to confession since I was like twelve years old." I had so much to confess, the priest would probably make me say like five hundred rosaries. I was dreading it.

"I haven't been in a long time either," Tarek said.

There was silence for a couple more moments. I was still trying to figure him out.

Then Tarek spoke. "So are you deliberately provocative?"

I didn't understand. "What do you mean?"

"All your bumper stickers. It's like you're deliberately trying to piss off ninety-nine percent of the population of this city."

"I'm sorry," I said, in mock seriousness. "You must have confused me with someone who gives a shit what people think about her."

Tarek laughed. "Pardon me," he said, putting his hand to his chest.

"Is that a dealbreaker for you?" I asked then.

"What?"

"My bumper stickers. Are they a dealbreaker?"

"What do you mean?"

Maybe he doesn't get the slang, I thought.

"Are they a dealbreaker? Are they something that would prevent you from being my friend?" I explained.

"No," he said definitively. "The contrary, actually."

"You're joking." I didn't believe him.

"No, I'm not."

"There's no way you agree with them."

"Why not?"

"No one like *you* would."

"What do you mean 'like me'?" His eyebrows were furrowed.

"Well—I mean—" I motioned toward him with my hand, "You're of Middle Eastern background."

"So?" He shrugged.

"No one from the Middle East would think like that," I said matter-of-factly.

"Oh, so you've met every person from the Middle East?"

"No, but, not if you believe the media."

"So you believe everything the media says?" Tarek asked.

"Wait, what?" I was confused. "*I'm* the one who always says that to Josh, that the media always tells the same old story, that he should branch out and read all kinds of news sources."

"People need to read everything. No source is objective."

"I completely agree." I looked at him.

I was in some alternate universe, with a Middle Eastern man who didn't believe the mass media, who agreed with my bumper stickers? I expected myself to wake from this dream any second.

"Look," Tarek said then. "For example, I don't completely agree with everything that President Bush did, but he did a good job of keeping the country safe after 9/11."

"Exactly," I agreed. "And the president's job is to defend this country. I hate how some people seem to think that a president's success is somehow measured by his popularity overseas. What the hell does that have to do with anything?"

"Foreign nations want a weak United States, that's the bottom line. When a U.S. president is weak, most foreign governments prefer that," Tarek said.

"That's what I've always said. When the U.S. president is strong and doesn't take any crap, that's when his popularity overseas goes down. But a president needs to protect American interests, not make them subservient to the interests of other nations."

"I agree. And by the way, I agree with what you said in class the other day."

I smiled, another genuine one, and looked at him. "Why didn't you back me up then?"

He looked at me. "I thought maybe it would have offended you somehow."

"It wouldn't have. It would have been nice to know I wasn't alone."

"Well, I'll remember that for next time." He smiled.

We were pulling into the Pentagon City area.

Tarek directed me to his apartment building, which was only a couple of blocks from the shopping center.

He told me to pull into the area in front of his building.

"This is a really nice building," I said. "All that oil money must really be working out for you."

He looked at me, and I half-smiled.

"You're joking again, oh my God."

"I do joke occasionally, you know? People say I should do it for my health." I put the car in park.

He looked at me. "You actually have a good sense of humor. I hadn't expected it."

"Yeah well, it takes too much energy to be a bitch all the time."

"You're not a—what you just said." He really did have a tough time cursing. Maybe I should temper my cursing around him, I thought.

We sat there for a moment. "Look," I began, "you asked me last Monday why I'm so closed off. Now you know. People in this town are totally intolerant of others' views. A couple of those bumper stickers—I've had to replace them three times. People keep ripping them off my car."

"I understand." He paused. "And I want to apologize for what I said the other day, about you shutting people out. It was rude." His eyes were downcast.

"It's OK. I was rude first."

There was another pause.

"Look," his eyes lowered for a second, "do you want to get a cup of coffee or something?" Then he quickly added, "Because I don't have anything else to do today."

I wanted to. I really did. But I had more reading to do. At this point in the semester, I needed to stay on track; otherwise, I would get overwhelmed really quickly. At least, that's what I told myself. But the real reason that I thought I shouldn't was because I was afraid. I was afraid of having feelings again. Having feelings meant being vulnerable, and I hated that.

"I'd like to," I said honestly, "but I can't today. But another time, sure." I glanced at him then looked away. The thought occurred to me that maybe he thought I was flirting, but I really wasn't. I was a bit nervous.

"OK," he said, smiling.

"Hold on, I'll help you with your stuff."

I got out and opened the trunk. He took his bag and I shut the lid down hard.

We turned toward each other.

"I'll see you tomorrow," I told him.

"See you tomorrow, Isabel."

I felt a thrill when he said my name. I got in the car and put it in drive. He waved to me as I pulled away.

Stranger things than that haven't happened for a long time, I thought, smiling.

I had been thinking about Tarek pretty much constantly since I dropped him off the day before. I still hadn't quite figured him out. He *seemed* interested in me, but was he really? Men who had been interested in me in the past had been pretty forward. They would ask me out, or kiss me, if we were in a bar or a club. I was confused, but even more intrigued than I had been when he had first approached me that day to ask me to study with him.

I had gotten to work early that day because I wanted to leave early. I wanted to get to campus way before class, so that I could corner Josh if I could. Mondays were the best day to do that. The later it got in the week, the more Josh would slack and the more time he would have to make up at work, and the later he would work. Typical Venezuelan, I thought, smiling. He would show up for class at exactly 6:00 p.m., slinking into his seat as the professor was starting class. Dinesh and I always made fun of him for it. But Josh was a really good sport and had a great sense of humor.

I was wearing a black suit today with a red silk, sleeveless blouse. Even though the suit material was lightweight, I was still warm. As soon as I stepped into the law school building, I found a small table to sit by myself and took off my blazer. After going to the gym at lunch, I had been lazy and had put mousse in my hair and let it air dry. It hung in loose waves around my shoulders and I kept pushing it out of my face. I needed a haircut.

Tarek usually got here before Josh did, so I sat in a corner, trying to hide myself from people walking along the halls. I sat past the area where the stairs and elevator were that led to the upper floors. I hoped that if Tarek came in before Josh, he would go straight upstairs to class and wouldn't see me skulking here.

After a few minutes, I struck gold. Josh came in, talking with some girl I didn't know. I got up and waved him over to my table.

"Hey," he said as he approached.

"Have a seat," I said. He sat. Then I dove right in. I didn't know how much time I had until Tarek showed up.

"Dude, you've been talking to Tarek about me."

Josh looked surprised at first, then smiled knowingly.

"It's not my fault," he said, holding his hands up.

"What the fuck does that mean? Did he torture you? Or do you mean you can't help gossiping like an old woman?"

"I didn't volunteer any information. He asked me about you."

"Oh, and you were forced to answer," I said sarcastically.

"What would you have preferred me to do? Plead the Fifth?"

This line of questioning was a waste of time. It had already happened, I figured. At this point, I just needed information.

"Tell me what he asked you, and what you told him."

"Why does it matter to you?"

"Josh, I swear to God, I will kick your ass," I told him in a low voice. "Tell me." Then I added, "Please." Sometimes Josh responded better to politeness.

"He asked me where you were from. He asked me if you were dating anyone."

"And you told him no?"

"Yes. I mean yes, I told him that you weren't. I told him that as long as I had known you, since the beginning of law school, as far as I knew you hadn't dated anyone."

"OK." That was a true statement.

"What else did you tell him?" I probed.

"I told him that you had excellent grades, and that you studied more than anyone I knew."

"Did he ask that specifically?"

"Not really. He mentioned that you seemed really into law school."

"What, like he thought I was a nerd?"

"No," Josh shrugged. "He seemed like he was impressed."

"OK. Did you tell him anything else?"

Josh thought for a moment, pursing his lips. "I don't think so."

"OK, then." I nodded.

"Isabel, why do you care?"

"I don't know that I do."

"Did you study with him this weekend?"

"Yes."

"And?"

I shrugged. "And what?"

"How did it go?"

"Really well. He's very smart."

"So you think maybe you've finally met your match?" Josh was grinning so much that lines showed around his brown eyes.

Maybe, I thought. I gave Josh a snarky look and shook my head quickly.

After a little while, we walked upstairs to class. Tarek was already in his seat. As I approached, he got up to let me pass and take my seat next to him. Josh sat in his usual space behind Tarek. Dinesh was there too next to me.

"What? Is Josh rubbing off on you?" Dinesh laughed. "You're going to start showing up late too?"

I shook my head and rolled my eyes, but I couldn't help smiling. "You're full of shit," I told him. Then I looked at Tarek.

"How are you?" I asked him.

"I'm doing well." He had learned proper English, at least. He had said 'well,' not 'good' like most people did.

"How are *you* doing?" he asked me then.

I looked at him and nodded, opening up my laptop. "Doing OK."

Then he said something that surprised me. "I didn't know that your hair was curly. I thought it was straight."

"Um, it's naturally curly. Today after the gym I didn't blow-dry it."

"It looks really good," he said.

"Thanks," I said. Your hair always looks incredible, I thought, like the rest of you.

"Yeah, who are you trying to impress today?" Josh said then from behind us.

I half-closed my eyes and shook my head to myself. I was going to kill him.

"No one," I said, then wondered why I had even dignified that question with a response. I could feel the color rising in my cheeks and knew that in a matter of seconds my face would be as red as my silk shirt. I looked at my laptop.

The truth was, I had been in too much of a rush to blow-dry my hair after the gym, and I hadn't thought about impressing anyone. But Josh's comment had embarrassed me.

Thankfully, class started and Josh and Dinesh were both forced to stop talking.

After class, I was packing up and asked Tarek if he was going to the metro. He said he was.

I told Josh that we would meet him downstairs.

"Josh always takes forever to leave," I told Tarek as we walked down the stairs. "He'll catch up with us."

Then I thought of something. "Hey, did you get your car fixed?"

"Yes, I did, thankfully.

"What was wrong with it?"

"The brake pads needed to be replaced, and one other thing."

"So you have a lead foot?" I smiled. "Is that why the brake pads needed to be replaced?"

"Maybe," he smiled and looked at me.

"That's the thing about European cars; the maintenance is pretty expensive. But they last a really long time."

We reached the first floor. Dinesh was with us. I introduced him to Tarek. We were chatting when Josh caught up with us. Eric wasn't coming, he told us. He had something to do.

"Let's go," I said then.

The four of us were walking out the door when this guy I sort of knew, Saul, passed us. I looked at him, and our eyes met for the briefest of seconds before I looked away. It made me uneasy.

Saul was a guy who I had had a brief fling with about a year ago. I had been horribly lonely and craving physical contact. He was just a guy I knew from one of my classes, but we hadn't really talked that much. I had been out dancing with Josh and Eric, I had run into Saul and I hooked up with him. We had slept together like two, no three, times. But then I didn't want to see him anymore. It had only been physical for me. Beyond that, I wasn't attracted to him on an intellectual level. We were too different. He, however, apparently had other ideas. He had wanted to keep seeing me. I knew for a fact that he had no intention of being with me long-term. However, he had wanted to keep sleeping with me, but at that point I was done. He had called and texted me for a while, and had tried to talk to me once in a while, but I hadn't been interested. I avoided him after that and had been fairly successful at it.

The worst part now was that Tarek had greeted him on the way out. So they knew each other. Dammit. Saul saw me with Tarek, so now what if he told Tarek about what had happened between us? Well, if he told him that, then it was my own damn fault.

It actually made sense that they knew each other. Saul was Turkish; they both spoke Arabic. I had noticed that all the Arabic speakers at the law school seemed to gravitate toward each other, like all the Spanish speakers seemed to do. Maybe Tarek and Saul didn't know each other well enough for Saul to dish. Although, I had to admit, as far as I knew men certainly liked to dish about their conquests.

I pushed the thought to the back of my mind. There was nothing I could do about it now.

The four of us chatted on the way to the metro. Luckily, we didn't have to wait too long for a train. The train was unusually crowded for being after 8 p.m.

"There are seats over there if you want to sit," Tarek told me.

"Thanks, but it's OK." I smiled. "I've been sitting most of the day."

Tarek and I stood holding on to the same rail by the train doors, as the train sped off.

"How was work?" he asked me.

"All right. I actually had to do a Catalan to English translation today. I don't get the chance to do Catalan very often."

"So Catalan is a Latin language, right?" Tarek seemed interested.

"Yes, it actually developed from the same strain of Latin that French developed from—from which French developed," I corrected hastily. "So there are a lot of words in Catalan that are similar to French words. For instance, 'window' in Catalan is *finestre*."

"Ah, like *fenêtre*."

"Right. And *formatge*—"

"*Fromage*?"

"Right. So since you speak French, if you read Catalan, you could probably understand a lot of it."

"Interesting. So, the company you work for—"

"It's a government contractor, so we do a lot of translations for federal agencies."

"Intelligence-related?"

"Some, yes. A lot of business-related stuff too, like contracts, employment agreements, etc. But we also have private multinational clients. We translate websites, marketing materials, even pharmaceutical research, all that. I also do some linguistic stuff. For example, if someone needs help identifying accents, mostly Spanish and Latin American accents." I paused for a breath. "I'm also a 'Senior Translator/Linguist,'" using my air quotes, "so I also review other translators' work."

"How long have you worked there?"

"A few years, since I moved back to the U.S."

"And before that, you were in—?"

"Barcelona."

He nodded. "What did you do there?"

"Mostly translation, interpreting, and some marketing work."

"Why did you come back to the US?"

Goddamn, he was asking a ton of questions. But I couldn't think of a good reason not to answer them. I was also starting to get tired.

"I wasn't happy with the employment market in Spain. It's difficult for women and foreigners to advance in their jobs." And I missed my mother and my sisters terribly, but I didn't say that.

"But you weren't a foreigner there. Your father was Spanish, right?"

"Yes, but I was born and grew up in the U.S. They treat you differently."

He nodded. "I know what that's like."

"It must have been similar for you in France," I told him, "because you *look* different."

"Yes, it was." He gave me a look of understanding then, almost like we were co-conspirators.

Then I overheard part of Josh's conversation with Dinesh. They were arguing.

Josh was Scalia-bashing. This was somewhat of a regular occurrence at the law school. To be fair to Josh, he wasn't the only one who engaged in it. But Dinesh usually didn't agree with Josh.

I felt the need to jump in. I almost always did. "Josh, look me in the eye and tell me that you don't agree with Scalia's opinion in *Kyllo*."

Josh and Dinesh both looked at me.

"Well, I—" Josh began.

This was typical, and it annoyed me. None of the liberals at school would ever say anything that could be construed as even remotely good about Justice Scalia. It was like they all took an oath or something.

I continued. "So you think the government should be able to use thermal imaging sensors to find out what you're doing in your house?"

"No, I—"

"So Scalia was right! Say it. Say it, Josh!"

"The *Kyllo* decision was correct, yes."

"Jesus Christ! Let everyone here remember the day that *you* agreed with Scalia!" I held my hands up skyward.

Dinesh laughed.

"Lower your voice," Josh whispered to me urgently. Other people on the metro were staring at us.

"Scalia's almost always right," Tarek said then. "Josh is upset because deep down, he knows it."

"I agree," I said.

"You wish," Josh said.

"Oh, so you agree that it's a matter of federal law whether to enforce a forum selection clause in a contract case?" I pressed. Many contracts had such clauses, which indicated, in the case of a legal dispute, the forum (i.e., court or alternative dispute resolution method, such as mediation), in which the case would be heard.

People on the train were still staring. They must be thinking about how lame law students were. They were right.

"What?" Josh said.

"Don't you remember the *Stewart* case from Civil Procedure?" I asked.

Dinesh was guffawing. "He doesn't remember the cases we talked about yesterday!"

I smiled. That may be true but it wouldn't stop me.

But Tarek answered before I did. "The question is, in a breach of contract case, is it correct for the court to transfer a case from state to federal court under 28 USC 1404(a) in order to enforce a forum selection clause, by framing the issue as whether or not to transfer a case under 1404(a), thus framing it as a procedural question governed by the Rules Enabling Act, when the real issue is—"

"Whether to enforce a forum selection clause, which is a question of state contract law, not federal law," I continued.

"So the Rules of Decision Act would apply instead," Tarek concluded.

"The majority applied the wrong rule," I said.

"That's arguably true," Josh said.

"OK, I'll take that," I told him.

"A federal rule did not govern, so the Rules of Decision Act should have been applied," Tarek was still going. "But the federal government wants to keep its hand in everything, and if it doesn't like a state law, it will try to get around it."

"Oh my God, I had no idea the Rules Enabling Act was so provocative," Dinesh was still laughing.

"OK, so that's two for Scalia. Let's keep going."

"I just think he's too socially conservative," Josh said. "And he said that the Constitution is a dead document."

"He means we should look at what the Founders intended," Tarek said.

"Let's not get off track," I said, then looked at Tarek. "Not that what you said isn't important." But if I let the conversation get off track, then the conversation with Josh would turn into a heated Latino discussion with both of us talking over each other. That was how our politically-driven conversations almost always ended. "*JEB v. Alabama*," I continued.

JEB v. Alabama dealt with peremptory strikes. When attorneys were selecting juries to hear court cases, they had a certain number of peremptory strikes they could use to kick jurors off the potential jury without stating any reason for it. The *JEB v. Alabama* Court held that it was unconstitutional to strike a juror for his or her gender. In a previous case, the Court had found it unconstitutional to strike a juror based on race.

"Why should you be allowed to use peremptory strikes to strike jurors from serving on a jury for any reason except for race or gender?"

"Because those are protected classes."

"So is national origin. So is age. So is religion. So I can strike someone from a jury for being Muslim or Sikh, or for being from France. How is that fair?"

Tarek went on for me. "And Scalia made the point in his dissent that you can use peremptory strikes to strike potential jurors for a variety of reasons, none of them necessarily good ones."

"Right," I agreed. "And now when you strike a juror, the opposing party is going to argue that a juror was struck due to race or gender, and hearings have to be held for the purpose of determining that, and that makes litigation totally inefficient."

"All at taxpayer expense," Tarek said. "That's one reason why people hate lawyers."

"But it's discriminatory to strike a juror based on race or gender," Josh said.

"But it's OK for me to strike Tarek from a jury for being Lebanese, or for being Middle Eastern? Litigators discriminate all the time when they use their strikes. No stereotypes are legitimate, so if none are legitimate, then you shouldn't be allowed to use peremptory strikes at all. You should be able to strike jurors from the jury for anything you want, or not at all."

"Also," Tarek continued, "every citizen has the right to serve on a jury. So Scalia's point is that everyone still gets that right. There is no discrimination because everyone can participate. After that, it's a matter of who gets to participate on a jury."

I nodded. I had nothing more to add. I couldn't believe Tarek remembered these cases from Civil Procedure, which was a first-year course. I had thought that *I* was the biggest law-school nerd I knew.

Josh changed his tack then.

"So you agree with Scalia's dissent in *Lawrence v. Texas*?" Josh asked me. *Lawrence v. Texas* was a famous case where the police entered a home with probable cause related to drugs and found two men performing homosexual acts. The acts violated Texas' sodomy laws, and the men were arrested. The issue before the Supreme Court was whether the state anti-sodomy law violated the Constitution. The Court had found that it did.

"I agree with the holding in *Lawrence*," I said.

"Consenting individuals should be able to do whatever they want in their own homes," Tarek said.

"Yes," I agreed. "It's not the government's business. But I agree with Scalia in his dissent to *Lawrence* when he says—"

"That it's the end of any law based only on moral justifications," Tarek finished for me.

I looked at Tarek. "So polygamy, as long as it's consented to by all parties, should be legal."

"Exactly," Tarek agreed. "Don't you think so, Josh?"

"No, I don't think that polygamy should be legal."

"Why not?" Tarek pressed.

"Well, it's a slippery slope—" Josh began.

"That's arguably true, but that's not a *legal* argument," I countered.

Josh didn't respond, and I weighed whether or not to press him.

Then Dinesh was laughing. I looked at him curiously.

In response to my glare, Josh said, "Oh my God, he's like a male version of you," motioning to Tarek.

I couldn't help smiling. "And you don't know the half of it." I was thinking about my conversation with Tarek in the car the day before.

We were at Pentagon City. I turned to Tarek. I suddenly had an idea and acted on it without reflection.

"Do you drink?" I asked him.

"Sorry?"

"Do you drink alcohol?" I specified.

"Yeesssss," he said slowly, as if he didn't know where I was going with this.

"I'm taking you out for a drink this Thursday after class, if you're not busy. It's on me." I winked at him.

Part of me couldn't believe the words coming out of my mouth. They were not something I would ever say to someone. "I'm taking you out for a drink?" My sisters wouldn't recognize me now. I had said them full of emotion at having someone around me who actually agreed with me instead of viciously arguing and telling me I was a reactionary.

"OK, thanks. I'll look forward to that." He smiled, his eyes twinkling as he exited the train. "See you tomorrow, Isabel."

I watched him for a little while, then the spell was broken when Josh spoke.

"Oh my God, Isabel, that's your man right there."

I couldn't help thinking that maybe Josh was right.

The rest of the week passed quickly. Tarek and I talked more and more, and rode home on the metro together, usually with Josh and Dinesh. Sometimes Eric was with us. If I got to campus early and Tarek was there, we would sit and chat together before going upstairs to class.

He was always polite and gentlemanly. I was nervous waiting for Thursday evening. It occurred to me that maybe he thought it was a date. I hadn't meant it like that. I had actually meant for us all to go out as a group, which was what Josh and Dinesh and Melanie and I usually did on Thursdays during our first year.

When Tarek and I got to class on Thursday, I turned to Josh and Dinesh.

"We're going out for drinks tonight, right?"

"Yeah, of course," Josh said.

"Sure," said Dinesh.

I looked at Tarek. He smiled and nodded. If he was disappointed that Josh and Dinesh were coming, he didn't show it. I inwardly breathed a sigh of relief.

God, when was the last time I had asked a guy out? Never, I think. At least, not that I remembered.

When class ended, we all got up to leave.

Tarek held his hand out to me, palm up. I looked at it, then at his face.

"What?" I asked, confused.

"Give me your Property book, Isabel."

"Why?"

"I'll carry it for you."

"Why? I can carry it."

"I know you *can* carry it. But I refuse to be seen with you lugging all that stuff and me not helping you."

I opened my mouth to say something but then had the feeling that I was about to engage in a losing argument. Instead, I handed him my book and smiled.

"Thank you," I said. "You could have just asked if I wanted help. *No tenias que ser mandon.*"

"What?"

"You didn't have to give me a command."

"The last time I asked you politely, you refused."

"I would not have refused this time."

"You say that now." He smiled and his eyes were playful. I let him have the last word.

We walked to our usual bar, right off campus. This bar was probably a former townhome. It had three levels. The first was a bar with the usual barstools and tables. The second floor was a more-or-less proper restaurant with tables and chairs and tablecloths. I suddenly remembered the fact that my mother always preferred to dine at restaurants with tablecloths. I don't know why I was thinking about her. I should call. I hadn't talked to her for a while. She would get antsy. Since I lived by myself, she liked to check on me.

We headed up to the third floor and crashed on the comfy couches there. I deflated as I dropped my backpack on the floor. I sat on the couch and leaned back.

Then I remembered that I was treating Tarek tonight. I stood up.

"What are you drinking?" I asked him.

"I'll get yours," he said.

"No, but—I invited you."

He sighed. "I'd like to get yours, please?"

"But now I feel bad. I didn't invite you so that you would pay for me."

"I know," he said. "And I appreciate it. I really do. But—just let me do something nice for you."

I was going to protest, or to (jokingly) say it was anti-feminist, but I actually liked the gesture. I did feel bad, though, because I was working and had a salary and he didn't. But I didn't want to bring that up. I made the decision that I would relent this one time and would try to make it up to him later.

That thought implied that there would be a later, as in we would go out again. I felt both elated and panicked simultaneously.

"OK, just this once," I agreed. I had a feeling it wouldn't be just this once, though. "And thank you."

I told him that I wanted a glass of Malbec.

When the four of us had our drinks, we began to unwind. Josh and Dinesh had ordered a couple of appetizers too, and we all picked at them. I noticed that I was really hungry then.

Josh liked to eat. I loved that about him, since I liked to eat too. I couldn't stand people who never ate, or who only ate salads. I mean, I liked to eat healthy foods, but eating only salads was no way to live.

Tarek and I were sitting on the couch, both of us leaning back, relaxing.

I looked at him and smiled. "If you're always paying for women you hang out with, then you must be broke."

"What do you mean?"

"Well, you must go out with plenty of women." I made a hand gesture, as if I were sizing him up physically.

He had a look of realization then. "Oh, that's right. You think I'm attractive."

"I've never said that." Wait, had I said that?

"Yes, you did. I think the term you used was 'gorgeous,' actually." He was grinning broadly.

"Oh my God, I can't believe you remember that." I felt mortified. I could feel my cheeks getting hot. Thankfully, the lighting in here is low.

"Isabel, it was only two weeks ago."

Oh my God, that's right. Why did it seem so long ago? The first day that we had actually had a conversation, other than in passing, and he had asked me to study with him, I had told him that just because he was gorgeous didn't mean that he could convince me to do whatever he wanted.

"For the record," I said then, "it was your intelligence that convinced me to study with you, not your looks."

"Oh, I know."

We looked at each other. I had no idea if he considered me attractive. He knew I thought he was, though. And he had seen me that day, raking my eyes over his entire body. I shuddered.

"Are you cold?" he said.

"No," I shook my head. I felt like I was giving all my cards away. He knew I thought he was both intelligent and sexy. And I still didn't know what he thought about me.

Then I quickly changed the subject.

"You never told me what you did before law school."

"You never asked," he smiled back.

"That's a lawyer's answer." I paused. "So now I'm asking."

"I studied Finance in undergrad in New York, and then became a CPA and was working for a business consulting firm in Miami before law school."

I laughed. It was a good belly laugh, the kind that made my abdominals ache. Tarek looked surprised. "No seriously, man," I said. "What did you do?

He was a little confused now. "I told you, I was a CPA."

"No, you weren't," I choked out between laughs.

"Yes, I was!"

"You don't look like a CPA!" I gasped, gulping in air.

"What is a CPA supposed to look like?"

"Like, nerdy, with glasses, not like—not like you!" I motioned toward him with my hand, still laughing.

He laughed. "Oh my God," he said, shaking his head at me.

"What did you say to her?" Josh asked Tarek. "She almost never laughs like that."

"Nothing!" Tarek said. "I didn't say anything funny!"

I couldn't stop laughing.

"What was in your wine?" Dinesh asked me.

"Must be some roofies," Josh said.

"Sorry!" I choked out, wiping tears of laughter from the corners of both of my eyes. I had finally calmed down and turned to Josh. "I'm OK now. I promise." Josh went back to chatting with Dinesh.

"I—I didn't peg you for a number cruncher," I tried to explain to Tarek.

Tarek was smiling, possibly waiting for me to erupt in laughter again. After a pause, he answered. "Well, it got a little boring, so that's why I'm in law school. I—I wanted to do something else."

"Actually," I said in all earnestness, calmed down now, "being a CPA is great to combine with a law degree. It's—highly sought after."

"I hope so. The economy isn't so great right now, to put it mildly."

"Yeah," I agreed. "At worst, I'll have to stay at my current job after I graduate."

"But that won't be so bad," Tarek said. "You'll have a job. I'm kind of regretting leaving my job to go to school."

"Yes, but I want to do more than what I'm doing now."

"I understand that." He paused to take a drink. He was drinking beer, like Josh and Dinesh. "What do you want to do after law school?" he asked me.

"I'd like to do corporate work. I—uh," I always felt like a nerd saying this, "I actually really like transactional stuff and contracts. I like getting involved in the details."

"That makes sense," Tarek said. "Translators are very detail-oriented."

I nodded, then continued. "Ideally, I'd like to work as corporate counsel for a multinational company. But—what I've been told is that it's very difficult to get a corporate counsel job straight out of law school. You should really work for a firm for a few years before doing that. So, I'm trying to get experience with a firm, but I'm not having much luck."

"Really? Even with your grades and your languages?"

I suddenly felt like unloading. This was the type of thing I would usually do with my sisters, or with Melanie, but they weren't around.

"The truth is," I began, lulled by the comfy couch and the wine. "I think I've been a bit naïve. I figured that with my work experience, my overseas experience and my grades I would land these great firm jobs. But I'm competing with much younger law students, and the thing is—I don't think that firms want to hire entry-level female associates in their mid-thirties. They figure that a woman my age will eventually have kids and leave the firm, and they don't want to invest in a person like that only to have them leave. Also, frankly, first-year associates do a lot of grunt work, and firms want to be able to work them eighty hours a week, to the bone. And people my age are less likely to take that shit."

Tarek was looking at me curiously.

"Sorry for the cursing," I said then. But that wasn't the reason for his look.

"Wait, how old are you?" he asked then.

"How old do you think I am?"

"I thought you were my age, around twenty-eight or so."

I half-smiled and shook my head. "No, I am thirty-four years old."

"I had no idea you were that old." He was genuinely surprised.

"Well, thanks," I said, bothered. "Thirty-four is ancient, I know. I shouldn't even be going to clubs anymore, right? I guess I should plan my funeral."

"No," he said, embarrassed. "I'm sorry. I meant that—you look a lot younger and—you act a lot younger."

"How does a thirty-four-year-old act?"

"Well, you curse all the time, and you say 'dude' a lot."

I couldn't help smiling. Lara had warned me about that. "People your age don't really say 'dude,'" she had said.

"Well," I countered, "*You* don't curse and *you* don't say 'dude,' so that must mean that you act older than your age."

"Yes, I agree," Tarek said. "And most people think I'm older. You're the only person who guessed correctly."

I pondered for a few moments. "Is thirty-four too old?" I blurted out.

"Too old for what?"

Too old for *you*, I thought. Instead, I said, "Too old for—law school."

"No, of course not. Why would you think that?"

I shrugged. "Because sometimes I look at these kids and I feel old."

"You shouldn't. You're just more worldly than they are. Most of the students here are too young to know anything about real life."

It was very easy to talk to him. And I was finding that, more and more, he was saying the right things.

"That's what *I* always say," I told him. He smiled.

"What do *you* want to do after law school, ideally?" I asked then.

"I was originally thinking politics, but I'm kind of turned off to that now. I think I want to stick with corporate, maybe regulatory. I wouldn't mind either working for a firm or for the government. I can't afford to be too picky in this economy, anyway."

"That's true," I agreed. "Are you going to do a summer associateship?"

"Yes, I hope so. I interviewed with a bunch of firms and am waiting to hear." He told me the names of the firms he had interviewed with. Some were in DC and a couple were in New York; one was in Miami.

"Well, I'm sure that any of those firms will be happy to have a CPA there," I told him.

"What will you be doing next summer?" he asked.

I sipped my wine. "For the moment, staying with my current job. I'm trying to see if I can get something, but it would have to be something with a salary, because I have bills to pay and an apartment to maintain." I smiled. "I'm too old to do an unpaid internship."

Tarek nodded and smiled. "If you tell me what you're interested in, I can keep my eyes open."

"Thank you. I appreciate that." Two weeks ago, if he had told me that I would have been defensive, and would have felt offended that he thought I needed "help." But now that I had more of an idea about what type of person he was, I did feel appreciative.

"It's no problem," he said.

I smiled at him then, a genuine smile. I was not liberal with giving them, and I hadn't intended to give him one now. He smiled back, his head leaning against the back of the couch, framed by his black curls.

"What's that for?" he asked me.

"What?"

"That smile," he said.

"You honestly believed I was only twenty-eight years old?"

"At the most," he said.

I shook my head. "Tarek Cordiez, there may be hope for you yet."

His grin widened.

We were on the metro on the way back. It was almost 10:00 p.m.

Tarek asked me if I would be OK all the way home to Franconia.

"Of course," I told him. "I do this all the time."

"OK," but he didn't seem convinced. "It's—you shouldn't be taking the metro home alone so late."

I smiled. "I'll be all right," then I added, *"Mom."*

He rolled his eyes.

"Are we studying this weekend?" he asked then.

"Sure," I said, trying to sound nonchalant but excited at the prospect of seeing him again. "Um, would Saturday be OK? Like, in the afternoon, maybe three-thirty?" That would give me time to read in the morning.

"Sure," he smiled. "Same place?"

I hesitated for a second. "Yes," I said.

We were at Pentagon City. "OK, then I'll see you Saturday."

"OK, bye."

He left the train.

Saturday came faster than I had anticipated. The day kind of ran away from me. I read in the morning, then around lunchtime started to make paella. It was something I could do while studying, because it had to simmer for a long time, and I could read and stir once in a while. I was making a ton, two pans, and figured I would have leftovers and could freeze some for later.

Then my mother called and my day started to be thrown off track. She had a million questions. As usual, she spoke in her *porteño* accent. She was forever asking me to slow down when I spoke. My accent was more Castilian. For some reason, I picked up my father's accent more than my mother's. Also, my time living in Spain had rubbed off on me. Even the Spanish thought that I spoke really fast.

First, she kind of laid me out for not calling her.

"It would be nice to hear from you once in a while," she said. There was sarcasm in her voice.

"Sorry, Mom. I've been busy since school started again."

"I mean, you live by yourself, Isabel. I need to hear from you once in a while. I have to ask Lara for updates on how you are, and she's busier than you are."

I was going to protest that, but decided against it. I mean, Lara was doing her medical residency, that was true. But I was working full-time *and* in law school. I figured I was as least as busy as she was, as far as Mom was concerned.

"I'll try to call more often, Mom." I'm thirty-four years old. I don't have to check in with you, for God's sake.

"How is school?" she asked then.

"Good, like always."

"Have you met anyone new?"

"I always meet new people every year, Mom."

"Anyone with possible boyfriend potential?"

"No, Mom."

My mother, God bless her, had been trying to set me up with a boyfriend since I was sixteen years old.

"I mean," she began, "your sisters have found men, and they're a lot younger than you. I can't believe that in your entire class there isn't one person that interests you."

Well, there may be one person, but I wasn't about to tell my mother that and have to suffer through her questions every week.

"There are a lot more eligible women than men in DC, Mom." I didn't know if that was true or not.

"You should go out more."

"I do go out, Mom."

"Aren't there any eligible men at work?"

"No, Mom." Not unless you wouldn't mind seeing me with an older or married man.

Then I changed the subject. "How is Mark?" I smiled to myself, thinking about what Lara had told me.

I still thought that my Mom liked the fact that she and Mark didn't live together. My impression was that she liked her independence but needed to have a partner. Mark was American, and he was a friend of one of Mom's coworkers. Mom taught Spanish literature at the local university, and had met Mark at a party the coworker had at his house. Mark was divorced, with no kids. He was retired military, and he was so nice to my Mom. I thanked God for giving her such a nice guy, so that she could spend time with him and bother her children less.

"He's doing well. We're going to visit his parents soon. They are getting up there in age."

Mark's parents were in their eighties.

I wondered why she didn't tell me what she had told Lara, that Mark had talked to her about marriage.

I looked at the time.

"Mom, I'm sorry but I have to go. I'm meeting someone."

That was the wrong thing to say.

"Oh, really? Who? Anyone I know?"

"No." If I wanted a quick exit, one-word answers were better. "Look, I'll tell you about it next weekend, when I see you."

Lara, Patrick and I had been planning to go visit Mom next Sunday for dinner.

I hung up with Mom. Then I stirred the paella, a little worried now that it wouldn't be ready in time for me to leave. I checked the chicken. It was almost done but still a little pink in the middle. I stirred it some more.

I thought about Lara and hoped she could still go next Sunday. I preferred to visit Mom with her and not by myself.

As usual, when I was thinking about Lara, she suddenly called me.

"Punk, I was just thinking about you!" I happily exclaimed.

"That's why I called!" she said.

Luckily for me, she was still free next Sunday and, yes, she assured me, she and Patrick would come with me to visit Mom.

We chatted about her week at the hospital. She had a bunch of interesting cases to tell me about.

Then she asked about Tarek. I had emailed her after our first study date and had told her everything. She really enjoyed reading my updates as a break when she got home from her shift.

"How are things with him?" she asked gently.

"Good. He's really smart. I think it was definitely a good idea studying with him."

"I bet it is!" Lara said, with some attitude.

"Oh my God," I laughed, "You think you're so funny."

"I am!"

"Speaking of Tarek, I'm meeting him this afternoon so I have to go, I'm sorry! I'm so glad you called!"

"Of course! See you next Sunday, and we'll talk before then. Let me know how it goes today."

"OK, love you!"

"Love you too!"

We hung up. Let me know how it goes today, she had said. How it goes studying or how it goes something else? I figured she probably meant the latter.

I looked at the time. It was 2:15. The paella was not quite done, but almost.

Oh! This is so frustrating! I started to panic. As usual, I had been too ambitious with my plans for the day. I didn't have time to finish the paella and be at campus at 3:30. And I didn't want to meet later than that because it would be too late. I wanted to get a lot of studying done today.

I made a decision then. I picked up my cell phone again and called Tarek.

"Hey, Isabel," he said in his deep voice.

"Hey," I began. "I was wondering—would you mind if—" I suddenly had trouble speaking, "um—can we meet at my apartment instead of at campus?" I felt the need to explain so he wouldn't think I was up to something. Wait, what would I be up to? Ugh, say it already! I told myself. "I'm sorry. My mother called, and then my sister called, and I did the reading but—"

"Isabel," he said slowly, "It's OK. I can go to your house. It's no problem."

"Are you sure?"

"Of course."

"OK, thanks." I sighed a sigh of relief. "If you want to take the metro I can pick you up at Franconia."

"No, I'll drive."

I gave him directions to my apartment building, and told him where he could park.

"I'll have to let you into the building," I told him, "So call me when you're here and I'll come down."

"OK. See you in a little while."

We hung up.

By 3:15 the paella was done and I had finished reading and taking notes on the remaining couple of cases. I was hoping to start with Property today.

Then I looked around my apartment. It was decent. I closed my bedroom door since my bed wasn't made. I also didn't want Tarek to see my bedroom. Thinking of him and my bedroom at the same time made me uneasy and a little turned on.

I looked around my apartment. I suddenly remembered that I had a lot of personal things out here, and that maybe I hadn't totally thought through having Tarek come over. Oh well. It was too late now. I couldn't uninvite him.

He would be here soon. I quickly washed my face and applied foundation, mascara and lip gloss. I was wearing dark skinny jeans and a loose, long-sleeved fuchsia top with a slight V-neck cut and an understated ruffle. I didn't like anything too ruffly, but a little bit was feminine enough.

When Tarek called, I was a little nervous. I didn't usually have people over at my place. Of my law school friends, only Josh and Melanie had been here. In fact, I was kind of amazed that I had invited him over. And I was excited to see him.

I ran down the stairs, then forced myself to walk slowly down the last couple of steps. I looked through the main glass doors, and saw him walking to the entrance from his car. I opened the door for him.

"Hey," I said.

"Hi, Isabel." I saw his eyes pop wide for a second, then they readjusted. Did he think I looked good? I couldn't tell. Stop overanalyzing, I told myself. It's probably from the dim light in the interior of the building.

I held the door for him. As he walked in, I got a whiff of his aftershave. But it was more understated this time. I smiled to myself. It smelled so good that I wanted to nuzzle my face against his neck.

He was wearing a button-down shirt today instead of a T-shirt, and jeans. His shirt was a deep burgundy. It looked great on him.

"Thank you for coming here," I said.

"It's no problem." He smiled. We started walking upstairs. "It's probably more comfortable here than at campus anyway."

"Not really, no. I don't have any furniture to sit on. I'm trying to save money. So we'll have to sit on the floor."

"What—" he started to say, then I laughed softly.

"Oh, you're joking, oh my God. Sometimes I can't tell."

"That's the idea." I looked at him; his eyes were alive, always turned on. He always appeared to be calm, but his eyes betrayed him. There was a pent-up passion there. I wondered if I would ever see it. I had the feeling that he was thinking all the time, like I was. I wondered what he thought about.

I opened the door to my apartment and we walked in. The aroma of paella permeated the entire apartment.

"What are you cooking? It smells so good," Tarek said.

"Just—um, paella."

"*Just* paella?" He asked. "It's a lot of work, isn't it?"

"No, not really."

I had cleared off the dining table. "We can study here if it's OK."

"Sure," he said agreeably. He started unpacking his laptop and his books.

"So . . . you said you were talking to your mother before?" he asked me.

"Yes." I paused. "She talks a lot, a typical Argentine woman. And then my sister called right after that."

"I didn't know you had a sister."

"You never asked," I gave him a playful look.

He smiled. "Where does your mother live?"

"About an hour south of here."

"Oh, that's great, so you get to see her often."

I nodded.

"Do you only have one sister?" he asked then.

"No, I have two. I'm the oldest." I checked the paella and turned the stove off. "Look, I'm going to make coffee, did you want any?"

"Oh, no, thank you."

"You don't drink coffee," I said then. It was a statement, not a question. Coffee was the ubiquitous life blood of all law students. It was obvious when someone didn't drink it. The rest of us, especially Josh and me, always had our takeout coffee so we could make it through class. I had noticed that Tarek usually had tea.

As though he had read my thoughts, he said, "No, I'm more of a tea drinker."

"I have tea. Would you like some?"

"Sure, if it's not a lot of trouble."

I looked at him and smiled. "It's not." I filled the kettle and put it on the stove. Tarek walked into the kitchen.

"Thank you." He was so polite. It reminded me of Santi. Santi was *uber* polite. He would leave me little notes. Isabel, he would say, I went to the lab to work. If you want to eat lunch with me, I'll be back at 3 p.m.

Tarek was talking. Wait, what did he say?

"I'm sorry, what was that?"

"Do your sisters live nearby?"

"My middle sister, Lara, lives pretty close, in Old Town Alexandria. She is actually a first-year medical resident at the hospital, at the same university we go to."

"Are you serious? So you get to see her?"

"Yes, although she works crazy hours, and she's married, but we try to see each other when we can. And we talk on the phone all the time."

I realized that I was quite nervous. Talking about my sisters helped me to relax, so I continued. "My little sister, Ariel, lives in New York. She finished business school recently and works for a consulting firm. She lives with her boyfriend."

"Ariel? That's a Jewish name."

"Yes."

"Is your family Jewish?"

"Is that a dealbreaker?"

"No, not at all. But you said you were Catholic."

"I am. I mean—my family is. Like I told you before, I don't really go to church, but I pray. I—I pray all the time." I prayed to forget, to have strength to keep going, to be too busy to think about things. "I mean—" I was totally rambling, so I stopped and took a deep breath. I didn't look Tarek in the eyes when I spoke. "My mother liked the name *Ariel*."

Then my eyes met his. Tarek had a strange expression on his face. "Why do I get the impression that you're constantly trying not to like me?"

I was floored. He was right. Part of me wanted to spend time with him, but another part of me, a more cynical part, a part that never believed I would have a chance at happiness, was telling me to get the hell away from him. That part was telling me that I would end up getting hurt. It was telling me not to trust a man, any man. And that part was looking for excuses for him not to like me. I kept thinking that he would see or hear something about me that he would hate, and then he would leave.

"I'm not," I lied.

"You're very—"

"Abrasive, I know. It's off-putting. It's by design."

"Why?"

"I'm used to people in this town insulting me for my beliefs and how I think." That much was true, at least.

"I'm not like that, Isabel."

"I know. I just forget sometimes. Force of habit. I'm sorry."

"Don't be sorry. It's OK."

We looked at each other for a few moments. Then he smiled.

"You are an impressive family, a doctor, a lawyer and a business major."

I smiled and shrugged, not really knowing what to say.

The silence made me nervous, and when I was nervous I talked more. "So you said before that you were in Miami before coming to DC?"

"That's right."

"How long had you lived there?"

"Several years. When we left France, we moved straight there. My mother and my sister still live there."

Of course, such a glitzy city. His family must come from money. I wondered about that. His father had been in the military, and could not have made that much money. And his mother's family fled Lebanon, so if they had money they must have made it afterward, maybe after coming to the U.S.

I kept talking. "Ariel lives in Brooklyn, in a tiny apartment. But Brooklyn is a nice area."

I noted that he said his *mother and his sister* lived in Miami, not his *parents*. I wondered about his French father but didn't say anything.

We were waiting for the tea. I was leaning against the kitchen counter, looking at him. My arms were still crossed because I didn't know what else to do with them.

"I'm surprised to hear that you have a sister. You strike me as an only child," I told Tarek.

"No. My sister is younger than me."

"Oh, really?"

"Yes, Zaida."

"Oh, that means Maria in Arabic."

"Yes, how did you know that?"

"I'm not an idiot, Tarek."

He looked surprised. "I didn't say you were."

I ignored his comment.

"I work with a bunch of Arab men. I listen to them chatting in Arabic all day. I figure these things out."

"Really?"

"Yes, I would say that my company translates mostly Arabic and Spanish. There's so much demand for Arabic translations."

"Oh, I'm sure." Tarek paused and looked at me curiously. "So is that why you have a bad impression of Arab men?"

"What do you mean?"

"You seem not to like Middle Eastern men. Some things you said to me." He paused, smiling. "I believe it was something like, 'you're a typical Arab man, freaking arrogant.' Something like that."

I was embarrassed. I deserved to feel that way. I didn't really know you then, I thought.

"Look, Tarek, if I offended you, I'm really sorry."

"It's OK, you didn't."

"It's just—" I paused. It was difficult to explain.

"Are the men at work rude to you?"

"No, not really rude—" I didn't quite know how to say it. "Some of them are nice. And some of them—"

"They kind of look at you?"

How did he know this? "Yes, they're very direct. Some of them like, study me, like I'm a lab experiment or something."

"It's because—they probably think you're very attractive, and—different."

"It's probably because I have a big nose or something."

He laughed. "It's not, I promise. They're—kind of—fascinated by you." He smiled slightly.

"Why?" I asked, not fully understanding.

He shrugged. "Because you're—" He struggled with how to articulate it. "You're direct," he said finally. "They're probably not used to it."

"You mean, culturally they're not used to it?"

"Yeeesss," Tarek said slowly, "that would be a good way of putting it. I mean, don't take this wrong, but for a Hispanic woman—"

"I'm very direct."

"Yes," he nodded.

I shrugged. "I know that. I—I'm not always comfortable with attention."

"Do they kind of flirt with you?"

"Some of them, but most of them are married."

"But the ones that do, you don't go out with them?" he asked carefully.

I gave him a hard look. "You've got to be kidding me. No, I don't go out with them. I don't need to complicate my life further by dating my co-workers."

He smiled. "It's rude of them to make you feel uncomfortable. In the U.S., staring like that isn't really socially acceptable."

Like the way I stared at *you* like a piece of meat the day you asked me to study with you? "I can deal with it." I smiled.

"Do you want me to talk to them?"

"Would you?" I cocked my head playfully.

"Gladly." He smiled broadly.

The kettle boiled.

I prepared his tea and my coffee. He took sugar, and I had to hunt for it, because I didn't usually use sugar for anything unless I was baking. I hadn't had time to bake in a while.

We sat down at the dining table. I was thinking about the paella, and thinking about Tarek at the same time. I had an idea, but I was nervous about it.

Darn my mother. I had spent my entire life telling myself I wasn't like her, but in the end I was the perfect mix of her and my father. Like my father, I was a loner. Like him, I was an intellectual. Like him, I was coldly logical. But like my mother, I liked people. I did, even though I didn't like to admit it. I loved little children, and I loved dogs. And the few friends that I did have, I cared about, and I had a good time with them.

And also like my mother, I couldn't refuse to offer guests something to eat. There was a small, maternal part of me. I wasn't sure if it was because I was like my mother in that way, or because I was a woman and, sooner or later, women became maternal.

I thought about the fact that Tarek didn't have a job and was paying for law school, his apartment and his expenses. I felt bad for him. It must be difficult. How much debt was he going to have? And he was so skinny. Was that because he didn't eat? I made a decision then.

We were both looking at our Property notes. I looked up at him, at his head full of curly black hair.

"Is—um—is there anything you don't eat?"

"Sorry?" He looked up from his notes.

"Is there any food that you don't eat?"

"No, I—I eat pretty much everything."

I hesitated. "Look, I made a ton of food. I always do." I smiled nervously. "Do you want to eat dinner later?"

"Sure, thank you," he said politely. "It looks amazing."

"OK. You can eat as much as you want. I never trust a man who is skinnier than me, anyway."

"I'm not skinnier than you." He smiled.

"And blind. I don't trust a blind man either."

Tarek laughed, showing his white teeth. Then we got down to organizing our Property notes.

It was 6:30 and we decided to stop and have dinner. I was experiencing the effects of the law of diminishing returns. My effort at studying was not producing an equal rate of return.

I was getting plates out.

"I'll help you," Tarek said.

"No, it's OK. You can finish outlining that case and then email it to me." I smiled at him.

"You know everyone stops outlining the cases after the first semester, right?" he said.

"Yes, but we're not everyone. Besides, by 'outlining' we're talking about pulling the rules and any distinguishing facts, not doing the one-page formal outline for each case like we did the first semester."

"True," he agreed. He moved his laptop to the side.

I came back with the plates. I had been sitting at one of the shorter ends of the table, the "head" of the table as it were, and he was sitting next to me, on the longer end. I reached over the table to set a plate down. Suddenly he completely averted his eyes from me, turning his face.

"What's your problem?" I said, confused.

"Nothing," he said quickly, but he wouldn't looked at me.

"What—" I looked down, and noticed that my flowing shirt was totally hanging open as I leaned over the table, exposing the tops of my breasts and my black bra!

"Oh, sorry," I said, smiling. "I didn't mean to offend your sensibilities." I stood up straight to correct my blouse. "Like you've never seen a pair of breasts before. At least I was wearing a bra." My words were careless and nonchalant, but inside I couldn't believe I had done that. I was so embarrassed. I hoped he didn't think that had been on purpose.

"Well, I've never seen a pair like that before, that's true." His eyes popped open for a second.

I opened my mouth in shock, reached over the table and playfully slapped him on the shoulder.

"Ow!" he protested.

"Dude, if I really wanted to hurt you, I would."

We quickly forgot the incident, ate dinner and chatted about our classes.

I thought of something then. "You're driving, right? So you don't want any wine?"

"Um," he seemed to think about it, "If you're having some I'll have a little bit."

"I only have reds, because I only drink reds. Sorry if that's a little uncouth since we're having paella with chicken. Is that okay?"

"Sure."

I poured Malbec for both of us. I preferred a Cabernet myself, since I liked the bolder reds. But a Malbec was a little lighter and probably more appropriate for the paella.

"Malbec is your favorite wine?" Tarek asked me then.

"No, but it probably goes pretty well with this dish."

"Oh. I thought it was, because that's what you had last Thursday."

I smiled then. I couldn't believe he remembered that. I didn't remember what type of beer he ordered. I had been too fixated on *him*.

"If I could, I would drink Cabernet all the time."

"It's quite bitter."

"Appropriate, don't you think?"

"How so?"

"Because I'm a bitter person."

"Are you? I hadn't noticed."

I looked at him with an expression of irony. "Oh, you're funny."

His expression changed, becoming a little wistful. "In all honesty, Isabel, I don't think you're really like that deep down."

"How the hell would you know what I'm like 'deep down'?" I said, using my air quotes.

"I don't know for certain. I'm speculating." He paused. "You know, I've never seen such a beautiful woman who cursed so much."

I was shocked into silence for a couple of seconds. Then I regained my composure enough to speak. "No one's ever accused me of being beautiful."

"Not to your face," he smiled a little. "Why would they? It's not like it would have any effect on you."

I was going to protest but he was right. It would not have had any effect on me.

"It would be a lie anyway," I ended up saying.

"You really think so?"

"I know so, Tarek. Men in this town look for bottle-blond superficiality in a woman, with a super skinny waist, narrow hips and amorphously large boobs." Like Sorority Girl.

His eyes were sparkling. I wondered what that meant. "Only stupid men look for that."

"And this city is full of them."

"I don't disagree." He paused again. I had the feeling he was still trying to figure me out. "Why do you care what the men in this town are like? Are you looking?"

"No!" I said immediately, a little too emphatically. "But I can't stand being surrounded by lameness."

"Well, that makes two of us then."

I looked at him. Was it him talking or the wine? I took a sip from my glass.

"My sisters got all the looks in my family." And I got the guilt.

"Isabel," Tarek started to say slowly, "I haven't seen your sisters, other than those family photos up there of them when they were younger," he gestured toward my television console, "but I highly doubt that."

"I told you before I don't respond to flattery." That was still a lie.

"I know. I'm stating a fact." Then his expression became a little contrite. "Look, I'm sorry if I offended you. You've been very nice to me, with dinner and everything."

"I also don't get offended easily." That was sometimes true, sometimes not. I smiled a little. "It's OK."

I decided to change the subject slightly.

"Speaking of 'looking,'" air quotes again, "I'm kind of surprised you don't have a girlfriend."

Tarek smiled. "What makes you think I don't have one?"

I gave him a look that told him not to mistake me for an idiot. "Because if you did, you wouldn't be hanging around with me. And—*she* would have driven you home after studying last weekend instead of me."

He smiled. "Maybe she's back in Miami."

I smiled back. I was going to call his bluff because I knew the answer. "Is she?"

He hesitated for a moment. "No. You're right. I don't have a girlfriend." He paused and seemed to be remembering something. I found myself wondering when the last time he had had a girlfriend was. Then I found myself wondering when the last time he had had sex was. Then I thought about having sex with him.

Get a grip! I told myself.

"So why don't you have a girlfriend?" I asked, just to say something and get my mind off sex.

"Why are you surprised that I don't have a girlfriend?"

"Why do you always answer a question with a question?"

"*I* always answer a question with a question?" He was amused now. "Well, it's like you said, we're studying to be lawyers, and that's what lawyers do, right?"

"You mean, they deflect questions they don't want to answer?"

In our own strange way, we were actually flirting. This wasn't lost on me. I had told him before that he was gorgeous; now he was telling me that I was beautiful. But the verbal parries were a new thing for me. In the past, when I was sexually attracted to a man and wanted to sleep with him, I would literally grab him. This interaction was more interesting, but also more confusing.

I decided then to answer his question because I was tired of the back-and-forth. If he wouldn't get to the point, then I would.

"I'm surprised because you're attractive and very smart and gentlemanly." I was not telling him anything new. I had referred to him as "gorgeous" the first time we had actually had a conversation. And he knew that I thought he was smart. And he obviously knew that he was gentlemanly.

"Sometimes I think women don't want a man who is gentlemanly."

"Well, they're idiots then." I took another sip of my wine. "I promise you, Tarek, you won't last long in this town. A single man like you—" My eyes went from his face to his chest and back. I was remembering seeing him in that tight-fitting black T-shirt. "You won't last long," I repeated.

"Hmm," he murmured. Then he answered my question, or started to. "I don't have a girlfriend because—" he seemed to be at a loss for words. I was intrigued since to date I had never seen him at a loss for words. "I just haven't met anyone, I guess." He looked at me. Then he added, "But I'm open-minded."

I could feel my pulse racing.

He was looking at me in a way that was slightly disconcerting. It was an intense look. I stared right back, right into his eyes.

"Isabel," Tarek began, "Why don't you have a boyfriend?"

I sighed. "Why do you ask? Because I'm old?" I knew that wasn't what he meant, but I was trying to avoid answering the question.

"No, you know I didn't mean that."

I hesitated. "It's like you said, I haven't met anyone."

He crossed his arms and appeared to be studying me. Or maybe he was deciding whether to say something. His brows furrowed.

"I get the impression you don't want a boyfriend," he finally said. His expression was serious and his eyes were intent.

I opened my mouth, but couldn't think of how to respond. I sighed and shook my head.

"Is that true?" Tarek continued.

I was thinking. "Not—not exactly." I suddenly felt a hole in my chest and looked away.

I opened my mouth again. "I mean, I'm so lonely." Then I realized what I had said and immediately regretted it. My voice had been so low that I hoped he hadn't heard.

Tarek uncrossed his arms and leaned toward me. "Isabel—I'm sorry—"

I whipped my head around to look at him, and our eyes locked. His eyes were on fire, and held me there so that I couldn't pull away, although I wanted to. For a second I felt like grabbing both his hands in mine and kissing them furiously.

"What I meant was—" I shook my head to break the connection, "I totally prefer to be alone than to be with just anyone. So the answer is yes, I mean—I don't—I'm not looking for a boyfriend."

In that moment I felt so exposed. I felt more exposed than when I had random sex with some random guy. That exchange with Tarek had been so intimate that it left me feeling raw. I spoke quickly again to fill the silence.

"I think most men are intimidated by women like me, anyway," I said, shrugging as nonchalantly as I could manage.

"What do you mean, women like you?"

"Women like me. Outspoken, a little aggressive, self-confident." I paused. "Abrasive. I don't take anyone's shit."

"Real men wouldn't be intimidated by that." Tarek smiled.

I could feel myself blushing. My face felt hot, and I was sure that it was almost the same color as my blouse.

Then he spoke. "I'm surprised you and Josh haven't dated."

I laughed. He had probably said that because Josh was attractive. "My mother asked me the same question. I love Josh like a brother. But he's not my type. I mean, I don't like him in that way. He and I also argue constantly about politics. It's just—I don't feel that way about him."

There was silence again between us for a few moments. Then Tarek spoke.

"I would bet that there are more men interested in you than you think."

I leaned across the table toward him. My wall was back up and I felt like myself again. "I highly doubt that. And if by some miracle you're right, none of them have the balls to do anything about it."

"Just wait. One of them may do something one of these days."

In spite of myself, my pulse quickened even more.

THIRD WEEK: **SUNDAY**

I was waiting for Lara and Patrick to pick me up to go to Mom's house. I couldn't stop thinking about Tarek. We had talked for a long time after dinner. He had left my house at around 9:30 after paella, wine, dessert (I hadn't prepared anything but I had some cookies) and tea.

We had each had about three glasses of wine. More than that, and I would have started getting giggly and I would not have trusted myself to keep my hands off him. I'm a cheap drunk.

I hadn't been able to tell if he had stopped at three glasses because he had to drive home or because he didn't want to drink more than me.

I was anxious to tell Lara all about my conversations with him on the drive down. When he had left last night I had walked him downstairs to the main door. He had asked me what I was doing today, Sunday. I had told him the truth, that I was going to visit my mother. I wasn't sure if he had asked because he wanted to ask me to do something on Sunday, or just to make small talk. Then he had thanked me for dinner and had touched my forearm. I had suddenly felt an electric pulse running through my veins.

I wasn't going to deny that I was hot for him. I had hardly been able to sleep after he left. I had kept thinking about him, and his eyes, and the way he moved, and how he had seemed so concerned when I had said that I was lonely.

I completely regretted that, letting my guard down like that. Maybe for a second I had thought—

No, he was just a hot guy. Being hot for him didn't mean, however, that I felt an emotional connection with him. I denied that I had any feelings for him other than the beginnings of friendship at this point. I would admit that I liked him as a friend, nothing more.

Looking back on it now, I don't know why I even bothered trying to convince myself.

Lara and Patrick stopped by my apartment building around 3 p.m. to pick me up. I didn't see the point in taking two cars, and I preferred to have their company on the drive down.

Lara called me when they arrived and I locked up and walked downstairs.

Patrick was driving. I got into the backseat, behind Patrick, and then greeted them both with kisses. Then I slinked against the back of the seat. This was my relaxation time. I didn't have to drive or think about anything. I needed to rest up for the visit to Mom's house.

"Mark's coming too," Lara told me then.

"OK, this'll be interesting," I told her. Then I had a thought. "Hey, you know, I talked to Mom on Saturday and I asked her how Mark was but she didn't say anything about what you told me, about him talking to her about moving in or marriage or anything. Why would she not tell me? It seems like it would be a big deal."

"I think she's probably nervous about it," Lara said. "She's been single since Dad died."

"Well, she's dated off and on," I countered. "You know what she should do? They should move in together for a trial period to see how it works out."

"Yeah, that would probably be a good idea—" Lara started.

"—seeing as how she's pretty hard to live with," I finished.

"Exactly. I think that's it. She's become so used to doing everything how she wants."

"Would your Mom move in with him without being married?" Patrick asked then.

"I don't know, to be honest," I answered. "But, seriously, at their age, I don't see what the big deal would be. I mean, she's fifty-nine and he's what, fifty-seven?"

"Yeah, I think he's fifty-seven," Lara said.

"He doesn't have any kids, we're grown up—" I started.

"That's debatable," Lara countered, smiling.

"Oh, yeah, well, you're the one who's not the grown-up."

"No way!" Lara protested. "I'm not the one who says 'dude' all the time!"

"Yeah, Tarek said he thought I was younger due, in part, to the fact that I say 'dude' a lot." I sighed. "I guess you were right about that," I added somewhat grudgingly.

"Well, since you brought it up," Lara began, but I could see her conspiratorial smile as she stole a glance sideways at Patrick, "How did it go with him yesterday?"

"Who?" I would drag this out a little. It was our little game.

"With Tarek! Who do you think I mean?"

"Oh," I answered, as if it hadn't occurred to me. "Fine. He's really smart. We got a lot of outlining done."

"Dude!" Lara exclaimed, impatient and perturbed. "I don't care about the studying part!"

"Who's saying 'dude' *now*?!" She was making the digressions too easy.

"What did you talk about?" She tried a different tack.

"You know. Property stuff, adverse possession, leases, nuisance law. Then Crim Pro, Fourth Amendment. . . ."

"Don't screw with me!" Lara looked at me, smiling and raising her eyebrows in mock anger.

"Oh, yeah, thanks for the reminder. We also had dinner and wine at my apartment, then we screwed!!"

"Oh my God," Patrick said in a minor panic. If we decided to talk about sex, he would have nowhere to go but the side of Interstate 95.

"Are you serious?!" I think Lara thought I was.

"No! Of course not!" I exclaimed. "Did you really think I would sleep with him?"

"I don't see why not!" she said. "You're single, he's—wait, is he single?"

"Yes, I found out last night that he's single."

"Interesting," Patrick mused. He also seemed relieved.

"All right, I'll tell you." I knew I would end up telling her every detail anyway; I always did.

"Yes, thank you!" She threw her hands up in the air. I could tell that she was more than a bit flustered with me.

I sighed. "We studied at my apartment. He came over at about 3:30. I had made paella for the week. So I invited him to stay and have dinner. We had dinner, wine and tea. We talked a lot. He left at about 9:30. Nothing happened," I said the last part emphatically. "We didn't kiss, we didn't—do anything." I paused. "When he left, he touched my arm, though."

"Ooo, the arm-touching," Patrick said. I couldn't tell if he was serious or if he was making fun of me.

"What does that mean, anyway?" I wondered aloud.

"What does *what* mean?" Lara asked me.

"What does it mean that he touched my arm? Or does it mean nothing?" I was musing out loud. Then I turned to Patrick. "You're a guy. What does it mean?"

"Well, I'd have to know the context and everything, what was said, his demeanor, all that stuff."

"OK." Then I proceeded to give them both a rundown of everything that was said last night, the 'good' stuff, as Lara said, not the law-school stuff. I didn't leave anything out.

"OK, let me get this straight." Patrick began. "He told you you're beautiful?"

"Yes," I answered.

"And he told you that real men like curvy women, all that stuff?"

"Yes," I said again.

"And he also told you that real men like assertive women, like you, and that real men wouldn't be intimidated by you?"

"Yes."

"And he told you that he thought there were probably lots of men interested in you?"

"Yes." I could see where he was going with this. All roads would eventually lead to my naivete.

"And he told you that maybe someday one of them would do something about it?"

"Yes."

"This guy is into you," was Patrick's conclusion.

"I agree," Lara concurred.

"But are you sure?" I wasn't convinced.

"Guys don't say stuff like that for no reason," Patrick said.

"Yes, they do," I countered. "They would say that stuff to get a woman into bed."

"They would say that to a woman they meet at a bar, or a party. They wouldn't continually try to hang out with a woman, all day Saturday, for example, just for a booty call."

I was more confused than before. "You guys, I haven't really dated for a while. I've only done hookups. I don't know the protocol. I don't know how to tell if a guy really likes me or just wants to hook up."

"You don't want to hook up with him?" Lara asked me.

"No, I mean—I do but—not yet. I only want to be friends with him. For now. I don't know." I didn't know how to articulate what I wanted. I was hot for him, but I was afraid that if we hooked up, then that would be it and I wouldn't see him anymore, just when I was really starting to enjoy hanging out with a like-minded individual.

"So you like him?" Lara asked, a bit incredulous, turning back in her seat to look at me. She had one eyebrow raised.

"Yes," I admitted.

"Do you *like* him, like him?"

"Dude, how old are you?!"

"Isabel, answer the question." Her tone seemed to be one she would use with one of our little cousins in Barcelona.

"It's a lame question." I was buying time to think of a noncommital answer.

Patrick clarified. "Do you have romantic feelings for him?"

Whenever I started to daydream about Tarek, my nipples got hard and I got turned on. Did that count? But I didn't say that. My sister wouldn't care but it would make Patrick terribly uncomfortable.

"I don't know," was the best I could come up with. "I plead the Fifth." I was at a loss for words, and I didn't like it.

"OK, so that's a 'yes.'" Patrick was relentless.

"That's a 'yes,' Isabel," Lara seconded.

I exhaled a long breath. "I'm not admitting to anything by this statement." I paused. "But guys, please don't mention this to Mom."

"Don't worry, we won't," Lara said, with a look that told me she loved me.

We made pretty good time to Mom's house. However, I was dreading the traffic on the way home. Sunday evenings were notorious for heavy traffic going north on Interstate 95. Everyone was coming home from their weekend jaunts.

Patrick pulled up to Mom's house. Mom lived in a nice neighborhood in Fredericksburg, Virginia. She had a huge, colonial-style house with a big fenced backyard. The entire lot was about a half an acre.

She didn't need a house this big. When she had bought it several years ago, I had asked her why she wanted such a big house.

"So that all my kids and grandkids have room when they come to visit," she had said.

To me, that made no sense. She was wasting her money on this huge house, when she lived by herself. It wasn't practical, in my mind.

But I knew that it was her choice. My philosophy was that I didn't criticize other people's decisions, and I expected that others didn't criticize what I did. However, the issue with my mother was that she always had an opinion about everything I did, from how my apartment was set up to my dating habits, or lack thereof. I had gotten pretty good at shrugging it off.

I took a breath before getting out of the car. The three of us walked up to the door.

My mother opened the door for us and we all walked inside the house, welcoming the cool air. Mom always had the air cranked up.

The foyer of the house was large, and the house had a pretty open floor plan. Beyond the foyer was the staircase, which wound to the left, leading upstairs to a hallway and four bedrooms. From the foyer, you could also either turn toward the back of the house and head to the kitchen and living room area, turn to the left and enter Mom's study, or turn to the right and enter the formal living room and, beyond that, the dining room.

When my sisters and I visited, we invariably spent most of our time either in the kitchen/living room area, or downstairs in the finished basement watching TV and goofing off.

Mom hugged each of us in turn. I entered the house last.

"Hi Mom," I said.

"Isabel, I'm so happy to see you! I haven't seen you in so long!"

"It's only been a couple of months, Mom."

At about 5 feet 7 inches tall, my mother was about a full inch taller than me. She had thick black hair, with some gray in it. She touched her hair up to cover most of the gray. She had just turned fifty-nine years old, but she looked no older than fifty. She had been beautiful when she was younger, and she was still attractive.

"I hope you guys are hungry," she said. "I made lasagna."

Mom's lasagna was legendary, and my mouth was already watering.

Then I saw what I considered to be the highlight of visiting Mom: her huge, furry dog.

Lola came bounding up to me. I liked to think that I was Lola's favorite, but in my head I knew that Lola unconditionally loved my Mom. Mom spoiled that dog rotten, going so far as to cook for her and hand-feed her when she wouldn't eat.

Lola was a pure-bred German Shepherd, and she weighed about eighty pounds. She was about twelve years old.

I squatted down and petted Lola with both hands, rubbing her furry Shepherd hair. Lola's ears went back and she licked me profusely, as always. I had read somewhere that dog's mouths and tongues were supposed to be very clean, and I wanted to believe that but really wasn't sure. Well, her kisses wouldn't kill me, I figured.

I straightened and looked at Mom. "I can't believe you made lasagna. I haven't had your lasagna in a while."

Mark was there and we all hugged him. Mark wasn't very tall, about an inch taller than Mom. He had thick hair that was completely gray, and he was always smiling.

After we greeted him, Mark continued setting the table. He was such a good guy.

Mom ushered us into the formal dining room to have dinner. The five of us would have fit at the kitchen table, but she preferred the dining room. Her house, her rules.

Patrick, Lara and I helped Mom and Mark carry casseroles, bread and salad into the living room. As usual, Mom had made a ton of food. That was a trait that I had inherited from her. I simply could not cook in small quantities. My freezer was, even now, packed with leftovers.

We all settled into our chairs at the dining table. Lola was not far away; she had lain down in the living room.

We all started to dip up our food. I was hungry. I took a huge helping of lasagna, bread and salad.

"Isabel, you look like you've lost weight," Mom told me. "Working too hard?"

I rolled my eyes a little bit. Mom *always* told me that I had lost weight, even if I hadn't.

"No, I haven't, Mom."

"So how much can you benchpress now?" Mark asked me, smiling.

I smiled back. "My max is only like eighty pounds," I told him. "It's all right."

"That's pretty good, for someone your size," Mark said.

"Isabel, I want to hear all about school," Mom told me then.

I sneaked a look at Lara. She half-smiled at me, but concealed it.

I was thinking about Tarek, and how I would see him in class tomorrow, but I wasn't going to tell Mom about him.

"It's going well so far," I told her.

"What classes do you have?" Mark asked me.

I told him.

"Criminal Procedure," he mused. "That will be very handy."

"Hopefully no one at this table will ever be arrested and will ever have to call me for help," I said, trying to smile a little.

"But you don't want to do criminal law, right?" Mark asked then.

"No, I—I'm hoping to do corporate law, transactional work, ideally." That kind of work would allow me to mostly work by myself, reviewing contracts all day. Kind of like now, except that I would be reviewing their legal contents and making legal recommendations instead of thinking about how to render them in a different language. "But," I continued, "the legal economy is not so great right now. So I'm open to a bunch of different options. I'm considering litigation, immigration, national security work, regulatory and other stuff."

"With your languages, you should be in great demand," Mark said. He was always so nice to me, and so positive.

"Why don't you stay with the government?" Mom asked then. Here we go.

"I don't work for the government now, Mom. I work for a contractor."

"Well, can't you just stay with your current company?" Mom asked. Here was where she started twenty questions.

"I could, and that is my fallback plan." She and I had already spoken about this. Why she felt the need to talk about it again, I had no idea. My mother was nothing if not insistent.

"Well, don't you have any contacts in the government, like at the Department of Defense or something?"

"I'm looking at all options." I considered what I was about to say, then went ahead. What the hell? "I'm applying all over the place."

"Really?" Mom asked. "Where?"

"I've applied to places all over the country, DC, New York, Miami, Delaware, Texas, for example."

"So you might move?" Mom asked.

"Yes," I answered. "I'm single, so I'm mobile."

"Maybe you'll meet someone at your new job," Mom wouldn't quit.

I closed my eyes and lowered my head a little bit, so Mom wouldn't see my expression.

"Yes, I'm ancient and my ovaries are about to dry up, so I guess I need a man, right?" I started to get a bit pissed off. "I mean, I can't be a real woman without a man and a couple of kids, right?"

"I didn't say that," Mom said.

"She didn't mean that." Lara was always conciliatory.

Yes, that is exactly what she meant.

"Mom, Lara and Ariel will give you grandkids. Don't worry about it."

"Not for a few years," Lara said. I shot her a look that said, you're not helping me right now!

"I'm not worried about *that*," Mom answered.

"Then what *are* you worried about?" I asked her point-blank. "If I meet someone, *bien*. If not, *bien tambien*. Not everyone wants kids and wants to be tied down, Mom. Besides," I paused for a breath, "You know something? You continuing to harp on my not having a boyfriend does not make it any likelier to become true."

Mom sighed, and shook her head a little bit.

"Don't pity me, Mom. I can't stand it," I told her.

Patrick asked for more lasagna. Mark cleared his throat. I picked at my dish. And she wonders why I don't come over here more often. That seemed to close the issue.

I was wrong.

"So—" Mom said then, glaring at me, a look of determination on her face. "Who was the person you were meeting to study with the other day when I called?"

Damn. My mother was so incredibly stubborn. I found myself thinking of my father for some reason. He had always tempered her moods a little bit.

"No one you know."

"Yes, you told me that on the phone. Who was it?"

"It doesn't matter."

"Is it a guy?" Mom asked then.

I was a jackass but I wouldn't lie. For some reason, I hated to lie. I considered it almost a sin. I didn't know why I felt that way.

"Yes," I admitted. Lara and I exchanged a look. My look was resigned. Her look was amused but I could tell she was also concerned about me. I smiled a little bit.

"You met him at school?"

"Yes, that's why we were studying." I exhaled sharply.

"Is he new to the school?"

"Yes, but it's his second year of law school. He transferred here from another school."

"He went over to your apartment?"

"Yes."

"I hope you cleaned it up, Isabel."

I couldn't help chuckling, but it was a mad chuckle, like the Joker. I didn't say anything in response.

"Her apartment is always clean," Lara defended me then.

"You should also get some more furniture," Mom told me then. "You need end tables for the sofa or something."

I rolled my eyes. We had had this conversation at least three times already. Then I suddenly thought of a way out.

"Hey Mom, Ikea is having a sale if you want to look at furniture with me sometime."

"Don't change the subject," Mom said gently.

Damn. Shut down. She was good.

"So what did you do?"

"What are you talking about?" I knew what she meant, but I played dumb.

"When this guy went over to your apartment, what did you do?"

"I told you, we studied." I was trying to remain calm, but it was becoming increasingly difficult.

"What does that entail?"

"You want to know what it means to 'study?'" using my air quotes. Now I was getting pissed off.

"Yes."

"We talked about the cases and did some outlining," I answered sharply. Why the hell was I answering all this?

"So then did you like, what, hold hands?"

"Jesus Christ, what the hell are you talking about?!" I started to lose it. "First of all, Mom, I am thirty-four years old! I'm not freaking fourteen! Second, it's possible to have guy friends that are just friends, not love interests! Jesus!" I blasphemed twice for good measure.

Mom looked at me, so I continued, trying to calm down. "He's a friend, that's it."

"Well, I'm sorry," Mom said. "What's his name?"

"I'm not telling you!" I looked right at her. "You know why? Because if I tell you, then you'll be calling me every weekend asking for updates. Isabel, how's so-and-so? Have you kissed him yet? Any chance you'll get married? Blah, blah, blah. I'm not putting up with that."

"So," Mom said, "to sum up, you have a new guy friend, and you're not dating anyone?"

I looked directly at her, raising my eyebrows. "That's right, and until I tell you differently, that is my relationship status."

"All right then," Mom continued. "You don't have to get all worked up about it."

I threw my hands up in the air.

We were all having coffee in the formal living room. Mom had made herbal tea for me, since if I had coffee at this time of the evening, I wouldn't sleep. Sometimes I didn't sleep anyway, but tonight I would at least try.

It was only 6:30 p.m. In Spain, this wasn't technically "nighttime" yet. But in the U.S., "nighttime" started at about 5 p.m. How curious.

I sunk back into the armchair I was sitting in. Mark was regaling us with stories of when he was in the Air Force. They always made us laugh.

"Isabel, did you get enough to eat?" Mom asked me.

"Yes, it was great," I told her.

"Can I get you anything else? Are you sure you don't want any cake?"

"No thanks, Mom." I felt bad about telling her off earlier. Whenever I erupted at Mom like that, I almost always felt bad later. But she was so insistent all the time. She would never take what I told her at face value. It was always, Are you sure, Isabel? But what about this? Have you considered that? It was as if she never heard my first two answers and by the third time she repeated her question, I was so exasperated that I would raise my voice at her.

I opened my eyes and listened to Mark for a while. He was so friendly. I hoped Mom married him. I would have to ask Lara later if there were any new developments in that department.

Then I looked at Mom, and caught her looking at me.

And there it was, the look that I dreaded. Mom was looking at me with a mixture of wistfulness and sadness. Her brows were a bit furrowed, and her mouth was a bit turned down. Her lips were pursed, and turned slightly inward. There was also pain in her eyes.

It was this look that I was avoiding when I didn't come to visit her. It was a look that told me that she still blamed me for Dad's death, and that she still thought about it.

It was a look that wished for something different, for something else. Was she wishing I had never been born? That can't be it. I can't believe she would want that, even if it meant that Dad were still alive.

The worst part was that I couldn't do anything about it. Dad had died, and I couldn't change that. And I couldn't do anything to get her to stop looking at me like that. The only thing I could do was avoid it.

Avoiding issues that I didn't want to deal with was one of the things that I did best.

On Monday morning I hit the ground running. Usually I tried to decide the night before what I wanted to wear the next day, so I wouldn't have to think about it in the morning. Last night, however, I had been tired. After preparing coffee for the next morning, packing my lunch and preparing my gym bag and school backpack, I fell down in my bed. Consequently, the next morning I didn't know what to wear.

This will be one of the days when I wear jeans. I pulled on a pair of black jeans and a black shirt. I put on minimal makeup, and started thinking about my conversation with Lara on the way home the night before.

The ride home had been fairly uneventful. I had asked Lara about Mom and Mark.

"No, I don't know anything besides what I told you the other day," she had told me. "But I'll let you know."

I had been silent for a few moments. Then I had said, "Guys, I'm sorry for getting worked up in front of you. Mom infuriates me with her questions."

"I know," Lara said in a conciliatory tone. She was forever the peacemaker in our family, at least between Mom and me.

"She's so insistent all the time," Patrick said then. "I don't know how you guys handle it."

"Apparently, I'm not handling it very well," I said.

Then I remembered something that Melanie and I were always talking about.

"Why do married people feel pity for single people," I asked Lara and Patrick, "the way Mom seems to feel pity for me?"

"I don't feel that way," Lara said.

"I know that *you* guys don't, but—people are so self-righteous, and they always think they know better than you," I said. "It's infuriating."

"That's this town," Patrick said. "It's full of self-important congressional aides and students working unpaid internships."

I agreed.

We were silent for a little while.

"You know, Tarek has a sister," I said then, completely out of the blue. I have no idea why I said it. I felt like talking about him for some reason.

"Really?" Lara asked.

"Yeah, just one sister. She's younger than he is. She lives with the Mom in Miami."

"He's from Miami?" Patrick asked.

"Yeah."

"I thought you said he was French?" Patrick asked.

"I thought you said he was Lebanese?" Lara said at the same time.

"Well, I guess he's both." Then I explained the story of his parents, and how the family immigrated to Miami.

"So what happened to his father?" Lara asked me.

"I don't know. He hasn't mentioned him and I haven't asked." I felt like it wasn't my business.

When they dropped me off, I gave them both big hugs.

"Good luck this week," I told my sister.

"You too," she smiled, her eyes twinkling.

The smile I gave her now was completely genuine, a reflection of how I felt when I was around her.

"Let me know how everything goes," she winked at me as she got back in the car.

I smiled again. I knew exactly what she meant.

Mondays were always busy at work. I finished a bunch of revisions and then hit the gym at lunch to pound the treadmill. It felt great after sitting down studying all weekend. After my run, I was rooting around in my makeup bag, wanting to do my face up a little bit. I found a new dark blue eyeliner that I had been wanting to try. No time like the present. I put it on, pleased with the effect. I smudged in some purplish eye shadow that had a little glimmer to it. I liked it. I finished the look with mascara and clear lip gloss.

When I went to the kitchen to nuke my lunch after the gym, several of my coworkers were eating there. Once again, the conversation stopped as soon as I entered. I could feel their eyes boring into my back as I grabbed my lunch from the fridge.

"Isabel," Abdul started, "do you have a date after work?"

"No," I said without turning around.

"Then why all the makeup?"

"No reason." So women need a reason to wear makeup now?

"It looks good."

"Thanks." I gave Abdul a quick look as I was waiting for my food to heat up in the microwave. The others were also looking at me.

"It looks *really* good."

Oh, God.

I pretty much successfully avoided everyone at work for the rest of that day. Tim was still somewhat pissed off at me after our conversation several days ago. Well, he would have to deal.

Luckily, the weather was starting to get a bit cooler. I still didn't need a jacket, but at least I wasn't sweating when I got to campus.

I was early today; I had managed to leave work at 5 p.m. and was at campus by 5:25 or so. When I walked inside the law school, I saw Tarek sitting by himself on a sofa by one of the tables in the back.

I could feel my heart leap at the sight of him. Oh God, this is *not* good.

He looked great. I noticed that he had tried to get his curls out of his face by moussing them back. But he had somewhat failed because he was holding them back with one hand as he leaned over his book reading.

I approached him and he saw me. He smiled instantly. I saw his eyes pop.

"Hey, Isabel." I also saw him look me over from head to feet.

"Hi. Do you mind if I sit here?"

"Of course not." He moved his book from the seat next to him. "Here, sit on the sofa, it's more comfortable."

"Thanks." I sat next to him and took out my Crim Pro book. I leaned back against the sofa.

"Did you finish reading for Crim?" I asked him.

"Almost," he smiled.

"OK, well, I won't bother you then."

"No, that's OK. I don't mind being bothered." His look was a little flirtatious. I wasn't sure if he meant it to be or not. I also wasn't sure if he gave that look to all women or just to me. I hadn't really seen him speak to any women other than Zara, and he hadn't looked that way at her.

"Actually," he said then, "I have a question for you."

"Shoot."

"It's about probable cause for a warrant."

"OK." A Crim Pro question. I loved those.

"So, if I understand correctly, there are two lines of inquiries, reliability and the information itself."

"Well," I said, "under *Spinelli v. Gates* the Supreme Court said that, to determine whether there was probable cause for a warrant, the inquiry was a two-prong test. You look at the reliability of the informant and the quality and type of information in the oath, i.e. whether it is corroborated. But the current test is expressed in *Illinois v. Gates*. That's the minimum test under the Constitution, but the professor said that some states provide even more stringent requirements."

"But you still consider basically the same elements as in *Spinelli*, right?"

"Right," I agreed. "When you look at whether there's probable cause for the search warrant, you still look at the reliability of the informant and also the type of information provided, and whether on its face it could be evidence that a crime had occurred or was occurring. But in *Gates*, the Court called it a totality of circumstances test. But you're right, it's basically the same test."

"And, to confirm, the problem in *Gates* was that the letter was anonymous and the police couldn't really verify the reliability of the informant?" His eyes went from my face, to his book, then back to my face. Then I realized that I was holding my breath.

I exhaled, then answered. "The way I read the case is that just because a tip is anonymous does not mean that there is *per se* no probable cause. It depends on how specific the information is. Possibly, if the information in the letter in *Gates* had been more specific, or more indicative of illegal behavior, and had been able to be corroborated, then there may have been probable cause."

"OK, so the other part is corroboration."

"Right, if the police can corroborate the information provided by the informant, that makes it more likely that probable cause will be found. The less reliable the informant, the more important corroboration becomes."

"OK, that makes sense."

"Here," I said. "Take a look at the cases after *Gates* to see how the test was applied." I took out my Crim Pro book. "They're helpful."

I opened the book between us and found the pages I was looking for. We both leaned a little toward each other to read. I noticed then that our shoulders were touching. I was a little unnerved at being so close to him.

"So the standard for probable cause is a fair probability," I continued.

"It's a lesser standard than preponderance of the evidence," Tarek said.

"Right." I looked at him. God, our faces were closer than I had thought. He smiled. "Thank you, Counselor."

I smiled back a little. "OK, you can't ask for my help and call me a nerd at the same time."

"I wasn't calling you a nerd," he said sincerely.

"Hey guys."

We both looked up immediately. It was Josh. Jesus, Sorority Girl was with him. For some reason she occasionally hung around Josh. I got the impression that maybe she liked him, or maybe she was nice to him in order to get his notes when she wasn't in class. *I* sure as hell wouldn't give her *my* notes.

For some reason, I felt like Josh had caught us in the middle of something, and I felt my face turning red. I don't know why. We were only talking about Crim Pro!

Josh and SG sat down. I didn't introduce her to Tarek because I didn't care about her.

But SG took the liberty of introducing herself.

"Hi, I'm Alyssa," she said as she reached out her hand to him. He politely shook it and introduced himself. I noticed her dark roots were starting to show. Why would she dye her dark hair that obviously fake straw color? Evidently, she was trying to be something she wasn't.

She looked at me, and for a second I froze, fearing that perhaps she could read my thoughts. Then she glanced at Tarek, and it dawned on me that she was trying to figure out whether he and I were together. I was going to let her stew for a while. I gave her a hard look, daring her to say something. She looked from me to Tarek, then back to me. I raised my eyebrows at her.

Then she seemed to resign herself. She looked at Josh and asked him, "Could you please send me your notes from last Tuesday? I wasn't here."

"Sure," Josh told her. He was too nice.

I was right. She was only nice to him for his notes. She probably couldn't get them from anyone else.

I got up then. "I'm going to get coffee before class, you guys." I grabbed my purse. "Does anyone want anything?"

"I'll go with you," Tarek said. "I'll get tea."

"No, I'll get it." I smiled and left before he could say anything. I knew he wouldn't let me pay otherwise. After all, the other day I had said *I* was going to treat *him* to a drink and he wouldn't let me pay for *that*.

Alyssa was looking at me as if she were going to say something, but my look shut her down.

She didn't honestly think I was asking *her* if she wanted anything, did she?

But she got me back big-time. As I was leaving, purse in hand, almost clear of the lounge area, I heard her say, "You know she sleeps around, right?"

Well, Goddamn. She figured she would 'out' me to Tarek, huh? Damn her. I knew she was talking to him. Who else would she say that to?

I continued walking like I hadn't heard anything. I walked outside what the students called the quad and across it to the university-run coffee shop. I would have preferred to get my coffee on the outside but there wasn't enough time.

I was angry at Alyssa, but, honestly, why would I expect anything else of her? She hated my guts.

I got my coffee and Earl Grey for Tarek and headed back. Alyssa was no longer there, thank God.

I handed Tarek his tea.

"Thank you," he smiled. "How much was it?"

"No problem. And if you try to pay me back, I'll be offended," I said then, grabbing my backpack.

Tarek looked at Josh.

"Oh, she will be," Josh nodded, with a look that said you really better not try it.

Tarek seemed resigned, but his eyes were playful. Again, I wondered what he was thinking about.

Josh, Tarek and I walked upstairs.

"I'm going to stay after for something today so don't wait for me," Josh told me.

"OK." I guess it would be Eric, Dinesh, Tarek and me on the metro.

"Awesome, maybe we'll actually get out of here on time for once since we won't have to wait for you." I was chuckling. I couldn't help it.

"Ha, ha," Josh said in mock laughter.

Eric and Dinesh were already in their seats.

Class began shortly after that. Today, the professor was still discussing search warrants and reasonableness.

I opened my instant messaging program. Josh was connected, too. I was dying to know something, and I needed to know right away. I sent him a message.

I heard what Alyssa said after I left. What did Tarek say?

You mean about you "sleeping around?"

Yes. What did he say after she said that?

Nothing.

Nothing?

He waved it off like he didn't want to hear about it.

He didn't say anything?

No. He literally dismissed it.

"Wait, she said that?!" It was Eric. He sounded incredulous. He was trying to keep his voice down, I could tell, but he was doing a poor job of it. Freakishly loud Brazilian.

I whipped the swivel chair around and glared at Eric. He was looking at Josh's screen. Pissed off beyond all measure, I slammed Eric's laptop down, catching his right hand.

"Ow!" Eric protested

I whirled back around as fast as I could, but not fast enough. Several people around us were looking at Eric and me.

"Ms. Vilanova!" It was the professor.

Shit. Shit, shit, shit shit.

"What do *you* think?" the professor asked me.

I opened my mouth but no words came out. I felt like hundreds of eyes were glued on me, probably because they were. "I'm sorry, professor, would you mind repeating the question?"

"Yes, what is the significance of the case *Warden v. Hayden*?"

Luckily, I knew the answer. "Um, the Court found that any evidence related to or associated with a crime could be seized under a warrant, not only the instrumentalities used or fruits of the crime, and not just contraband. That is, any evidence can be seized."

"Yes, very good."

I sighed with relief; I had just dodged a bullet. I looked at my screen. Tarek had written to me, *Is everything OK?*

Yes, I answered. Then I shut down the instant messaging program.

At the one-hour break, I stood up.

"Jesus, what was that for?" Eric asked me, also standing up.

I whirled around. "For snooping. If you have a question for me, just ask!"

"OK," Eric's face suddenly had a look of determination, which was uncharacteristic.

He leaned toward me and motioned me closer with his index finger. Hesitantly, I leaned in so our faces were close.

"Why do you care what he thinks about you?" Eric spoke in a low tone and motioned toward Tarek as he asked me.

"I don't know," I whispered.

"OK, I can see that's an honest answer," Eric seemed satisfied.

"I have a question for *you*, Eric."

"Yeah?"

"Why do *you* care why I care about what he thinks about me?"

He paused, as if weighing something. "Maybe I don't want to see you get hurt." His eyes changed; they got a little misty for a second. Then he was his usual self again.

"We're friends, right?" I asked him.

"Yes," Eric said.

"I'm sorry about your hand." I smiled.

"I'm sorry for snooping." He smiled back.

At the end of class, Eric said that he was going out that night with some friends, so he wouldn't be walking to the metro with us. Dinesh had driven, so he wouldn't be going with us either. That left only Tarek and me. My heart started to race a little bit as we left together.

*   *   *

Tarek and I walked into the metro station and down the stairs. I was starting to get sleepy and watched my feet so I wouldn't fall.

It was just the two of us. We reached the platform and I turned around to face him. I didn't say anything at first. He smiled.

"So what's with the all-black clothing today?" he asked in his mild French accent. Had I always found the French accent sexy, or did I only find *his* accent sexy? I couldn't tell.

"Oh, you know. I'm mourning the deterioration of our society into a welfare state, the deterioration of language and grammar skills, the emasculation of men, all of the above."

He chuckled. "Don't worry about any of that."

"Why not?"

"Because governments, and the latest fads, come in cycles. It won't always be like this."

"I'm not so sure," I answered honestly. I had a lot to say on this subject, but I figured I would save it for another time.

"And the rest of what you said," he continued, "There are still enough intelligent people in the world to make sure that society doesn't completely degenerate."

"I wish I could be as optimistic as you." These were the things I worried about at work, and at night, when I tried to fall asleep. "I always think the worst about everything. That way I'm not disappointed later." Eventually, I was always disappointed. It never failed.

I looked at the electronic sign that announced how long we had to wait for the next train. We had twelve minutes. I sighed, then looked at Tarek again.

I really wanted to know what he thought about what Alyssa had said, but I was afraid to ask.

Then I steeled myself. I was way too old for high-school shit. I was going to take the direct route. What the hell? I figured I would play one card. I had plenty left.

"So Sorority Girl told you that I sleep around, huh?"

"You heard that?" he said, looking at me quizzically.

I nodded and rolled my eyes. "She's an idiot."

He looked at me, a bit cautiously. "So is it true?"

"What? That I sleep around?"

"Yes," he said, still cautious, like he was treading lightly.

I paused, weighing my words. "Well, that depends . . . on your definition of 'sleep around.' How would *you* define it?"

He hesitated. He seemed to be thinking about whether I was serious or not. "That's very lawyerly of you, answering a question with a question."

"Well, I *am* training to be a lawyer and all." I paused and looked intently at him, weighing how honest I should be. "But," I began, "if you tell me how you define the term, I'll answer honestly."

"Fair enough," he was still looking at me warily, like he didn't quite trust me to be honest. "To me," he began, "if you sleep with random people—"

"Define 'random,'" I said immediately.

He sighed, feigning impatience, or maybe it was actual impatience; I wasn't sure. "If you sleep with people who you don't know really well, who you aren't dating, who you only intend to have a one-night thing with," he looked at me, waiting for an objection.

"OK," I said. "By 'dating,' you mean more than one date?"

He considered for a moment. "More than two. That's why I included the term 'one-night thing.'" He crossed his arms. "Isabel, you're stalling now."

But I didn't give up. "Hmm, so you would expect a woman to have sex with you after two dates?" I was baiting him, but he was smart; he saw it.

"Objection, Counselor," he smiled, "As this line of inquiry is irrelevant to the main issue. But I'll answer the question." He paused. "I would never *expect* a woman to have sex with me, even if I hoped for it."

I thought of all kinds of questions to ask regarding his answer, but I decided against saying anything. I let him off easy, because his definition actually helped me, since that would mean I could include fewer men in my response. Under his definition, since I had hooked up with Saul three weekends in a row, I had 'dated' him. At least, that was how I figured it.

"OK," I said. "Continue."

"I would say—" he continued. He seemed to really be thinking about it now. "I would say that if you do that more than once a month, more or less, that is 'sleeping around.'"

"Interesting," I said. "Well, based on the term, as you've defined it, I do *not* 'sleep around.'" I held up air quotes for 'sleep around.' "Not that there's anything wrong with it, or with anyone who does it."

"I didn't say there was, necessarily."

We looked at each other. I smirked a bit.

"So you sleep with 'random' guys, as I've defined it, less frequently than once a month?"

"That is correct." I said slowly, wondering where this was going.

"So how often do you do that?"

"Less than once a month," I parroted. "That is all you need to know, not like you need to know any of this." In fact, I wasn't sure why I was telling him about my 'sleeping' habits.

He smiled back. "Do you ever date them?"

"Who? The men I sleep with?"

"Yes."

"No."

"No what?"

"You're slow tonight," I said, watching his reaction. He was actually keeping me on my toes, so that I had to think two steps ahead, but I wasn't going to let him know that. He smiled and continued to look at me, waiting. Oh good God, I'll answer the damn question and be done with this.

"No, I do not typically date the men I sleep with."

"But you do date sometimes?"

"Not really, no." I hesitated. "I mean, I'm not averse to it. I just haven't—'dated,'" using air quotes again, "anyone for a while."

Our train arrived then. We got on and sat down next to each other. I thought that maybe he wouldn't say anything else, but that was wishful thinking.

"Why not?"

Damn. Was he asking me all this because I had told him that I was lonely the other day? I should not have done that.

My hands were in my lap. I looked at them, thinking. Tarek didn't say anything.

I began to get lost in my thoughts, and started thinking about Santi. I don't know why. He was the last man I had really been in any semblance of a relationship with. "It's too painful," I blurted out, without thinking. Idiot. That's what happens when you're overtired!

Tarek's face changed; he looked concerned. "What happened?"

"Nothing!" I was beginning to get miffed.

But Tarek wouldn't let it go. I would learn soon enough that this was typical of him. He never let me off easy. "What you just said," he moved closer to me, "that was from the heart." There was a crease in his forehead. "You don't usually do that. You're so—"

"Guarded?" I offered, "suspicious?"

"I was going to say closed-off, but you are those things too."

"Yeah, well—that happens sometimes. Every once in a while I say what I really feel."

"You say what you feel all the time."

"No," I shook my head. "I say what I *think* all the time, that's true. I never say what I feel."

He nodded in agreement. Then he said softly, "You must've been in love with somebody, at some time—"

"I never said I haven't been in love," I snapped.

He ignored my snarkiness. It irked me that my general impoliteness had little to no effect on him. "And I refuse to believe that no man has ever loved you, I mean, a woman like you—" He stopped, and seemed a little embarrassed.

Wait, a woman like me? What did that mean? I considered embarrassing him further by saying something snarky, but I decided to leave him alone.

"I did once, I mean, I was in love once, with someone who was in love with me, a long time ago." I was wistful, and started getting lost again. I had again spoken without thinking about what I was going to say. Any more and this is going to become a bad habit.

"Well, then," Tarek said, his smile broader this time, his eyes twinkling, "Isabel Vilanova, there may be hope for you yet."

"You're an optimist," I scoffed.

"Yes."

"Well, then, you won't be a good lawyer. The law is one of the few areas where pessimists outperform optimists."

"Well, you will be an excellent lawyer then." He paused for a moment. "So you're not going to tell me what happened?" he asked.

"What do you mean?" I played dumb. I knew what he meant.

"About the man you were in love with."

I wanted to say something snide, but instead I told him straight, "That's too personal."

We sat in silence for a little while. Then Tarek looked at me and said, "I'm your friend, you know?"

I looked at him, taking in his huge dark eyes and long dark lashes. I could get lost in those eyes if I wasn't careful. I smiled, but not in a mocking way. It was a warm smile, a genuine smile. "The jury's still out on that one."

He smiled back, his eyes laughing.

We talked about Crim Pro until Pentagon City.

I don't know why I had said that. I really did consider him a friend. But I didn't know if he was interested in only being friends with me or in something more.

I was on my way to campus, walking up H Street, trying not to overthink things. I was attempting to distract myself by mentally going over the cases we had read that night for Crim Pro. It was only minimally working. Although I was trying not to be, I was excited to see Tarek tonight.

He confused and excited me at the same time. On the one hand, I was really glad to have another person to talk with not only about the law, but also about politics. I was also glad to have someone to talk to about my international experiences, and how I always felt slightly out of place in the U.S., even in DC, but how I also felt out of place in Spain and in Argentina. When people asked me where I was from, I never knew how to respond. I always paused, weighing how much to tell them and making a snap decision on it.

I was trying to figure out how I felt about Tarek. We were friends but we were also like law school soulmates. I had told him that we would never get together romantically, but I was starting to think that maybe I had spoken prematurely. I was hot for him; I was no longer denying that. I wanted to kiss him badly. What if I did? What if he and I had a one-night thing? Somehow, that seemed unfulfilling, like I would be left wanting more. I usually had no problem spending one night with a guy, but Tarek was different because we had connected on a higher level. If we did that, then things would be weird between us and we would probably spend less time together, and that thought was anathema to me.

I had almost reached the law school. I was a bit early and there weren't as many students around as usual, running up the stairs late to class. Ahead of me there were two women pulling a red wagon with three or four kids inside. They must be daycare providers taking care of those kids. The women were chatting and the kids were enjoying the nice weather.

One of the kids was a little blonde girl. She was about seventeen or eighteen months old, and wore one of those helmets on her head, probably to help her cranium form properly, I guessed. She was so cute. I was at the bottom of the steps that led up to the school's main entrance. I smiled at her, a big, broad smile. I couldn't help myself. The little girl smiled back, a huge smile that lit up her entire face. I kept looking at her as I walked up the steps, and waved at her. She waved back. I was at the top of the steps and could still see her. I kept smiling and waving and she smiled and waved back, *super contenta*. I waved at her until she was out of sight.

I was sad then. Her parents probably missed her when they were at work, but in this town you really needed two incomes to make ends meet.

Then an unbidden thought crept into my head that started to make me feel downright depressed. I would never have kids. I'm thirty-four years old and unmarried with no significant other. Not that I minded being alone. Like I had told Lara and Ariel countless times before, it was better to be on your own than to be with someone who was not a good partner for you. But I would never have a little mini-me, someone to teach everything to, someone to watch grow up, someone to cheer for.

I was still standing there, thinking, when someone greeted me.

"Hey, Isabel."

I turned at the sound of Tarek's voice. I must have had a sad expression on my face, because he looked instantly concerned.

"Are you OK?"

"Yeah," I lied.

"I saw you, you know?"

"Saw what?"

"I saw you waving to her. She was really cute."

"Yeah, she was."

"I didn't know you liked children."

"I don't—I mean, I don't like them particularly. I—" I was suddenly at a loss for words, and didn't like it. "My cousins in Spain have kids. I'm just used to them." I looked pointedly at him. "And there's a lot you don't know about me."

For once, he didn't press me. He could tell I didn't want to talk about it. He changed the subject and I loved him for it.

"Did you read for class tonight?"

"Yes, did you?"

"Everything except the last case."

"I'll fill you in during the break."

"Thanks." He held the door open for me. I had my hands full, since I was carrying my Property book. We didn't have Property class tonight, but I had been reading for the next day, since I was behind. I had been daydreaming too much.

When we stepped inside the building, Tarek said to me, "Let me get that."

He then took my Property book gingerly out of my hands, like he was afraid I would bite him or something. "How was work?"

"It was all right." I decided to keep up the conversation, partly as a distraction but partly to get his opinion on something. I was going to change the subject again.

"Turkish men are really direct, aren't they? I mean, in general."

I had run into the Turkish guy again near my job. He had asked me to go out for coffee but I had said that I was busy. I had also told him that I had a boyfriend. I didn't know why he was so insistent. I was tiring of it.

His interest was piqued. "What do you mean? Is there a Turkish man you're interested in?"

And why would you want to know that? I thought.

"No, I wouldn't say 'interested in,'" using my air quotes. "There's this guy I keep running in to in Crystal City. He doesn't work where I work; he works somewhere else. But he keeps asking me out."

"And you've been turning him down?"

"Yes, well," I was a little embarrassed because I would have to admit that I had lied. "I told him I was dating someone."

"You lied?" Tarek smiled.

"I wouldn't usually, but he was so insistent."

"And you don't want to go out with him?" We were walking up the stairs to class.

"I mean, he's good-looking, but I don't know him. I told him I was dating someone and then he asked how long I had been dating this guy, and whether the guy I was seeing was jealous."

"And what did you say?" Tarek seemed a little too interested in the details.

"That my supposed boyfriend is jealous, and that it wouldn't be a good idea." Why was I telling Tarek so much? I had only planned to ask him about Turkish men. I decided to get back to my original question.

"I've never dated a Turkish man," or slept with one, I thought, "hence my question to you about Turkish men in general."

"Well, they are *very* direct," Tarek said. "Also, even if he thinks you have a boyfriend, or a husband for that matter, that won't necessarily stop him from asking you out."

"OK," I was pensive. "So you would say that they're intense?" We walked into the classroom.

"Yes."

"OK," I said. "Like maybe they would stare at a woman from head to toe? That kind of thing?"

"Yes."

"Oh, OK." I rolled my eyes.

"What?" Tarek asked.

"Nothing." My subtle jab was lost on him, or so I thought. Yesterday, Tarek had been looking at me from my toes all the way to the crown of my head. I had felt thrilled by it.

"I was already leaning in that direction, anyway," I told him.

"In what direction?" Tarek seemed confused.

"In the direction of not dating that guy." We sat down in our seats. I took out my laptop and switched it on.

"So you're dating now?" Tarek asked, half-smiling. "I thought you said you didn't really date."

"That is true, as a general rule," I said carefully. Tarek, please don't ask me out now, I mentally panicked. I'm not ready for it. However, my heart was dying for him to ask me out.

"So are you telling me that you were only thinking of doing that guy?"

"Doing? Where did you learn that expression? It's slang."

"I know what it means. And you're not my only source of slang."

"Really?" I was interested now. "Who have *you* been doing recently?"

"No one. Who have *you* been doing?"

"None of your damn business," I said, perturbed. Then I let out a long breath. "But no one." That was partly the problem. I was so horny. I was like a man, thinking about sex during the day. Jesus.

Then I had an afterthought. "Why are you so interested in my love life, anyway?"

"Isabel, you asked me who I was doing first," Tarek countered.

"You didn't answer my question," I parried. "And my asking that question is not relevant to the issue of why you are so interested in my sex life." I said the last part a bit too loudly and the people behind us looked at us.

Tarek sighed, then looked at me. "Men can be dogs sometimes."

"Yeah, well, women can too. So be careful out there."

"Don't worry. I have no prospects."

"Well, I don't either, so we're even," I said. I looked at him, and we both smiled at the same time. He was gorgeous when he smiled. He flashed white teeth, prominent against his darker skin. His dark curls were carefully arranged, and he had recently trimmed his goatee. He looked incredible. Inside, I was salivating.

Although I recognized that I might be blinded by his good looks, I also had the impression that he did care about my welfare on some level. I had no idea why. I hadn't always been the nicest person to him.

I opened my mouth then and said something without thinking. "You're a good friend."

His smile broadened. "You are too, in your way. But I thought you said the jury was still out on whether we were friends."

"Well, I thought about it, and I hereby declare that we are friends now."

He was still smiling. "Well, OK, then, *friend.*"

Class started then, and I looked at my laptop. I was smiling inwardly, and my heart was fluttering a little.

I was rushing to campus, running as fast as I could while carrying my backpack and Property book. I had worked at home that day so that I could wait for the maintenance man to come fix the air conditioner. It was still warm enough outside during the day that not having the A/C was problematic. He was able to fix it, but it took longer than I had anticipated.

On top of that, I had woken up earlier than usual to be able to finish my translations on time. But I still hadn't been able to do everything that I had wanted to do. And I hadn't finished the reading for Property. And I had to make it to campus for my 3:50 class. Boo. I had been too ambitious today.

I made it to the Franconia metro station and hopped on the train as the doors were closing. I was sweating already. Fantastic. At least I remembered to put some makeup on, foundation, mascara and lip gloss. For some reason, I always wanted to wear makeup now. My hair hung in waves around my face. It was getting too long, and there was too much of it, but I didn't have time to go to the salon. I had left it wet and slapped a ton of mousse on it so that it wouldn't frizz out.

I looked at my phone to see the time. If I made it to class on time, it would be by the skin of my teeth, assuming that the metro wasn't delayed.

I took out my phone and sent a message to Tarek.

Will be late. Don't wait downstairs for me.

We had kind of gotten into the habit of meeting downstairs in the lounge area before class. I didn't want to inconvenience him.

Dinesh was right, I thought wryly. I was turning into Josh, getting to class right as it started, Latin time.

Growing up, my mother was late to everything. She was late to movies, to dinner, to everything. She continually operated on Argentine time. In

Argentina, if someone told you to show up at 7 p.m., you showed up at 9 p.m. In the US, that was pretty offensive. It had constantly driven me nuts growing up, so much so that I always told my mother that I had to be somewhere an hour before I really needed to be. The party starts at 7 p.m., Mom, I would say, when it really started at 8 p.m.

I tried not to be late, but sometimes I slipped.

My phone blipped, showing a message from Tarek.

OK. Am getting tea. Would you like anything?

Yes! God bless you! I hadn't had any coffee since 8 a.m. and I was dying for a caffeine fix.

Yes, please. Small coffee. Thank you!

After a minute I received his response.

OK, will do. Since you said please.

Everyone is a comedian, I thought, smiling to myself.

I ran out of the train at the metro station, up the escalator, breathing heavy by the time I reached the top. I was carrying at least fifteen to twenty extra pounds with my backpack and Property book. As I ran past the quad, the clocktower tolled forty-five minutes past the hour.

I was barely going to make it!

I ran up the main steps, throwing the glass doors back. I didn't even bother with the stupid elevator. I ran up four flights of stairs as fast as I could and finally got to the classroom.

I slowed down a little and exhaled. I got to International Law class just as Zara did. She looked at me and seemed unsure of something.

"Hi," I told her, panting, my chest heaving.

"Hi," she smiled back. She still looked uncertain, but I didn't know about what. I shrugged it off. I didn't have time to worry about random stuff like that. For all I knew, I had something on my face.

The professor was already there but he hadn't started speaking yet.

I slinked into, or tried to slink into, my seat next to Tarek. It's difficult to be surreptitious while carrying a laptop bag, purse and law school book. I sat down and exhaled a giant breath.

Tarek and I looked at each other. He was leaning on his left elbow, resting his chin in his left hand. He slid my coffee over to me, shaking his head with a smile as he did so.

I smiled back. "Thank you," I whispered.

"No problem," he whispered back.

I wasn't sure why I was whispering. Class hadn't started yet, and everyone was still chatting.

"Is everything OK?" Tarek asked me then.

"Yes—it's been a long day."

I opened my laptop and switched it on.

Class started and I tried to pay attention.

As I was opening my notes, a message from Tarek appeared on my screen.

Casual day at work today?

I smiled. I was wearing jeans and a black T-shirt with my red Pumas. It was pretty casual for me.

Technically, there is no dress code at my job.

But you always dress up.

Well, thank you for noticing. Then I wrote, I worked at home today. Had to wait for the man to come fix the A/C.

Did it get fixed?

Yes.

"Ms. Vilanova!" It was the professor.

I almost jumped out of my seat. Holy shit. Did he know that I was chatting online? I hardly ever chatted during class. 98 percent of the time, I paid attention and took detailed notes. I usually scoffed at the students in front of me, chatting, looking at the New York Times and online shopping.

I looked at the professor. "Yes, sir?" I thought if I was *uber* polite, he would be more forgiving if I didn't know the answer.

"What do *you* think?"

What did he ask? *Dammit.*

As I was pondering what to say, another message appeared on my screen from Tarek.

Avena case.

Oh, right! We had read the consular cases for today.

In the so-called *Avena* case, the Mexican government brought a suit against the U.S. in the International Court of Justice, on behalf of several Mexican citizens who had been detained in the U.S. The issue concerned the Vienna Convention on Consular Relations, to which both Mexico and the U.S. were parties, and which required that foreign nationals arrested or detained in a signatory country be notified without delay of their right to have their embassy notified of their arrest. In the particular case, a Mexican national had been arrested for rape and murder in Texas, but had not been notified of this right under the Vienna Convention.

The International Court of Justice had found that the U.S. was required to notify the detainee of this right and, since he hadn't been notified, that Texas should retry the criminal proceedings.

To enforce the ICJ judgment, the detainee brought suit in Texas. That case was *Medellin v. Texas*. The case eventually went to the U.S. Supreme Court, where the Court found that an international treaty or agreement was not binding domestic law unless Congress had enacted implementing legislation or the treaty was self-executing. Since Congress had not done that here, and since the United Nations Charter and the statute that had created the ICJ, had not been implemented by Congress as part of domestic U.S. law, and they were not self-executing, the ICJ *Avena* judgment was not binding on the states. Medellin was eventually executed for his crimes.

I looked up at the professor. "The Avena case?" I asked hesitantly. "*Medellin v. Texas*?"

"Yes," he said. "What do you think about the Supreme Court holding?"

"I agree with it. Since Congress had not enacted implementing legislation, the Vienna Convention isn't binding on the states."

"What about the Court's finding that the ICJ decision wasn't binding either?" The professor continued.

"I also agree with the majority. The Court found that the ICJ statute and United Nations Charter are not self-executing due, in part, to the fact that Article 94 of the Charter indicates that signatory nations will "undertake to comply," suggesting, as the Court found, that the Charter is aspirational in character. I mean," I paused, thinking, "these international agreements are meant to be commitments, unless, of course, Congress has enacted them into law."

The professor continued. "So the idea that nations are subject to the jurisdiction of the ICJ—?"

"It's not practical. First, as we've discussed before, there are no enforcement mechanisms. Second, no nation would be willing to fully subject itself to the jurisdiction of a supranational body. It's never going to happen."

"Does the fact that President Bush issued a Memorandum instructing the Supreme Court to comply with the ICJ decision change anything?"

"No," I answered. "The judicial branch is separate from the executive branch, and the Court is supposed to consider cases independently." Then I added, "That's not what I think. That's what the Constitution says."

Another student spoke up then. "Well, then, the U.S. risks other countries not providing the same consular rights to U.S. citizens who are arrested overseas."

"Absolutely," I agreed. "That's a diplomatic issue and it's a risk. The president is generally in charge regarding diplomatic affairs, but he has very little authority, if any, regarding Supreme Court decisions." And thank God for that. The Founders certainly knew what they were doing.

"Thank you," the professor said. He then moved on to something else.

A message popped up on my screen. It was Tarek again.

Toma!

I smiled. He was writing in Spanish now. Maybe I was rubbing off on him.

I'm signing out, I told him. I needed to pay attention.

So far, I was two for two that week, with a little bit of help.

We were walking to Property class. We only had ten minutes until class started. Tarek once again insisted on carrying my Property book, as I was trying to juggle it and my coffee at the same time.

"You drink your coffee so slowly," he commented.

"Because it has to last until at least 8 p.m.," I explained. "One quick shot won't help me." My days were so long, I lamented.

Then I added with a joking expression, "I don't have the luxury of sleeping in like some people."

Tarek chuckled. "Well, I can't sleep in tomorrow."

"Why not?" I was curious.

"I have a call-back interview with a firm here."

"In DC?"

He nodded.

I was elated. I wanted him to stay in DC next summer instead of going to New York or Miami.

"Which firm?"

He told me the name of the firm. It was a huge firm that did a lot of lobbying and regulatory work. It was probably a good fit for him.

The call-back interview was a big deal. After the initial twenty-minute interview with the firm, where the interviewer got to know the candidate, if they liked you enough they would call you for the call-back interview. At the call-back interview, you would interview at the firm's office, typically with several different attorneys, who would then take you out to lunch. The call-back interview was meant to impress the candidate. As if the attorneys were telling you, look, all this can be yours. But together with the fine dining and a prestigious associateship, you would also be working eighty hours a week and having random assignments thrown in your lap at the last minute, all while being treated like a lackey.

"Well, congrats," I told him.

"Thank you." He smiled. Then, "Hey—"

I looked at him. He seemed to be remembering something.

"You never told me how the visit with your Mom went last Sunday."

"Oh," I sighed, "It went OK. My sister is doing well, but she's busy with her crazy schedule. I wish I could see her more often."

I noticed that my voice sounded lonely. Maybe because I was lonely.

I continued. "My sister told me on the way down there that my mother is considering marrying her boyfriend."

"Really?" Tarek's eyebrows shot up.

"Yeah, I know."

"How long have they been together?"

"They've been dating a few years, but they live separately."

"Do you like him?" Tarek asked me.

"Yes, very much. He's really nice." And he loves my Mom, I can tell. How she found another man to put up with her, I don't know. Then I felt bad for thinking that. My Mom was really independent, and did pretty much whatever she wanted. It would take a strong, secure man to deal with her.

"I hope they do get married," I said then.

We walked into Property class and got to our seats. Tarek handed me my book.

"Thanks," I told him.

Melanie was sitting behind me and looked at me then, raising one perfectly manicured eyebrow over her designer eyeglasses. One side of her mouth was curving up into a half-smile.

I rolled my eyes. With that look, she was asking me what was going on between me and Tarek. I wasn't going to answer her, even if the answer was "nothing."

Then she seemed to remember something. As I sat down, she said, "Oh, hey, Isabel."

I swiveled around in my chair. "Yeah?"

"Will you go to the Feminist Forum meeting with me tonight?"

"Um—I don't know." I had never gone to the Feminist Forum meetings. The Forum was another of the law school's many extracurricular clubs.

"Pleeeaaase. I don't want to go by myself. And they'll have food there."

"I don't know. It'll be late." It had been such a long day, but I hadn't spent much time with Melanie since the new semester began.

"Please? It shouldn't take long."

"Oh, OK," I told her.

"Great! Thank you!"

Class was about to start. As I turned on my laptop and opened my textbook to the first case for that day, Tarek leaned toward me.

"So you consider yourself a feminist?" He was smiling.

I chuckled. "Yes." The answer was more complicated than that, but that was all I had time to say for the moment. Then I added, "Why? Is that a dealbreaker for you?" I looked at him from beneath my lashes.

"No, not at all." He was still leaning toward me. I was a little unnerved by it. I inhaled a deep breath and then let my chest fall as I exhaled. From the corner of my eye, I thought he may have sneaked a look at my breasts. It was difficult to tell, however.

"I can wait for you after your meeting if you want," he said then.

I would like that. I looked at him then, with a flirtatious half-smile. I didn't mean to be flirtatious. Well, maybe I did. I was having difficulty reconciling my feelings as of late.

"It's not a good idea to walk around here that late by yourself," he continued.

"OK, if you don't mind."

"I don't mind."

"But you have the interview tomorrow, right?"

"Not until eleven a.m."

"OK, then." I paused. "Thank you."

"*Ningun problema.*"

"You never told me that you speak Spanish," I said accusingly.

"Only a little. You can't escape it living in Miami."

I nodded. "I'm going to have to watch what I say around you."

"Have you been talking about me behind my back?"

"Don't flatter yourself." He would notice that I hadn't answered his question.

Class started then. I felt a little flush.

After class Melanie and I proceeded to the meeting. Tarek said that he would wait for me downstairs in the lounge area.

Melanie and I found the room and grabbed seats in the back. Then we helped ourselves to pizza. It was already 8 p.m., and I wouldn't be home until 9:30 or 10 at the earliest. At least there were only two more days left in the week.

We sat down with our food.

"So tell me," Melanie began. She was always so direct. "What's going on with you two?"

When people asked me those kind of open-ended questions, I usually played dumb to drag out the conversation. However, it was late and I was tired and Melanie was my friend.

"You mean between Tarek and me?"

"Yeah!"

"We're just friends."

"Well, you look like more than just friends to me." Then, "Do you like him?"

"Yeah, I like him. I like Josh, Dinesh and Eric too."

"That's not what I mean."

"I don't know." I was being honest. "I'm—attracted to him, yes. But—"

"So what's the problem?"

"I like him too much as a friend."

"You don't want to ruin that." She said it as a statement, not as a question.

"Right." At least, I don't want to ruin that for now.

"But I will say," Melanie continued, eyebrows raised, with one finger in the air, "that I think that he's interested in you."

I wanted to tell her everything that I had told Lara and Patrick the last time I had talked to them. But we didn't have enough time. Later, I figured.

"I—I don't have enough recent dating experience to figure these things out," I said then. It was a totally honest statement. I was frustrated with myself.

"Hey, you don't need experience to know when a man is into you," Melanie said knowingly. She was like five years younger than me, but she was wiser than me in this. All of a sudden, I felt like an eighteen-year-old.

I sighed. "I guess," I said.

The meeting began.

The Feminist Forum was a group of, I would soon find out, ardent left-wing young women who all pretty much subscribed to the same beliefs. I had hoped that the group represented women of various ideals who came together to support female empowerment. But, as most things in this town, it was a group of women who assumed that you believed the exact same things as they did.

The meeting began and the President of the group had each of the participants give a short introduction of themselves. There were at least thirty young women there, so this would take a while.

Most of the women were first-year students. They looked so young to me. Of course, I thought, most of them are about twenty-four to twenty-five years old. Jesus Christ, I'm old.

One by one, the women (I guess they were technically women, but I actually thought of them as girls), introduced themselves. The President had asked them to say their names (state your name and serial number for the record, I chuckled to myself), and state why they went to law school.

That got me thinking to why I had gone to law school. Hmm. I had better think of something fast. The real reason that I had begun law school, because I had had too much free time and was starting to depress myself with my thoughts, was probably not appropriate.

I listened to the other women. Every single one of them gave pretty much the same reason for going to law school.

"I want to save the world."

"I want to make a difference."

"I want to protect human rights."

"I want to help people."

And variants thereof.

Melanie and I looked at each other. She raised her eyebrows.

The issue with these responses was, they were all fine and good, but how were these girls going to repay their student loans and afford malpractice insurance after they graduated, if they all were going to work as volunteers or for nonprofit agencies?

It appeared that these girls were going to forsake making a lot of money in order to "save the world." However, the fact was, these girls may scoff at rich lawyers who worked for firms, but rich people kept the world moving, and rich people not only created employment, but they also donated vast sums of money to help others. The Bill and Melinda Gates Foundation is one example. Who did they think donated money to research new medicines for the developing world? Rich people!

Melanie was next.

"Hi, my name is Melanie. I'm in the evening program. I went to law school because I want to work in legislation, hopefully on the Hill."

Good answer.

I was next, and I was the last one.

"Hi, I'm Isabel. I went to law school because—um, I'm too anal retentive and not social enough for business school." That was totally true. "And because I'm highly analytical, and law school was a good fit for me." There, that was a truthful but relatively innocuous answer.

The President went on to talk about their upcoming events.

"We're having a rally in support of reproductive rights."

Wait, I thought. So in order to be a feminist, I have to be pro-choice? I didn't really consider myself pro-choice. I mean, I didn't know whether I was pro-choice. But why couldn't I be a feminist if I wasn't pro-choice? I thought that feminism was about women doing and believing whatever they wanted to.

"And then," the President continued, "in the spring we have our big event where we have a bake sale. We charge women 72 cents for each item and men $1 for each item, since women only earn 72 cents for every $1 that men earn."

I had a lot to say about that as well, but now was not the time. Besides, I was tired.

I really didn't get it. Feminism was about women making their own choices, right? I guess for this club, it meant that women could make their own choices as long as they made the correct choices, right? Correct according to this group.

At that moment, I felt that I couldn't say anything. If I said what I really thought, everyone here would dismiss it, like I was some freak. That's what this city did to you.

I was suddenly reminded of something that my mother had told me a while ago.

My mother, like me, also considered herself a feminist, and she had said something to me once that made sense.

"The truth is," she had said, "Back in the 60s, when feminism first started to be popular, women were sold a bill of goods."

"What do you mean?" I had asked her, intrigued.

"Women were told that they could do everything. They could work, have fulfilling careers, have and raise children, do volunteer work, travel, take care of the house, etc."

"OK, so you're saying that 'having it all,' as they say, isn't possible?"

"Right. My point," she had said, eyes intense and wagging her finger at me, Argentine-style, "is simply that women cannot possibly do all those things and do them *well*. By that I mean, they can't do them all the way they would like to."

Instead of dismissing my mother's comments, as I often did, I had actually listened to her that time, because what she said was logical. Also, she would know, I figured, since she had worked and raised three kids by herself after my father died.

"If you work," she had said, "you put your kids in daycare, so maybe you won't raise them how you would like them to be raised."

"I get that," I had said, thinking back to when I had taken care of my cousin's newborn in Barcelona when I was about twenty-two years old.

"So now women are expected to do all of that," my mother had continued, "and to do it all perfectly. There are a lot of expectations. Not only that—" she was looking more and more bothered, "after more women started working, since families had two incomes, prices for everything went up, from airfare to food to clothes. Everything!"

That made economic sense too. If people are willing to pay more for stuff because they now have two incomes, prices rise.

"So you think women shouldn't work?" I had asked her, surprised. The thought of staying at home without exercising my intellect was anathema to me.

"No, I'm not saying that," she had responded adamantly. "I mean, *I* work and I'm glad to be working. I'm saying that what I've described are the logical consequences of what happened."

I sighed, thinking of that past conversation. I was disappointed at the club meeting. However, I was glad that I had gone. It only reinforced my opinion that people in general were lame and illogical and didn't think for themselves anymore. Instead, they were told, "If you're a feminist, this is what you think." They wanted to be feminists, so they adopted the ideas that these "feminists" told them. But in doing so, they really weren't being feminists because they weren't thinking for themselves.

Ah well. I'm only one person. I wasn't going to convince anyone anyway.

Then I smiled. The other good thing was that I would get to go home on the metro with Tarek, just the two of us.

Then my heart froze. The scary thing was that I was going on the metro with him, alone! Jesus, what had I been thinking? Also, the later at night it got, the lower my inhibitions always became. It was like I was drunk with sleep.

Well, it was too late to go back now.

When the meeting was over, Melanie and I left together. As we walked down the stairs to the lounge area, she said, "I thought there would be more substantial food. Sorry about that."

"That's OK. I'm glad I went."

"Really?" She seemed surprised.

"Yes, I know it's not a club for me."

Melanie sighed. "I know, they all think one way."

That was why Melanie and I were friends. We were on different sides of the political spectrum, but we respected each other's beliefs. She wanted to work on Capitol Hill. It would be good for someone like her to be in politics.

"I mean," she continued, "you can still be a feminist and be pro-life."

"Right," I said. We walked downstairs. "But not according to the people in that meeting."

"That's because for them, 'feminist,' with a capital 'F,' is equated with a certain set of beliefs."

"You got it," I responded.

"See," Melanie wagged her finger for emphasis, "That's why people like you and me should join groups like that, to educate them."

"Hmmm," I pondered, not sure what good that would do. "Are you taking the metro?" I asked her.

"No, I drove." Melanie lived in Maryland. She leaned toward me and lowered her voice. "So you two can be alone." She smiled.

"Oh my God," I felt my face getting hot. I took a deep breath.

We said goodbye and I walked to the lounge area. When I saw Tarek, my heart leaped.

That's only because I think he's attractive, I told myself. He and I both know I think he's attractive; that's no secret.

He had his laptop open and his earbuds in.

I approached slowly and waved. He saw me and smiled.

"Hey," I said.

"Hi, Isabel. Ready?"

"Yeah."

He was chuckling as he packed up his stuff.

"What's so funny?" I asked, curious.

"I was chatting with my sister. She has a new boyfriend."

"Really?"

"Yeah, but, she'll probably break up with him by the time I'm home for Christmas."

"She's a heartbreaker?" I asked, amused.

"Not really, at least I don't think so. They're never very serious for her."

"Well, she's young, right?"

"She's twenty-five."

"Yeah, so that's probably understandable."

"She dates mostly Latin men."

"Well, then she and I have something in common."

"Really? You only date Latin men?" He asked curiously.

We walked out of the building and down the stairs.

"Not consciously. That's just how it's turned out." I paused. "It's not like a rule or anything."

"So they're your type?"

You're my type. Then I organized my thoughts.

"I don't know. I don't know if I have a 'type,'" using my air quotes.

I decided to turn the tables on him.

"Tell me, what's *your* type?"

He looked at me and smiled. "I don't discriminate."

"So, basically, she has to be breathing?"

He laughed. "Basically," he mimicked my word choice, and I wasn't sure if he had done it consciously or not, "I like women who are self-confident. That's about it."

I nodded. "Makes sense."

I felt a tension between us then, not a bad tension, like an electricity. We were both walking pretty fast. He always matched my pace, and at first I had thought that he was walking fast because I did, but then I had remembered that even before we started to hang out, I had seen him walking fast.

It was starting to get cool outside and I didn't have a jacket. The wind had also picked up. I shivered, but I wasn't sure whether it was because of the wind or because of him.

"So how did the meeting go?" he asked.

"OK, I mean, it was kind of a bust from my point of view. It's not a group I'm interested in."

"Really. Why not?"

We were entering the metro station. I stood on the right side of the escalator, so that we could talk. The right side was for people who stood as opposed to the people who walked down on the left.

"If I tell you, it involves me—unloading a little bit. Do you mind?"

"No, of course not." I could tell by his smile that he really didn't mind. In fact, I got the impression that he was glad for some reason.

I told him my impressions of the group, and how it was obvious that they considered that everyone who called themselves 'feminists' had to have certain conformist beliefs.

"It's disappointing," I concluded.

We were at the platform. Our train would arrive in about ten minutes.

"So you're not pro-choice?" he asked me.

I hated when people asked me this question, because they usually asked me in order to argue with me, not that I necessarily thought that was Tarek's reason for asking it. The other reason I didn't like the question was because I really didn't know the answer.

"OK, so—" I began, trying to organize my thoughts, difficult at this late hour and after the hectic day I had had, "the short answer to your question is not really, I mean, I am pro-choice but—" I looked around. "Let's walk further down the platform." We turned and walked and I lowered my voice. "I mean, I think an argument can be made that at the time the country was founded, the Founders considered that abortion was permissible during the first trimester, around the time when the baby's first movements could be felt. So if you look at the question only from that viewpoint, maybe you can make an argument for it during the first trimester."

"But not for after the first trimester."

"Right. But," I continued, looking around again, "my issue with abortion is what is the right protected? If the right is the right not to be a mother, then you can give the baby up for adoption when it's born and you don't have to be a mother. And if the issue is the right not to be pregnant, or the right to do whatever they want with their bodies, then women can either abstain or use birth control. That's their choice." I stopped and then clarified. "And I'm not talking about rape because, obviously, that's not the woman's choice."

We had stopped and were looking at each other.

"So," Tarek said, "the choice is whether to have sex or not." It was a statement, not a question.

"Right, that's what I think." I was a little unnerved when he had said 'sex,' but I continued nonetheless. "This is not the nineteenth century. Women don't have to give men sex whenever men want. The choice is thus when a woman chooses to have sex, protected or not." I was switching to my in-class tone, using 'thus.' "Women can't control when they ovulate, but they *can* control when they have sex and whether they use protection or not."

"I agree."

"So, I guess technically I am pro-choice but, like you said, the choice is whether to have sex or not, specifically, whether to have unprotected sex or not. I mean—" I was even more unnerved talking about contraception with him. "If you use it right, protection is almost always effective." I paused. "So if we all have to take sides, I guess I'm pro-life, but I can't tell anyone that."

"Why not?"

"Look around you. They call pro-life people anti-choice or anti-women's rights. It's difficult to have a conversation when that's your starting point."

"Right," Tarek agreed. "Optics are everything in this city."

"But all they're really doing is telling women that they can't make their own decisions. They can't decide when they have sex, that they're always forced to do it, so they need help." I paused for a second. "Some people say that abortion is necessary because many women can't afford contraception."

"But they can get it free at several places."

"Yes, that's one argument."

"And they can also say no."

"And that's another argument. All women have free will."

Our train arrived. We boarded and found two seats together. At this time of night, it usually wasn't that crowded.

"Interesting," Tarek murmured.

"What?" I could feel my eyebrows furrow together.

Tarek smiled. "I haven't met very many women who agreed with me on that."

I couldn't help smiling then. "Oh, we're out there. We just can't say anything."

We looked at each other for a moment. His eyes held mine for longer than I would have liked.

I eventually broke the silence. "There's more, too," I said provocatively.

"Oh?" He leaned toward me, feigning great interest.

I proceeded to tell him about the bake sale, where they were going to charge women 72 cents and men $1 for the goods. I told him why they were doing that, and then I explained what my mother had said to me several years ago.

"Yes, I see that," Tarek agreed.

"I don't necessarily think that it's fair—"

"But that's the economic reality of it," Tarek finished.

"And, life isn't always fair anyway."

"That's true."

I laughed.

"What's so funny?" he asked me.

"I'm so used to arguing with people all the time. I'm not used to people agreeing with me."

"Would it make you feel more comfortable if I argued with you?"

I was still smiling. "If you want. I can take it."

The next stop was Pentagon City.

"Have a good night," Tarek told me.

"You too."

"Can I ask you something? It's kind of like a favor."

I was instantly nervous. What would he ask? "Sure."

"Will you text me when you get home? So that I know that you got home OK."

"Sure."

"OK." The train stopped. "See you tomorrow, Isabel."

"See you tomorrow."

I got home in one piece and made a sandwich. It was too late for anything heavy. I was so tired. Then I remembered. I took out my phone and sent Tarek a message.

I'm home. And I forgot to tell you, good luck on the interview tomorrow!

After a couple of minutes my phone blipped.

Thanks. I'll let you know how it goes. Good night, Isabel.

Later, I lay in bed, thinking. Then I started daydreaming about Tarek. I thought about kissing him. Oh, my God. This is NOT helping me sleep.

I took a few deep breaths and eventually fell asleep.

My alarm clock went off on Thursday morning and woke me out of a deep sleep. I had slept like the dead that night, with no dreams. I felt oddly rested.

My first thought was for coffee.

My second thought was about Tarek and our conversation at the end of the night before. I then realized that I hadn't thanked him for waiting for me and escorting me on the metro. I should have thanked him.

Well, I would see him later today. I was excited.

I grabbed a sleeveless black sheath-type dress with an embellished collar and a black jacket. All black again. It was easier.

I put my hair back in a bun. I was going to shower later at the gym anyway and would wash my hair then.

As I headed out the door, I saw my neighbor John with his little dog. Next door there lived a young couple. They were younger than me, probably. They had a cute Beagle. Beagles could be temperamental and, the first time I had seen him, I had wondered how he dealt with apartment living. But, apparently, he was OK with it since I didn't hear him bark that much. Sometimes he howled, but he was usually fairly quiet at night. Of course, I wasn't home during the day, so I didn't know if he barked then.

I bent down and petted him. His ears went back and he stretched out his neck toward me. He loved attention. I liked to think that he had a soft spot for me.

"How's it going?" I asked John.

"Pretty good. How's school?"

"It's going OK."

"I can't believe you're in law school and working. That's crazy." He shook his head.

Everyone said that.

"It's not so bad. Plus, I only have this year and next year, and I'll be done."

"And then the bar," John said.

Ugh, don't remind me. I wasn't even sure where I was going to take the bar. I didn't even know where I was going to end up.

"Yeah, well," I hedged, "I don't have to worry about that for a little while longer."

We said goodbye and I left to walk over to the metro.

Seeing that little dog was the only good thing that happened that entire day. As we say where my family is from, *el dia fue de Guatemala a Guatepeor.*

Work started out like any normal day, but then Martin called me into his office.

Martin was a nice guy, and a decent boss. I respected him because he was a good translator, but, in my opinion, he needed to be more assertive.

Every time he called me to his office, I got a boot-in-the-gut feeling. 99 percent of the time, it was something positive, or something entirely innocuous. I had no logical reason to feel that way when he called me; I guess I was conditioned ever since I had attended Catholic school as a little girl and the nuns would call me into the main office for poor handwriting, daydreaming too much or other such horrible crimes. When my father died, since my mother didn't work at the time, we didn't have enough money for my sisters and me to continue in Catholic school. We had all started going to public school then. That had been a rude awakening. I had had to deal with my father's death and with the transition from Catholic school to public school. It wasn't a good mix for an introvert like me. We had worn uniforms in Catholic school, so I hadn't had an extensive wardrobe. In public school, it was all about the clothes that you wore. I had had a really difficult time the first couple of years. After that, I had cared less.

Remembering all this at the time, I tried to stay calm when Martin called me into his office.

I walked inside and he told me to close the door. That's not a good sign.

Martin was about fifty years old and had dark hair with a lot of gray. He was attractive and I was sure that he had been a real looker when he was younger.

"Isabel, Tim came to talk to me," Martin began.

"OK." I decided to listen for a moment. Plus, he hadn't asked a question.

"He didn't agree with some of your revisions."

That was an understatement.

"OK," I nodded.

"He thinks you're abnormally hard on him."

Was that a *double entendre*? Martin and I went way back, and I almost made a joke, but thought better of it.

"I'm not. I treat him and his work the same way I treat the others and their work."

"I know."

"OK." I was confused. "So what's the issue?"

Martin sighed. "A couple of the others have made similar comments."

I cringed. Tim wasn't the only younger Spanish or French translator working there.

"Martin, you've seen their work. Am I wrong?"

"No, I don't necessarily think so."

"OK, so—?" I left it hanging.

"Isabel, you're one of the best translators here, and certainly the go-to person for Spanish. The others aren't up to the same standard as you."

"OK." I agreed. I wasn't seeing where this was going, though.

"But you should try to be diplomatic with them."

I was confused and now beginning to get upset.

"I *am* diplomatic with them." Of course, Martin hadn't witnessed any of my conversations with these people. Who knows what Tim and the others had told him?

"I'm sure you are, just—just try to go easy on them."

"Martin, look," I began, frustrated, "I'll try but I have to be honest with them too. To do otherwise is a disservice to them and to our clients."

"I know," Martin said. Then he began to look a bit sheepish. I wondered what was coming.

He continued. "Isabel, there's something else too."

I waited, without saying anything.

"I'm going to shift some of Tim's clients over to you."

I was in shock for a few seconds. "Wait," I said. "Martin, you know I'm bogged down as it is. I have my own workload plus I'm reviewing other people's work."

"I know, Isabel, but I don't have anyone else, and—and Tim isn't as experienced as you."

"You mean he can't keep up?" Maybe that was overreaching but Martin wasn't going to fire me over it.

Martin gave me a strange look. "Something like that."

"So, maybe you should fire him and hire someone else, or send him for more training."

"You know how difficult it is to get people who are qualified and who pass the background checks. If I let Tim go, it will be a while before someone else can start."

I was starting to get downright angry. "Let me get this straight." My hands went to my hips. "I perform better work than Tim, and my reward is that I get dumped on and he has less work to do. Is that right?"

"I need to provide high-quality work to the end clients," Martin was exasperated and he knew this wasn't fair. It was a business need.

"So you're saying that we should all strive for mediocrity?"

"No, but you should be more diplomatic with the others and just try to get the work done."

"That's what I've been trying to do," I said, seething inside but remaining calm for now. I had to say something else. "OK, well, I hope that this will be reflected in my performance review."

"Of course. Don't worry about that."

I wasn't convinced, however.

I left our meeting thinking that I should give glowing reviews to the others when I reviewed their work. That way, no one would complain. But then I wouldn't be doing a good job and I wouldn't be able to sleep at night. And if one of the clients at some point had a real complaint, and it was discovered that I hadn't caught it, then it would be on me, and I couldn't deal with that.

Despite what I had said to Martin, I didn't mind so much that he was dumping Tim's work on me. That was a business necessity. However, I did mind that Martin was putting up with inferior work from Tim without replacing him. Because that wasn't good for the company. I was trying to help the company by producing quality work, and Martin should be doing the same. He was the boss, after all.

I was going to have to seriously start looking for another job.

At lunchtime I grabbed my bag and headed over to the gym. I got on the treadmill and cranked it up, blaring my own playlist of electro Latino/

techno music in my ears. I pretended that I was running away from something that was chasing me. Before I knew it, I had run for forty minutes and my legs were sore. I stretched and then showered. I immediately felt better after running. I guess the good thing about being pissed off was that you worked out harder.

I left my hair wet and slathered mousse through it. I put on some eyeliner, foundation and mascara, just the basics.

I was calmer when I got back to the office. I went to the kitchen to nuke my lunch and again encountered my Middle Eastern coworkers. This time, Tim and a couple of girls were in the kitchen as well.

I walked right in and smiled generically at everyone.

"Like this one!" Abdul said that, motioning an arm toward me.

I turned toward him. What the—

"She is?" another of the men asked.

Is what? But I didn't say anything.

"Yes, haven't you seen her bumper stickers?" Abdul said.

Aw, *fuck.* I knew I would get into trouble for that here someday.

Abdul continued, much to my chagrin. "She has all these conservative bumper stickers! She probably even likes George W. Bush!"

"Of course she does," one of the girls said. I looked at them.

Tim and the girls were smiling at me with condescension. It was enough to make me want to go over there and punch them all in their faces. God, I wanted to so badly.

I had never felt so alone. At least when my father had died, I had been surrounded by family members for a while after that. I had stewed in my own thoughts during the night, but during the day I had been with people who loved me. Here, in this city, except for Lara, I was alone, and I didn't see Lara as much as I needed to.

This was a city where I could never really be myself. It sucked. All day, every day, I had to listen to my coworkers and fellow law students belittle my beliefs, and talk about how great the welfare state was, and how capitalism was on its way out the door. And all I could think about was how my parents had fled totalitarian regimes so that they could have the opportunity for success, an opportunity that only capitalism could offer. And it made me utterly depressed. My family had been successful, and for what? To be taxed to death. I was glad that I was wearing all black today.

All of a sudden, I felt like I wanted to totally lose control. I wanted to just flail around like mad and duke all these people. For a moment I thought that it may be worth it not to ever be able to practice law. Several assault charges would probably prevent me from being barred in any state, unless I could maybe plea temporary insanity.

Then the logical part of my brain kicked in. These people are *so* not worth it. I would feel good after punching them, but then what?

No way. I'm not going to give them the satisfaction of having me arrested, or of seeing me lose my job, or even of seeing me lose control. This game isn't over yet.

I put on a nonchalant look and looked at Abdul. "When did you see my car?" I almost always took the metro.

"When you drove in one day," he answered. I hoped he wasn't stalking me.

"And?" I said with an annoyed look. "So what?"

"You must be the only person in this city that likes Bush!"

I heard Tim snicker. Of course. She likes bush. What a jackass.

I turned on Tim then. "How the fuck old are you?"

Everyone in the kitchen was immediately silent at my use of the f-word. He thought it was a real question, the idiot. "I'm twenty-six," he said.

"Well, you act like you're fucking ten years old, with an IQ of about four." Then I went on looking at everyone else, "And if you're all liberal 'progressives,'" using my air quotes, "as you say you are, then aren't you supposed to embrace tolerance?" I was raising my voice, but still trying to control my anger. "You guys are a bunch of intolerant bigots."

As usual, Peter saved me. He came into the kitchen right at that moment.

"Why is everyone so silent?" he said in his usual carefree manner. "Were you all talking about me?"

"Well, they were talking about Bush," I motioned to Abdul and the others. Then I remembered to grab my lunch from the fridge. I shoved it in the microwave.

"*Esta todo bien?*" Peter asked me, sliding in next to me.

"*Mas o menos,*" I said, lowering my voice since Tim and the girls spoke Spanish.

No one said anything else after that. Peter and I left together.

Peter and I were of the same political ilk. That was another reason why we got along so well. We walked back to my desk together and I told him what had happened in hushed tones.

"Don't worry about them," he told me.

"I know, but—it's the same old thing every time." And now everyone here would know my political bent.

That didn't seem to bother Peter. Peter talked about politics all the time with almost everyone; where he stood was no secret. I loved him for it. I wanted to be more private, but I guess that was over now.

I was going to leave at about 3:15 to make it to class by 3:50. Before I left I checked my personal email. I had more bad news.

I had two emails from law firms. I had had initial interviews with both of them. Now I had rejections from both of them. Both emails said more or less the same thing.

> *Thank you for interviewing with such-and-such firm. So-and-so enjoyed meeting with you. Unfortunately, we will not be able to invite you for further interviews.*

They should have just said the truth. If they had, the emails would have gone something like this:

> *You have an outstanding resume and we could certainly use your language and analytical skills. You also have excellent grades and significant work experience, much more so than the average first-year associate. The fact that you belong to a minority group is also a plus since hiring another minority law student would look good for our firm, especially since we hold out as making an effort to hire minority candidates.*
>
> *However, you are too old to be a first-year associate. We want someone that we can grind into the floor, making them work eighty hours a week. We also want someone who will accept menial, thankless work without complaining. We don't want to hire first-year associates with too much experience, because they are less willing to take our crap.*
>
> *And although we say that we prefer to hire diverse candidates, by "diverse" we mean the typical first-year associate who will be about twenty-five to twenty-six years old, who was on Law Review, who likely did a summer associateship with our firm for a summer (because why would we hire someone without trying them out first?) and who happens to be from a traditional minority group.*
>
> *We're sorry, but you don't fit this profile.*

Then, to add insult to injury, both firms had emailed me the Minority Form to send back to them. Law firms wanted to interview a certain number of minority law students each year so that they could say that they interviewed them, even though they may have no intention of hiring them. The forms asked you to state the minority group to which you belonged.

There was no way in hell I was going to complete those forms so the law firms could hold them up and say, "Look! We interview diverse candidates!"

I clicked out of my email account and began packing up my stuff. Now I was a little sad. It looked like the law firm thing wasn't going to work out.

I pushed my sunglasses onto my face and left the office. Usually I said goodbye on my way out to the people around me. That was a Spanish thing. In Spain, when you got to the office in the morning you greeted everyone, and on your way out at the end of the day, you said goodbye to everyone. Hardly anyone did that in the US.

I got on the metro and sat down, dejected and gloomy.

A couple of minutes later, the train stopped. People got off and on. The lady sitting next to me got up. It wasn't too crowded since rush hour had barely started. I still had my head bent, looking at my book.

"Hi, Isabel."

I looked up and saw Tarek. I opened my mouth without thinking.

"Oh my God, you look good!"

He was wearing a dark suit with a dark red tie. I had never seen him look so good. His hair was perfectly coiffed into tight curls. He must have used an entire bottle of mousse to get his curls to cooperate.

"Thank you." He smiled and sat down next to me.

I forgot my own troubles for a moment. "How did the interview go?"

"Um, I think it went well," he said. "I think they're considering me for the corporate or regulatory practice groups."

"That's what you want, right?"

"I—I think so."

"Well, that's great. I'm happy for you." I wouldn't tell him about the rejection emails I had received that day. I was a little jealous of him, though. I couldn't help it.

"Thanks."

I couldn't take my eyes off of him. "Well, you look really nice."

"Thanks," he smiled again.

Then I realized that I had already told him that. I felt incredibly stupid.

"How was your day?" Tarek asked me then.

"Um—fine, normal," I lied. Let's see. I got worked dumped on me, I had a tiff with my coworkers, I almost lost it at work and then I got rejected by two law firms in the same day. All in all, it was a terrific day!

We talked mostly about our classes for the rest of the trip.

As we emerged outside, near the law school, I saw a young kid (I say kid, but he was probably about twenty-one or twenty-two years old), displaying both a clipboard and a goofy grin.

I scoffed.

"Jesus Christ," I blasphemed.

"What?" Tarek said.

I tried to avoid the kid by walking around him but he got all up in my curtilage.

"Miss, aren't you worried about climate change?"

That was basically the straw that broke the camel's back. I was so pissed off. And I was so tired of these people being in my face all the time.

"Yes, that's why I'm wearing a jacket. In case the climate changes and it's cold, I'll be prepared. If it gets hot, I'll take off my jacket."

"Do you want to sign our petition—"

"No, unless it's a petition supporting the idea that advocating for the 'climate change problem,'" I said, holding up air quotes, "is just a way of raising taxes on unsuspecting taxpayers, exploiting naïve kids, kids who have no idea what it's like to live and work in the real world, and not live on Mommy's and Daddy's dime to be able to have money to throw at neo-liberal causes, because they think that by firehosing money at the problem it will go away."

The kid looked scared, but I wasn't done.

"And because they think that by throwing money at these poor people, like immigrants, they are actually helping them, but they're really being condescending jackasses." I paused, but the kids said nothing. "In short, I don't need your help, and you can stick that petition up your—"

"All right," Tarek said, "let's go." I shot Tarek a hard look. How dare he interrupt my diatribe! Once I started, there was no stopping until I decided to stop.

He leaned toward me and said, "Is he worth getting worked up about? He's just naïve."

I looked at Tarek, then looked at the kid. I guess I was done. I huffed and turned away.

Tarek shook his head.

"What?" I said.

"You're incredible."

"Excuse me, but *he* approached *me*. Are you saying you agreed with his position?"

"No, I agree with *you*, but—"

"Someone has to shake these idiots out of their reverie."

"Their what?" We were crossing the street.

"Reverie. *Tu ne parlais pas le français?*"

"*Oui, mais—*"

"It's an English word, too," I said. "Thank the Norman Conquest for that." We were back on the sidewalk on the other side of the street.

"Yes, but," Tarek began, "everyone is naïve at some point in their lives and, sooner or later, like you said, when they start working and paying bills and having kids, they will get out of their *reverie*," he heavily accented *reverie* and he also used the term incorrectly, but I let it go, "and they will see it wasn't as easy as they thought, and their priorities will change."

"Well, I'm tired of everyone thinking I'm crazy for speaking the truth. I'm also tired of everyone assuming that everyone else in this town has the same beliefs as they do."

"Because they're still naïve and they don't have the experience that we have. Isabel, even *you* must've been naïve when you were younger—"

I lost it then. I was like a stick of dynamite and his comment was the match that lit it. Under normal circumstances, I might have laughed it off. But I was in a shitty mood.

I was cogent enough to consider that Tarek might not deserve the on-coming outburst but it didn't stop me. I stopped and faced him. We were looking at each other, with our faces very close.

"I have *never* been naïve. Don't pretend to know me, Tarek." I was angry now, and it showed. I got right in his face. "When these kids were in diapers, you know what I was doing? I was doing the family finances and making sure my mother didn't crack up. I was cooking and cleaning for my sisters and making sure they ate their dinner." I was raising my voice. "When I was sixteen and got my driver's license, you know what I did? I carted my sisters around to school and drove them to appointments. I didn't go partying and messing around like the other lame students I went to high school with. I was old before my time and I know that your life can change in a matter of seconds. These kids know shit about life! Everything

I have, I have had to work my ass off for! All these kids do is party on their parents' dime and brag about their unpaid internships on the Hill!" Then the *coup de grâce*, "Do *not* purport to know me, Tarek! You know shit about me, so don't stand there and pretend that you do!"

I had not expected him to respond, but he surprised me.

"You think I judge you?" Tarek asked, almost as worked up as me. I was a little taken aback by his shift of demeanor, though, looking back on it, I shouldn't have been.

"Of course you do. Everyone does."

"Isabel, you've prejudged me since the day we met. You thought I came from a rich oil family. You thought I was Muslim. You thought I was a snobby French elitist. You think that me offering to carry your stuff and hold doors for you somehow treats you as an unequal."

"If I prejudged you, it's only because I know your type!" My face was closer to his now.

"And what type is that?!"

"Arrogant, like showing me up in class!"

"It was one time, and it was only so you would talk to me, because apparently you're too intelligent to talk to others who you think are intellectually beneath you!"

"It was several times, Tarek! It was all week long!"

"JESUS, WHY DON'T YOU KISS HIM ALREADY?!"

Tarek and I were both shocked and turned to look at the heckler. It was Eric, who was walking past us on the sidewalk toward the law school.

I held out my right arm in Eric's direction, giving him the middle finger, holding it up high for everyone in the world to see. "SCREW . . . YOU!" I shouted. Several people turned and looked at me but, as usual, I didn't give a shit what other people thought.

Eric was past us now. "I think you'd rather screw *him*!" Eric said, not missing a beat.

I half-smiled. Eric was more right than he knew. "Well, I'd rather screw *him* than you, that's for sure!"

Eric laughed and continued walking. "Well, at least you admit it!"

I couldn't think of a retort. I put my hands on my hips and shook my head. A smile was creeping on my lips; I could feel it. I tried my best to stifle it.

I looked back at Tarek and we smiled at the same time. This time when I spoke I lowered my voice.

"Look, Tarek," I began. For all Eric's faults, he seemed to have unwittingly defused this situation before I said something I would later regret. "Maybe I did prejudge you, and—I think—perhaps somewhat unfairly."

Tarek looked at me, but he appeared more relaxed, and a little surprised.

"And for that, I'm sorry," I said. "I am. You didn't turn out like I was expecting." And I was trying to figure out what to do about that.

He smiled. "Wow, an apology from Isabel Vilanova."

"I rarely apologize. You should feel honored."

"And you say *I'm* arrogant."

I love the fact that you're a little arrogant, I thought, but I wouldn't tell him.

"It's OK," he said then. "I'm sorry I thought you were ever naïve."

I sighed, weighing what to say. I figured telling him a partial truth couldn't hurt. "You were right, though. I was naïve once. But I stopped being naïve long before most people stop."

"Isabel, I understand that. It must've been difficult for you."

"And I want you to know something."

"Tell me."

"I've never thought you were intellectually beneath me. In fact, I think the opposite." I smiled. Then I hedged a bit. "Why do you think I tolerate your presence?"

He smiled. "That means a lot, coming from you."

I exhaled. As usual, after an outburst like that I felt bad about it.

"Look, I'm really sorry for going off on you like that. I—" I felt a little emotional but held it together. "I had a really—crappy day today. It was—a bad day."

Tarek looked concerned. "Isabel, I'm sorry."

"Not that that's any excuse," I added quickly. "I didn't mean to take it out on you," I told him. "I shouldn't have."

"It's OK."

"It's not OK, but—thanks."

There was a pause for a moment.

"What happened?" Tarek asked gently.

"I'll tell you later. It's kind of a long story."

But maybe telling him one other truth wouldn't hurt, either. I would show one more card. I had a fair amount left. "And by the way," I said a little playfully, my face even closer to his, so close, in fact, that I could smell his musky scent and even the mousse he used on his hair, "for the record, I *love* the fact that you carry my books and that you hold doors for me. Honestly, I really do. Any girl who wouldn't is an idiot." How's that for the truth?

He grinned and touched my arm. It was electrifying in a way that both excited and disturbed me.

"Come on, we'll be late," he said. Then, as if an afterthought, "And give me your books."

We made it to International Law class on time. Today the professor was discussing territorial sovereignty and the right to self-determination.

The question came up as to whether the U.S. interventions in Iraq and Afghanistan were justified under international law. The class was made up of American students plus several foreign students, some LLM candidates. It was mostly the American students who spoke up in class. One of them was speaking now.

He said, "The U.S. was wrong to invade those countries because it violated their national sovereignty."

I sighed a long sigh. I could see where this discussion was going. Tarek noticed because he glanced at me and smiled.

"Isabel, what do you think?"

This was typical. The professor always asked me my opinion at least once every class. I assumed it was because I almost always had different opinions from everyone else, and he wanted to stimulate the discussion. I wasn't really in the mood today but didn't have any choice.

"I think the argument goes like this," I began. "The U.S. is attacked and has evidence to believe that the terrorists are living in a foreign country, but the country harboring them won't help the U.S. find them. So the U.S. acts to protect in own citizens. It may be a violation of national sovereignty, but it is arguably justified under international law through self-defense."

The guy who spoke first countered me. "But the U.S. shouldn't have violated the national sovereignty of another nation in protecting itself."

I was frustrated but I kept my calm. "So what should the U.S. have done instead?" I asked him.

"Well, I don't know, but not that."

"So, you basically got nothing. You would have had the U.S. as a sitting duck, and terrorists could kill people on U.S. soil and run and hide in other countries."

"Well, uh—" the guy stammered. Of course he has nothing to say.

Tarek raised his hand then, and the professor called on him. This was interesting, since Tarek rarely volunteered to speak in this class.

"The thing is also that all national governments act in their own self-interest, as they logically should, and even if the U.S. action is a violation of another nation's sovereignty, there is nothing that the international community could do about that. Also, it likely would be considered an action in self-defense under international law."

"OK, thank you." The professor moved on to another topic.

I looked at Tarek and caught his eye. I smiled without meaning to. He winked at me.

Later, we walked into Property class together with our caffeinated drinks. I had been dying for coffee since I had left the office, and we had gotten drinks right after International Law. Tarek wouldn't let me pay. When we got to Property, Josh and Eric were talking animatedly.

"Saturday night, right, Isabel?" Eric asked me excitedly as I sat down.

"Sure thing," I answered.

"What's going on Saturday night?" Tarek asked me.

Josh answered before I could.

"We're going out dancing," he told Tarek. Then he smiled a bit conspiratorially. I wasn't sure if that smile was meant for me or not. "You should come, Tarek. It's worth it to see Isabel dance."

"Oh, come on," I said, suddenly feeling a little shy.

"She's a great dancer," Eric agreed. "And it's the only time she's ever really in a good mood."

I smiled in spite of myself, then looked at Tarek. "You should come—if you want."

He smiled back and his eyes were sparkling and alive. "I wouldn't miss seeing you in a good mood."

I could feel myself blushing.

Josh, Dinesh, Tarek and I were on the metro. Tarek and I were sitting together and Josh and Dinesh were sitting across from us, chatting about patent stuff, as usual.

"So do you want to talk about what happened today?" Tarek asked me.

"No, it would take too long," I said, looking at him. God, he looked good in that suit. And his hair was gorgeous. If he invited me to his house tonight for "coffee," I would totally go. Then I was startled at my own thought.

"If you want to talk, call me when you get home," he said then.

"OK, thanks. How late are you up?"

"Late."

"Oh that's right. You don't have a job to go to tomorrow," I said sarcastically.

"That's right, I can do what I want."

What *do* you want? He kept his cards fairly close to his vest, and I felt like I was using mine up.

I got home and closed my apartment door behind me, locking it. What a day. Thank God I didn't have class after work tomorrow. I would sleep in a little and get to work around 9 a.m.

I glanced at my watch. It was only about 9:30, still early.

After nuking some leftovers, I grabbed a glass of water and sat down on the couch.

I opened my laptop and checked my email account. I had an email from Ariel. She was going to try to call me this weekend, she said. Other than emails, we hadn't talked for a while. She was incredibly busy at work. I really wanted to talk to her. She and her boyfriend had only been living together for a few months. I wanted to know if things were still going well. I had no doubt that they were. Ariel's boyfriend was a real gentleman and it was obvious that he loved her.

Thinking about that got me thinking of Tarek. He had been so nice to me tonight. And I really wanted to talk to someone about what had happened today. I needed to unload. I didn't want to bother my sisters midweek. It would be too selfish of me.

I rationalized that Tarek didn't have a job so he could stay up later. I smiled to myself at how I could use logic to justify almost anything that I did.

I took out my phone and sent him a text message.

Are you awake?

I brushed my teeth and put on my pajamas. Then I went and sat on my comfy couch. I lay my head back against the soft pillows.

My phone showed a message.

Of course. You think I'm asleep this early?

I could literally hear the sarcasm through the phone. I texted back.

Do you mind if I call you?

Next thing I knew, my phone rang. It was him.

"Hey," I said.

"Hi. Is everything OK?"

"I guess." I exhaled slowly. "Tomorrow will be better, right?"

"Of course it will be. Tell me about it."

"Tarek, I don't mean to unload on you."

"It's OK. I don't mind."

"I'm sure you have better things to do with your time than listen to me complain."

"Not really." I could hear him chuckling through the phone. I laughed a little bit too. It was a good way to disconnect from the day.

"Actually," Tarek continued, "I really enjoy talking with you."

I could feel a broad smile spreading across my lips, and the color rising in my cheeks. I was glad he wasn't here to see me blushing.

"Well, then you must be a glutton for punishment, as they say."

"I must be."

"Tarek, again, I'm sorry I blew up at you today. I feel really bad about that."

"Isabel, don't worry. We all have bad days."

"My day was horrible. It got worse and worse." I proceeded to tell him about my conversation with Martin. In speaking about it, the pent-up feelings I had seemed to ebb. I took a couple of deep breaths.

"I was so pissed off," I concluded.

"I think he probably figures that it's necessary from a purely business point of view," Tarek said. "However, it's not a good business decision because he's not motivating employees to work efficiently."

"Exactly, and I told him that he seems to be saying that we should all strive to be mediocre. I don't want to be like that."

"Right. So now Tim knows that he works less and gets rewarded with less work. You do better work and get rewarded with more work. It's a disincentive for both of you."

"I agree," I said. "I mean, I kind of felt bad about talking back to Martin a little but—"

"You shouldn't. If you don't say anything, then he won't understand that he's not motivating his employees. Not being fair is one thing. You and

I both know that life is not always fair. But it's also poor management. If it takes that long to hire and train a new translator, then maybe the company should review that process. It's inefficient."

"Thank you!" I agreed. "You're absolutely right."

"Of course I'm right."

"Oh, you're so modest," I said sarcastically.

Tarek was laughing. "What would *you* know about modesty?"

"By modesty, do you mean how I dress or how I behave?"

"Isabel, you're trying to trap me."

"You're not answering my question."

"Oh, my God."

There was a pause in our conversation. I could see that he wasn't going to answer my question. It had been half in jest anyway.

Then I spoke. "You're right anyway, Tarek. I don't know a lot about modesty, in any sense of the word."

I wished that I could see his expression right now. I was so curious.

"Modesty is a relative term, anyway," he said.

Ain't that the truth. But that was another conversation for another day.

I exhaled and leaned further back into my couch. "Anyway," I continued, "things got worse from there."

I told him about being verbally assaulted in the kitchen at work, and what Tim and the others had said.

"I mean, people are so intolerant," I said. "If you don't believe exactly what the masses believe in this town, then you're an outcast."

"I know. Our law school classmates are not much better."

"Oh, I totally agree."

"Have you noticed," Tarek said, "in our International Law class, how the foreign students and immigrants tend to be more pro-American than the American students?"

"Yes!" I agreed, maybe a little too exuberantly, as I then thought about saying "Yes!" in a different context entirely. "Thank you!"

"It's like you've said before. They have had everything handed to them, and most of them have gone straight to law school from undergrad without having a real job—"

"And they don't think about things logically," I added, " about how things play out practically."

"Exactly. They think in only idealistic, theoretical terms. Like, health care should be free for everyone—"

"Without considering how to pay for it," I said.

"And without considering that standardizing or capping compensation for medical providers will push them out of the market."

I thought about one of my cousins in Argentina, who had been a physician, but who had stopped practicing medicine. His salary as a physician had been regulated by the government, and for all the years he had invested in education and training, his salary was unbelievably low. Instead, he had been able to obtain another job where he worked as a government employee reviewing medical records, without having to work long hours.

"You do realize," I told Tarek then, "out of all our friends at school, you and I are probably the only ones who have lived under socialized medicine."

"Yes, and we're the only ones who are against it, apparently."

"That's my point, precisely."

"But no one wants to hear from people like us."

"Because no one is interested in the truth. It's what I've always told you." I punctuated my words carefully.

Tarek laughed. "Yes, I know."

I laughed too. "I know, I'm so modest."

"Oh, my God." I could imagine him rolling his eyes right now.

"Anyway," I continued, "And then my day got even worse."

"What else happened? This is like a soap opera."

"I know. Welcome to my life."

"Is your life always like this?" Tarek asked me.

"God, no," I answered automatically. Then I reconsidered. "Well, maybe sometimes."

I paused then. "Tarek, I feel like a jerk for complaining about this, because I'm glad that your interview went well today. But—I got two rejection emails from firms today. So no callbacks thus far."

"Isabel, I'm sorry."

"It's OK. It's just ego-bruising. And if I don't get a summer associateship, then it will be nearly impossible for me to get a job with a firm when I graduate."

Law firms are very regimented in how they recruit. They generally hire law students to work as summer associates while in law school. Then, if they liked the summer associates, the firms would make them permanent offers at the end of their stint. If the students accepted, then they would start working as first-year associates for the firms after they graduated. The summer associateship was a good way for firms to "test" students before making them permanent offers. If you didn't do a summer associateship, then it was difficult to get a permanent position with a firm after graduation. The first-year associate salary in the DC area was generally anywhere from $120,000 to about $160,000, but that was a base salary. The associate also got bonuses. Of course, they would also work about sixty to eighty hours a week and had to bill a minimum of 1800–2400 hours per year. Associates were expected, however, to bill more than the minimum number of hours.

"What's always been ironic to me," Tarek said then, "is that most lawyers say that they're so liberal, but the law firm culture is so reactionary in how it operates and recruits. Many firms will only hire from their summer associate pool and would never consider other candidates."

"Right. It's the argument that, this is the way we've always done it." I sighed. It felt really good to get this all out. "It's just—it's a lot of work to prepare for interviews, travel, etc. And I'm starting to feel that these firms are only interviewing me to say that they interviewed a minority candidate. And it is a monumental waste of my time."

"Were these firms in DC?" Tarek asked.

"One was in DC and one was in Delaware."

Wilmington, Delaware had been one of my top picks since it was a hot spot for corporate law. Many corporations were registered in Delaware due to tax advantages. Delaware judges were very knowledgeable about corporate law and the Delaware bar included many corporate law experts.

"So you want to move to Delaware?" Tarek asked, surprised.

"It would be great if I could. I mean, the corporate work there is really interesting. The cost of living is a lot lower. I wouldn't mind. But it's a moot point now, anyway."

"So how many firms are you waiting to hear from now?"

"A couple in DC and one in New York."

"You'd move to New York?"

"I might. The bonus is that my sister Ariel is there."

"I understand that."

"And if Lara were going to stay in DC permanently, I would likely stay here. But she doesn't know where she'll end up after her residency." I paused. "What about you? How many more firms are you waiting to hear from?"

"One in DC, one in New York and one in Miami."

"So which one is your top choice?" I found myself wishing he would stay in DC.

"I'm not sure. And I can't really afford to be picky in this market."

"Tarek, you'll be fine."

There was a pause for a moment.

"Isabel, you know the fact that you didn't get callbacks with those firms, that it doesn't reflect on you, right?"

"I know; it's their loss."

"Exactly."

I realized then how tired I was. Our conversation had helped me to relax. "Thanks for listening to me rant."

"Anytime."

If he were here, I would give him a hug right now. Then I thought that it was a good thing that he wasn't here, because I would probably end up dragging him into my bed. Then I had a visual of that scene. I said something to distract myself.

"I'm looking forward to going out with you guys on Saturday night," I said.

"I am too," Tarek said. "Look, Isabel." He paused for a second, and seemed to be thinking about something. "Let me take you to dinner on Saturday, before we go out."

I froze. Did he mean like a date? I wanted that, but I also didn't want it.

"Just me and you?" I asked.

"Yes."

"Like a—a date?" I choked out the last word.

"No, no, no, no, no," he said quickly, and a little too emphatically. "Just—just as friends."

I pondered for like a millisecond. I was afraid that if I thought about it for too much longer, I would say no. "OK, I'd like that."

"OK, then." I knew he was smiling when he said that.

I was blushing.

We talked for a few more minutes. We planned to do some outlining at his apartment on Saturday morning. Then we hung up.

I had always thought that my life was boring, but it was beginning to get kind of interesting.

I felt like I hadn't really played any significant cards that night. In any case, I had plenty left. However, I had no idea how quickly all my cards would be used up.

Saturday came around faster than I had expected. I was on my way to Tarek's apartment. We had planned to study in the morning until around 1 p.m. Then my plan was to get home, have lunch and go get my hair done. I was going to have it highlighted today. It had been a while and I felt like my hair was too dark. I was looking forward to getting dressed up for tonight. I still had no idea what I was going to wear. Maybe I would try to call Lara later. Was she working today? I didn't remember. Maybe I would call Ariel. Both my sisters had good taste but Ariel tended to dress more like I did, in really dark colors and form-fitting fabrics.

Oh geez, I already had butterflies in my stomach. We're going out as friends, I said to myself.

I got to Pentagon City at right about 10 a.m. and walked over to Tarek's apartment building. This was my first time at his place. I was curious.

I was wearing dark jeans and a short-sleeved white blouse with a bit of a ruffle around the collar. I had put on some light makeup and lip gloss. I never left the house without makeup now.

I toted my backpack, purse, and thermos filled with coffee on the street. It was a nice day, not too hot. I was really looking forward to the fall weather. I hated the sweaty DC summers.

I found his apartment building. It was pretty posh. He must have help paying for this.

I walked into the lobby and found his apartment number. He had told me that he would have to buzz me in.

I pressed the button.

"Hello?" It was a hello of expectation.

"Hey, it's me."

"Me who?"

Dude, who else was he expecting?

"Your worst nightmare unless you open this door."

"Look, unless you're a half-Spanish, half-Argentine girl who's somewhere to the right of Genghis Khan, don't bother coming up."

"Oh my God, you're hilarious," I said with mock enthusiasm. But I couldn't help laughing.

Then the buzzer sounded.

I took the elevator upstairs and he was waiting for me at his apartment door.

"Dude, everyone's a comedian now," I told him.

"But it made you laugh." He was smiling.

"Mildly, yes."

"Good."

He was wearing jeans and a black T-shirt, just like the day he had first really talked to me. His curls were also arranged. I wanted to reach out and touch them, but I dared not do that. It would only make me want to touch him again, and in other places.

I walked in. "So this is your place?"

"Yes, *bienvenida*." He spoke Spanish with a French accent.

His apartment was a one-bedroom and it was very tastefully decorated.

"Something tells me that a woman helped you with the decor in here," I told him.

"What, you're saying I can't have good taste?"

"No, it was only a guess."

He smiled. "My mom and my sister were here to help me move in. They have very good taste."

"Yes, they do," I agreed, looking around. His place was also very neat.

"Dude, this place is so tidy. You've must've thought my apartment was a hazmat site."

"I did not think that," he laughed.

It was true; I wasn't the tidiest person. I usually washed my dishes (eventually) and never left laundry on the floor, but I didn't care if my bed was unmade or if I had left my shoes in the living room. My mother was always getting on my case about that.

I also noticed that there weren't a lot of appliances in his kitchen, or much of anything on the counters, really.

"You don't cook?" I asked.

"I do but it's difficult to cook for only one person."

"Yeah, I never really figured out how to do that either; that's why I always have tons of leftovers. Oh—" I had noticed something. "I'm glad I brought my coffee because you don't have a coffeemaker."

"I don't drink coffee."

"And you never expect to have anyone over who does?" I raised one eyebrow and looked right into his eyes.

He sighed. I thought how beautiful his eyes were, and his long lashes. I considered getting closer to them. Then his eyes were looking into mine.

"It's an American social custom. Get with the program," I said, to distract myself. "So where are we studying?"

"At this table, if it's OK."

He was like me; he didn't have a proper office or study desk.

I pulled out my laptop and turned it on.

"Isabel, can I get you anything?"

"Um, just some water."

"I have a Crim Pro question for you," Tarek said then, as he went to the kitchen.

"Shoot."

"At the end of class the other day, we were talking about the fact that police officers can arrest you for any crime, even for minor crimes that aren't punishable by imprisonment?"

"Yes, that's correct."

"That's crazy. So, even for speeding?"

"Technically, yes. They can arrest you for failure to use a turn signal, or speeding, or driving without a license. You have to understand, they wouldn't usually do that, but they would get a free search because officers get to search you upon arrest."

"So they also get to interrogate you while in custody."

"Exactly. And I imagine, if you piss them off enough, they'll arrest you just to punish you." I looked at him. "So it never pays to be rude to a cop. Just saying."

He brought me a glass of water. I thanked him.

He sat down at the table too, in front of his laptop. "How do you remember all this stuff?"

"What stuff?"

"The case names and the rules and everything." He was serious.

"I just do." I shrugged. "I love this stuff."

"Josh says you were born to be a lawyer."

I half-smiled and shook my head. So he and Josh were still talking about me when I wasn't around. I made a mental note to talk to Josh alone as soon as I could.

"Josh says a lot of stuff," I said, a bit annoyed. "But he's right about that. At least, that's how I feel. Whether I'll be a good lawyer is still an open issue."

"Oh, I have no doubt that you'll be a good lawyer," Tarek said, smiling.

I was suddenly thirsty and drank my water. When I put my glass down on the table, I could feel myself blushing. I looked at Tarek and he was still looking at me; his eyes were alive. It made me smile. It was a smile that took over my entire face. I felt it spread until I couldn't look at him anymore. I looked down at my laptop keyboard but I could still feel him looking at me. The silence was getting to be almost unbearable.

Then Tarek said something that surprised me.

"You should smile more often."

"What?"

"You hardly ever smile. But you should."

"I do smile."

"You usually force a smile, but you never smile like you did right now."

"Why? What's the point?" Indeed, what the hell was there to smile about?

"Your entire face lights up when you smile like that." He paused and seemed a bit sheepish. "You look gorgeous."

I was going to give him kind of a scowl, but somehow it ended up being a grin, then a broad smile that ended up in a chuckle. I closed my eyes, in half embarrassment, half flirtation. When I opened them, I found myself looking up at him from beneath my lashes, something I never did.

"Did I embarrass you?" Tarek was smiling broadly now.

"You—discombobulate me," I said.

"What does that mean?" His eyebrows furrowed.

"It means—to cause confusion, like, you make someone confused."

"Why do I cause you confusion?" It was a serious question.

I shook my head to clear it. "I—you just do, sometimes. Look, are we reading Crim Pro or are we discombobulating?"

"Well, apparently, we're doing both. And I love that word. I'm going to start using it."

"Great, I've created a monster." I threw my hands up in the air, much like my mother would do when she was frustrated with something that *I* had said.

Then we started with Crim Pro.

We were taking a break.

"How old do you think our International Law professor is?" I asked Tarek.

"He looks young, like he's about thirty or so."

"I think he looks like he's about twenty-five, but he's probably like a young-looking thirty." I sighed. "That's so depressing."

"What's depressing?"

"That he's most likely younger than me."

"Oh, *please.* Thirty-four *is* young."

"Yeah, but I'll be thirty-six when I graduate."

"So?"

"I'll be staring forty directly in the face." Sometimes I started to dwell on my age. It sucked. The years were passing by at warp speed, even more so because I was in school and working and was so busy. I liked to be busy, but it made the time pass that much more quickly.

I decided to change the subject.

"So tell me why you transferred here."

Tarek sighed and looked at me. We were standing in the kitchen. He had refilled my water glass and I was drinking.

"This is a better-ranked school." He shrugged.

Rankings meant about everything in the law-school world. If your school fell a couple of notches in the national rankings, it was bad news. All in all, it was better to be at a top-20 school, best to be at a top-10 school. Law firms looked at where you went to law school, and also at your class rank. Certain government agencies, like the Department of Justice and State Department, also focused on rankings, as if they were white-shoe law firms. It was pretty well-known that the State Department's Office of the Legal Advisor mainly hired first-year attorneys from the Ivy League schools. Recently, the Office had hired a couple of new attorneys from our school, and that was a big deal since those positions seemed more attainable to us mere mortals now.

The thing was, of course, really good attorneys came from all over, not only from the Ivy Leagues. But now the chips were down and the legal market wasn't so hot. Starting in 2008, the year when the economy started to go under, law firms began laying off attorneys and non-attorney staff. Some firms and federal agencies weren't even hiring entry-level attorneys. I remember that the university's Career Center addressed my class in 2009, telling us that it would be challenging to find the jobs we wanted. They made it sound like now the rankings were more important than ever.

Whatever. I was ranked in the top of my class at a top-20 school and it wasn't helping me.

"So you only care about the rankings?" I asked Tarek, raising my eyebrows.

Tarek looked at me in a way that told me that he didn't only care about that.

"There are also a lot of job opportunities in DC," he said then.

I thought that I was pretty good at reading people, and I got the impression that there was something else he wasn't telling me. But I disregarded it for now. If he didn't want to tell me, there was no sense in pushing him.

I was leaning with my back against the kitchen cabinets, thinking. What would make him leave Miami for DC? I decided to change my line of questioning.

"So Zaida is your only sibling, right?"

"Yes. And I like how you say her name."

I had known a couple of Zaidas in Spain. It was actually a pretty popular name there, due to the country's close proximity to Morocco and the Arab influence. But in Spain it was pronounced "Thaida," with the Castilian accent, pronouncing the z's and c's with a 'th' sound.

"My coworkers call it the Castilian lisp." I smiled.

"I knew some Spanish people in Paris. They talked like that." He drank from his glass.

"What was your impression of them?"

"They were a bit arrogant." Now Tarek was smiling. "But they loved life, and they knew how to have a good time."

"That's about right," I agreed, then continued my questioning. "You get along with your mom?"

"My mom and my sister and I are very close." He paused. I noticed that it was a meaningful pause, as if he was weighing something. It suddenly made me on edge, like he was about to tell me something very important. "We've always been close, but more so since my father died."

Time stopped for me. The flirtatious half-smile I had had on my face disappeared instantly. How had I not known that?

"Tarek," I said accusingly, "You never told me that."

He shrugged. "It never came up. It's not something I would just—say like that."

"I'm so sorry." I could feel my brows furrowing in concern.

"Isabel, it's OK."

"When?"

"When I was twenty-two."

"I'm so sorry," I said again. I couldn't think of anything else to say. When my father had died, people had kept repeating that to me. I'm sorry, I'm so sorry. Is there anything I can do? Do you need anything? And I knew they were trying to help, but they didn't know how. And you didn't know how they could help.

Tarek continued. "He had AVMs. It stands for—um—arterial venous malformations. It's apparently something you're born with. But it can burst later in life, which is what happened."

I looked at him. I put my glass of water on the counter and crossed my arms. I felt like a jackass. When we had first met, I had assumed he came from a family of money, a full-time law student who was like a kept man. I again thought that he must be digging himself into over six figures of debt with law school tuition and with this apartment and with no income. It made me feel bad, and I didn't usually feel sympathy for people. I was usually too wrapped up in my own thoughts.

"He knew that when they told him. He was trained as a medic in the military. That's how my parents met. My mother was a nurse."

I was wondering at all the machinations that had to have happened for the two of us to end up right here, standing in his kitchen. Somewhere, God must be pleased. Maybe he was even laughing.

I was so sad all of a sudden. I felt the urge to go over to him and take him in my arms and hold him. I wondered what it would be like to feel him against me.

But I didn't do that. I was too scared.

His next question broke me out of my thoughts.

"Isabel," Tarek asked gently, taking a step forward, "what happened to your father?"

"Car accident," I lied. That was what I told everyone. That's what Josh, Melanie and Eric believed.

"I'm sorry."

"It's OK. It was a long time ago."

The mood was too sad. I had to think of something to lighten it up. I inclined my chin over to his bookcase. There was a photo there of him with two women. If the older one was his mother, she looked pretty young. But I assumed that was the case. "Your sister kind of looks like you."

"Yes, we both have our mother's hair." He smiled.

"Unruly? Difficult to tame?" I smiled.

"Yes, very."

"I like it, though." I smiled, and suddenly my smile became one of those huge smiles that he liked. I looked away from him, slightly embarrassed.

He continued, maybe to keep me from feeling embarrassed. I wasn't sure. "My sister's skin is lighter, though, like our father's."

"She's gorgeous. Your mother is too."

I got the courage to look at him again. He was looking at me intently. But then, his eyes always seemed to be intent.

My cell phone rang then. I had left it on the dining table.

"Sorry," I said. "Let me see who that is."

"No, that's OK."

It was Lara. "Speaking of sisters, that's mine now." I looked at him. "Let me tell her I can't talk."

"You can talk to her if you want," Tarek told me, waving his hand in a gesture saying that he didn't mind.

I answered.

"Hey you."

"Hey, hey! What's up?" Lara was always so chipper.

"Not much. I'm out right now. Can I call you back?"

"No problem. Where are you?"

"At a friend's house."

"The friend you told me about?"

"Yes."

"Interesting." Lara's tone was playful. "Actually, I was calling because today is my day off and I wanted to know if you wanted to go out to dinner with us. A bunch of us residents are going out, including that guy I told you about."

"I would love to, but I have plans tonight. I'm going out with the guys."

"The guys?"

"Yeah, you know. Josh and Eric and—someone else you don't know." I saw Tarek smiling out of the corner of my eye. I didn't think he knew I could see him.

"Well, well, where are you going?"

"Out to dinner and then dancing." I didn't tell her that I was only going out to dinner with Tarek.

"Well, have fun and I'll call you later."

"OK, you have fun too. Is Patrick going with you?"

"Yes. He wouldn't miss it!"

"All right. Love you."

"Love you too. Bye."

We hung up.

"My sister Lara," I explained to Tarek. "She wanted to know if I wanted to go out with her and some of the other residents tonight."

"Well, you have a busy social life."

"No, not really. This is just a fluke." I weighed whether to say more. "She's trying to set me up with one of the guys in her residency."

Tarek suddenly seemed really interested. "Really? What, like a blind date?"

"Oh, no!" I put my hands up. "I don't do blind dates. It's more like, she was going to invite me out when the rest of them were going out, like in a group."

"And you would go out with him?"

I laughed. "I don't know him. This was my sister's idea. Anyway—" I looked at him playfully. "I'm going out with you tonight so I can't go with them."

"Lucky for me."

I was trying to read his face. It was difficult. His expression was neutral but his eyes kind of gave him away. I thought I saw longing there. It was hard to tell. I bit my lip.

"Yeah, well," I told him, one edge of my mouth creeping upward into a smile, "you *should* feel lucky."

At 12 we had sandwiches and by 1 p.m. I was packing up to go.

"I have to be somewhere at two-thirty," I had told him. The metro was always unpredictable on the weekends, so I would leave with plenty of time to spare.

"Where?" he asked, curious.

"It's a surprise," I told him. That would leave him wondering.

He chuckled.

I got a little nervous then. "So what time are we going to dinner?" I asked him. He had his arms crossed. He was lean but really muscular. Oh my God, would I be able to handle tonight?

"Can we meet at eight-thirty?"

"Sure. Where? Oh, and Josh said to meet him and Eric at the club at eleven. But Josh is always a little late, FYI."

"We can meet here, but in the metro station if you want. That way you won't have to leave." He meant that way I wouldn't have to exit and pay again upon reentry. The DC metro was pretty expensive, especially if you lived at an end-of-the-line stop like I did. I wouldn't have had a problem with it, but I had to admit that it was considerate of him to think of that.

"Text me when you're on the metro and I'll meet you," he told me, as he walked me to his apartment door.

"OK." Then I remembered my manners. "And thank you for lunch."

"Oh, please. I mean, it's not paella but—"

I smiled broadly. "See you tonight."

He opened the door for me. "See you tonight, Isabel."

I smiled nervously and left.

Tonight was going to be very interesting.

I left my house at about 7:45 and drove my car to the metro. Parking was free on the weekends. The problem with taking the metro on the weekends was that there was almost always trackwork. I had checked the schedule for this weekend and there might be some delays but the high-traffic metro stations were all going to be open, so that was OK.

At 2:30 I had had my hair done. The lady who always did my hair was Vietnamese, and she was a firecracker. However, thankfully, she never let me look bad. After much debate, I decided to get dark red highlights done. Then she had trimmed my hair, leaving it in long layers. It looked good; I was happy with it.

After that I had called Ariel and had found her at home.

"Isabel, *que alegria! Cuanto tiempo! Que tal estas?*"

It was a very curious thing but Ariel and I almost always spoke in Spanish, but Lara and I spoke like a mix of Spanish and English. I guessed that was because Lara's husband didn't speak Spanish, but Ariel's boyfriend did.

As soon as I heard her voice, I realized how much I missed her. "When are you coming to DC to visit?" I asked her.

"Uff, I don't know. I'd like to, but things at work are crazy. I've been working really late. Can you come up?"

"Maybe over Thanksgiving," I said tentatively. "Hey, are you coming home for Christmas?"

"I'd like to. I'm not sure. We were kind of planning on it. Javier's parents are going to Mexico City."

The father of Ariel's boyfriend, Javier, was a Mexican diplomat who worked in the New York consulate of Mexico. Ariel had studied her MBA in New York City and had met Javier at school.

"They wanted us to go with them, but I'd rather see you guys. Frankly, we see his parents pretty frequently since they live here."

"I hope you can come," I told her. Then I had an idea. "But if you do end up going to Mexico City over Christmas, maybe I can go with you guys—if you don't mind."

"Oh, Isabel, that would be great! I miss you so much!"

"I miss you too."

Then her tone changed slightly. "Hey, I have a question for you."

Oh no. Her tone suggested that she was going to ask me a question that I wouldn't like. I knew my sisters too well. I mentally braced myself.

"What?" I asked hesitantly.

"Lara said that you're seeing some guy."

Oh my God. I loved Lara, but she could not keep a secret to save her life.

"That's not accurate," I said carefully.

"So you're not seeing anyone? But you're interested in someone, right?"

"No—I mean, I don't know. I have a new friend."

"But not a boyfriend?"

"No." Not yet, I thought, if I was even sure that I wanted him to be a boyfriend.

I decided to tell her straight. I didn't talk with her that often because of our schedules and I wanted to tell her about my life, or as much about my life as I felt like I could share with her. "I met a new friend at law school and we've been studying together and—kind of hanging out together."

"Hanging out?!" She was incredulous.

"Not the Millennial version of hanging out!" I corrected her quickly. "Not as in a quickie once in a while! I meant, you know, the Gen X'er version of hanging out—like, hanging out at school."

God, I was really going to have to remember what word choice I used with Millennials. As Melanie often said, when a Millennial guy asked you to hang out, he often meant for casual sex.

"Just as friends?" Ariel asked me.

"Yes!" I was a bit too emphatic. For some reason then, I felt the need to dish. "Although, we're going out dancing tonight, me, him, Josh and Eric, and he asked me to have dinner with him before going to the club."

"Just you and him?"

"Yes."

"So it's like your first date?!" It was cute that she was so excited for me.

"No, not a date. In fact, I asked him if it was a date and he said it wasn't, that it was as friends."

"Oh." Ariel sounded confused. "Isabel, it sounds like maybe he wants a friends with benefits situation with you."

"I don't know."

"Would you do that with him? I mean, would you have that kind of arrangement?"

I was completely truthful with her. I felt like I always had to be truthful with my sisters. "No, I don't think I could do that—with him."

"Oh, Isabel." There was concern in her voice. "You really like him."

"I don't know," I told her again. I was kind of embarrassed now. "I told him the first day we studied together that it would only be studying, nothing else."

"Oh, well that changes the inquiry." Ariel was logical, like me. "You told him that at the beginning, but now you like him. Maybe he's afraid you'll reject him if he asks you out on an actual date."

I was more confused than ever.

"How old is he?" she asked me then, curious.

"Twenty-nine."

"Oh, you cougar!"

"Oh please!" I resented that term.

"Of course, maybe he's intimidated because you're a real woman who knows what you want."

Well, I wanted *him*. At least, I wanted to sleep with him, but I wasn't sure that it was a good idea.

"I don't know what I want," I told her instead. That was the truth, too.

"Well, maybe tonight you can start to figure it out," she had told me knowingly.

I was smiling as I got on the metro train, thinking back on that conversation with my sister. Sometimes my sisters helped me see things much more clearly than I saw them myself. However, after talking with Ariel, and trying to think through things logically, I felt more confused than before.

Did Tarek like me? I mean, did he want to date me? If so, why didn't he ask me out on a real date? Did he think, as Ariel suggested, that I wouldn't go on a date with him? Was he afraid that I would reject him? He couldn't think that I didn't like him. I was spending more time with him than with anyone else lately.

Maybe he thought I only liked him as a friend. *Wait.* Why did I care whether or not he asked me out on a date? Indeed, what would I have done if he had said that tonight was a date?

My answer to myself surprised me. I would have said the same thing. "OK, I'd like that."

But would I have said yes to have a booty call or because I wanted to go out on a date with him?

I stopped myself. I didn't need to go out on a date with a guy in order to sleep with him. I would just sleep with him.

So did I want this to be a date? Yes, I told myself, because then I would have an excuse to touch his arm and whisper in his ear and maybe hold his hand.

I surprised myself with that answer. I wanted this to be a date. I did. Oh my God, oh my God, oh my *God*. I *liked* him. Holy shit. My palms started to get a little sweaty.

Wait a second, I stopped myself. Did I really like him or was this merely lust? When was the last time I really liked someone? What did that feel like? I couldn't remember. Maybe I would ask Lara. Wait, if I had to ask someone whether I liked Tarek, then that meant I didn't really like him, right? Right?!

I started to organize my thoughts to stay grounded in reality. First and foremost, I was a rational actor. And this wasn't a 'date.' So thinking about whether I liked him or not was a waste of time at this point. OK, so I would make sure that I didn't act like this was a date. How could I act like this was *not* a date?

Rule Number One, no arm-touching. Rule Number Two, no whispering in his ear. Rule Number Three, no hand-holding.

Then my mother's voice came back to me from the other day. "So what did you do, hold hands?"

Oh my God, I was going insane. I stifled a laugh on the metro.

From my seat I caught a couple of Latin men eyeing me. I looked away without smiling.

The truth was, I looked hot tonight. I didn't think I was the most attractive woman in the world, but there were times when I surprised even myself. Tonight was one of those times, at least, in my mind.

I had given a lot of thought to what I would wear that night. I wanted to be able to dance comfortably but I also wanted to look feminine. In the end, I had put on form-fitting black pants with a low waist and a sleeveless burgundy top with lace at the bust. The top was comfortable. Over that I wore a black blazer with a bit of black lace at the cuffs. It looked a bit Goth and I liked that. I wore black pumps with a low heel. I was a decent dancer but I was clumsy enough that if I wore heels that were too high, I might fall.

After I had had my hair done, I had washed it again at home and had blowdried it straight. I had also put on a little bit of black eyeliner and smudged in some shimmery purple eye shadow, nothing too outlandish. I finished off the look with mascara and clear lip gloss.

I had a small purse with me, the kind that had a long strap and that I could wear around my shoulder. As the train left the station I took out my phone and sent a message to Tarek.

On my way, leaving Franconia now.

And a couple of minutes later, the response:

OK, when you get off the train, wait at the platform. I'll meet you there. See you soon.

I suddenly realized that I was nervous. What was going to happen tonight? I couldn't deny the possibility that I would kiss Tarek tonight. I also couldn't deny the possibility that I would sleep with him tonight.

Wait, I stopped. He had said this wasn't a date. So no kiss for him. And I had already laid the ground rules, remember, Isabel?

Wait again. I wanted to kiss him. Didn't I always do what I wanted?

OK, so I won't sleep with him tonight. That's final and nonnegotiable. My other three rules were also still in force.

The kissing was still on the table, though, I decided. I would see how it went. I rationalized that maybe he wanted this to be a date, too. If that were the case, and if the moment seemed right, a kiss would be appropriate.

I was basically rationalizing my way to what I wanted.

Oh my God. My stomach was in knots.

I exited the train at Pentagon City. There were a ton of people, many with shopping bags. The Fashion Center at Pentagon City was a popular shopping destination in the area. It was metro-accessible; indeed, you could walk straight from the underground metro into the mall without stepping outside.

I got off the train and walked past the shoppers and other people going out for the evening. It was already dark outside but you wouldn't know it here underground.

I decided to get out of the crowd and wait, a little apart, instead of looking for Tarek. I figured once the crowd cleared a little, I would see him. I hung back against the cement wall at the back of the platform, and took out my phone to have something to do. Lara had emailed me.

Have fun tonight!

I emailed her back.

At the metro now. Will let you know how it goes.

As I hit send, I heard, "Hi, Isabel."

I looked up. There he was, looking so hot I wanted to jump him right there. He wore a white button-down shirt with a black blazer, and dark jeans. His hair was, as usual, carefully arranged in dark curls that framed his face.

As I looked up, I noticed that he had been smiling. But as I faced him, his face turned and he had kind of a strange expression.

Oh my God, what?!

"What?" I asked him. Did my makeup smear? Did I have something in my teeth?

"Nothing," he said, regaining his composure a little.

"Tarek, what? Tell me!"

"You look—amazing." He exhaled. "What did you do to your hair? It wasn't like that this morning, was it?" His expression told me that he was thinking that he would have noticed it if it had been like that.

"I went to the salon, I had highlights done." I put my phone away.

"Oh."

Then he looked at me from my head down to my feet.

"You look great," he told me, looking at my face this time.

For not being a date, it seemed that this was beginning like one.

"So do you," I smiled. "Where are we going?"

He seemed startled out of his thoughts. "Um—we have a reservation at nine." He told me the name of the place.

"Reservations?" I asked. "Am I dressed OK?"

"Of course."

"But this is a sleeveless top." I opened my blazer at my shoulder. "Am I too casual?"

"No, you're fine."

"Are you sure?

"Yes," he smiled.

"OK."

We walked to another platform to take another train.

I sensed a little bit of nervous tension. But this isn't a date, right?

"I talked to my sister Ariel today," I told Tarek, just to say something.

"How's she doing?" he asked me.

"She's doing well, very busy at work. She and her boyfriend work for different consulting firms."

"I can imagine how that is in New York." Then, "How long has she known her boyfriend?"

"They met in business school. I think they've known each other about three years."

"How long have they been dating?

"About two years. They've been living together for a few months." I paused. "She's very happy." I guess everyone will be happy except for me.

"So they knew each other for about a year before they got together?"

"Yes," I smiled. Our train would arrive in a few minutes. "It's kind of a funny story."

Tarek smiled too. "Tell me."

I continued. "So her boyfriend, Javier, is the son of a Mexican diplomat who works at the Mexican consulate in New York. He's a total gentleman, and also a little shy. Apparently, he was like in love with my sister from the moment he met her, or so he says." As I spoke, I stepped in closer to him and lightly touched his arm for emphasis. That was a Latin thing. For the life of me, I could not talk without using my hands.

There went Rule Number One. Hadn't I said that I wouldn't touch his arm because this wasn't a date? Oh well, that didn't mean anything.

I went on. "But he was apparently too shy to say anything to her. So they hung out with friends for almost a year, and she liked him the entire time, but she didn't think he was interested in her. Then near the end of the school year, their first year, they all went out dancing with their friends, and he had a couple of drinks and she had a couple of drinks, and then she told him how crazy she was about him."

"And the way he tells it, he was all like, 'I'm the luckiest man alive,' blah, blah, blah."

"That's romantic," Tarek said, smiling.

"Even *I* have to admit that it's kind of romantic," I told him.

"You're not a romantic?" Tarek tilted his head a little as he asked the question.

"No, not really." It was only partly true. "I think that most romance is totally lame." That *was* true.

"I thought Latin women liked romance."

"What do *you* know, or think you know, about Latin women?" I smiled coyly.

He smiled back but didn't say anything. I was tempted to not say anything and see which one of us spoke first. But, as usual, I couldn't stand the silence with him staring at me.

"Well—," I was trying to think of a way to explain it without embarrassing myself. I looked around and leaned in a little more closely. What the hell? I would tell him what I really thought. "I think sex between two people who love each other should be romantic, and by that I mean hot, like having that connection with that person in that moment is literally the best thing in the world. And—" I continued to talk without thinking. "Kissing should be romantic, like you're always kissing someone for the first time."

I noticed that his eyes were charged, almost on fire, in fact. So I continued on a more mundane topic. "But a guy buying me flowers or making a book for me about the story of how we got together, that's totally lame."

"Really?" Tarek seemed a little surprised.

"Dude, what the hell did flowers ever do for anyone? And if a guy has the time to make a book or a photo album for me, then he's got time to cook me dinner, clean the house and listen to me complain about my crappy day."

Tarek started to chuckle and it turned into a laugh. In fact, I didn't think I had ever seen him laugh so hard. "So you—" he was trying to stop laughing. A couple of people turned to look at us. "You prefer a man to cook and clean for you?"

Yes, and take the initiative in bed once in a while. But I didn't say that.

"Damn straight," I said. "Because if he does things for me, that shows that he cares about me. He tries to make my life easier because he cares about me." What I wanted was a partner, not a guy who sat around and brought me flowers and waited for me to get into bed with him. I mean, if I *wanted* to be with someone now, I would want a partner. Not that I wanted to be with anyone right now. "And I would do the same for him, because I care about him."

"Does buying you dinner count?" he asked suddenly.

"Yes, of course, that counts." Oh, wait. Was he talking about tonight?

Tarek smiled at me knowingly and I looked away. I was starting to blush again.

Thank God our train arrived then, and we got on.

It was crowded with people going out and tourists going back to their hotels late. We were standing and both holding on to the same pole. It was noisy and we had to lean in close to hear each other.

"So how do you like DC so far?" I asked Tarek, changing the subject.

"I like it," he nodded.

"I imagine it's not as glamorous as Miami," I told him.

"Have you been to Miami?"

"No, but I'd love to go."

"I think you'd like it." Then he added, "It can be a bit over the top, but it's fun. If you like to go dancing, you would like it." He paused. Then he asked, "So what do you do for fun around here?"

"Umm—" I considered it, "people usually go out drinking. A lot of people do the free concerts on Fridays at the sculpture garden at the National Gallery of Art. But I'm not sure if they only have them in the summer. Some people may go to exhibits at the galleries. There are a lot of good restaurants. People go out to dinner a lot."

Tarek was chuckling.

"What?" I asked him. "What did I say?"

"That's not what I meant."

"Jesus, what did you mean then!?"

"I meant, what do you, Isabel, do for fun?" He touched my arm as he said my name.

Our train had stopped in the tunnel and the conductor announced that we would be holding there for a few moments. That could be anywhere from five seconds to twenty minutes.

"Oh," I was surprised. What did I do for fun? "Law school," I told him.

"Come on. You must do other things."

I sighed, then looked at him. "Occasionally, go out dancing, like to-night, um—go out to dinner with my sister and her husband when we can."

I thought some more. I didn't know what he would think about the thing that I did most often "for fun," other than hook up.

"That's it?" he asked me.

"Actually," I went on, "you wouldn't believe what I do most often for fun."

"What?" By the semi-shocked expression on his face, I could tell that he assumed it was sex-related.

"Get your mind out of the gutter," I told him sardonically.

"It wasn't in the gutter!" he protested.

"Whatever," I said, looking away for a moment.

"Tell me," he said.

"Tell you what?"

He sighed. He knew I was stalling. "What you do most often for fun."

I leaned in close, and broke my second rule for the night. I whispered in his ear, "Go to the shooting range." I leaned back.

His eyebrows shot up. "Really?"

"Yes." Then I leaned toward him again. "You thought my NRA sticker was all talk?"

When I leaned back he was looking at me intently, and there was that intrigued look in his eyes again.

The train started moving again.

"Is that a dealbreaker for you?" I asked him. The question was a challenge.

"No," he told me. "*Au contraire.*"

Then he was looking past me, past my shoulder. His expression didn't really change but he was fixated on something.

I turned my head and looked with him right into Miguel's face. He was standing right next to me.

Holy shit. This could get interesting. Of all the places this guy could be right now, he's here.

"Isabel, I thought that was you," Miguel said. He was dressed to the nines, with a sportcoat. I could smell a ton of aftershave on him.

"Hey," I managed to say.

"Is this your boyfriend?" Miguel looked from me to Tarek.

I decided to ignore the question. I looked at Tarek. "This is Miguel. He and I work for the same company," I told him.

Tarek introduced himself and shook Miguel's hand.

"Where are you from?" Miguel asked him curiously.

"Miami," Tarek answered. I smiled.

"Where are you two going?" Miguel asked, still looking at Tarek.

"To dinner," I answered.

"Where?" Miguel continued. God, he was nosy.

"We don't know yet," I answered quickly. Tarek stole a look at me.

I had had enough of this. "Where are *you* going?" I asked Miguel. Because I will avoid that place.

"I'm meeting friends." He told me the name of the bar. "You guys should stop by after dinner. We'll probably still be there."

"Maybe," I lied.

Miguel left at the next stop, thank goodness.

"You do realize," Tarek said carefully, leaning toward me, "that he thinks I'm your boyfriend now because you didn't answer the question."

"I'm not answering his damn questions," I said. "And I don't care what he thinks." Then something occurred to me. "Oh my gosh, Tarek, I'm sorry if you care about that. I thought he was joking when he asked that." I really didn't think he had been joking, but wanted to offer an excuse as to why I hadn't disputed Miguel's assumption.

Tarek smiled. "Oh, I don't mind, Isabel."

"I'm sorry."

"Don't be." He looked amused. Then his expression changed and became more serious. "You don't like him." It wasn't a question.

"He's all right; he's always so inquisitive. And the more I answer his questions, the more questions he asks. It's—annoying." I had almost said *fucking* annoying but stopped myself. "And he keeps asking me to go out with him and his friends, and I always say no, and he keeps on asking."

"Well, maybe he'll stop now that he thinks you have a boyfriend."

I smiled. "I think I may owe you one."

"Oh, that's OK." Tarek smiled too. "I can think of worse things for people to think about me."

"Well, I can't." We both laughed then.

We exited the train at Gallery Place. There was a crush of people getting on and off. Tarek protectively touched the small of my back as we left together.

The restaurant we went to was in the Gallery Place area. It was one that I had been to before. It was really nice, and quite busy on Saturday night.

Our waiter, like an inordinate amount of waiters in this town, was Hispanic. I chatted with him briefly. He was from El Salvador. He asked me where I was from and I told him, "Barcelona." I also told him that Tarek was from Miami, at which point he looked at Tarek curiously.

He took our order and left.

Tarek looked at me. "You like doing that, don't you?"

I was confused. "What do you mean?"

"You like discombobulating people by telling them I'm from Miami, like with your coworker on the metro."

"Hey, *you* told him you were from Miami," I countered. But I was amused that he had used the word discombobulated, since I had taught it to him.

"*Touche.* But you didn't correct me."

"Who am I to correct you? If you want to say you're from Miami, you can say that. Technically, it's the truth. You've been living there for a long time, right?"

"True."

But he was right about something. I did like causing confusion in people. By that I mean, I liked making people think about things. He knew me a little bit. We hadn't known each other that long but we were figuring each other out. The thing that bothered me was, I was showing my cards before he was showing his. I felt like he knew more about me than I knew about him. I made a decision then to try to work on that.

"So," I said then, trying to read his face, "if people ask me where you're from, what do you want me to say?"

He smiled, leaning his elbows on the table. I was leaning forward with my arms folded. It was noisy (almost every restaurant in DC is noisy) and I leaned forward a little more to hear him.

"You can say whatever you want."

That was no answer.

I knew what his issue was with answering the question where he was from. It was the same issue I had. If someone whom I barely knew casually asked me where I was from, to tell the entire truth I would have to give them this long explanation. My mother is from Argentina. To which they would ask, "Then why do you speak Spanish with a Castilian accent?" To which I would answer, "My father is from Spain." To which they would say, "But why don't you speak English with a Spanish accent?" As if the fact that my parents are non-native English speakers means that, by definition, I'm unable to speak English without a foreign accent.

Or they would say, "So are you from Spain or Argentina?" It was annoying and I didn't like to play twenty questions with people who were practically strangers.

I was starting to get lost in my thoughts. Then Tarek said, "So you consider yourself from Barcelona?"

I looked at him. "Where do you think I should say I'm from?"

"Can't you answer a question directly?" He didn't miss a beat.

"Sure, when *you* answer one directly," I said a bit accusingly. I huffed and then leaned more closely toward him. "Tarek," I explained, "I asked you where you think you're from and you didn't answer me. So why should I answer your question any differently?"

He didn't say anything for a moment. "You're right. I guess I don't know how to answer the question."

I softened a little bit. I had been right. "Look, I feel the same way. It's easier to say I'm from Barcelona because of my accent. That way people don't keep asking questions like, how come I speak with a peninsular accent if my mom is from Argentina?"

"So you answer the question in a way that requires no further interrogatories?"

"Yes, pretty much. It's for efficiency's sake."

"You're very logical."

"Yes, I'm the consummate rational actor." Indeed, it was the only way I knew how to be. But there was something else. "But it's also—" I hesitated.

Tarek was listening intently. Then he said, "You don't necessarily want people to know your whole story."

"Exactly." I nodded.

If he wondered about that, he didn't say anything to the effect.

"But where do you really feel that you're from?" he asked me. From his eyes, I had the impression he was trying to figure it out for himself.

"From here."

"The U.S.?"

"Yes, I was born here. It's the best place I know of to live. But—" I paused, wondering how to say this. "I have the impression that many people don't consider me American. And when I go to Spain, I have the impression that they don't really consider me Spanish either. And in Argentina they don't consider that I'm Argentine because of my accent. So it's like I told you the other day, it's a loaded question. But I'm American, with a little Spanish and Argentine thrown in. That's how I feel."

Tarek smiled. "That's how I feel too. From here but with some other cultural influences."

"A lot of people don't understand that," I told him.

"For example, if I tell people that I'm from Miami, they ask me where I'm 'really' from."

I laughed. He had used air quotes for 'really.'

"What's so funny?" Tarek asked me, curious.

I was trying to hide my smile with my hand, but wasn't doing a good job of it. "You did this," I said as I mimicked the air quotes.

He smiled. "I usually don't do that. You must be rubbing off on me."

"The next thing you know, you'll be dropping F-bombs."

"Oh, I don't think I can do that." He smiled.

"Anyway," I continued with our conversation, "Sorry about the detour. You were saying that people ask you where you're really from." I didn't use air quotes because I was afraid I would start laughing again. "It's because of your looks."

"Oh, I know."

"People tell me all the time, 'Oh, you're not Hispanic,' or 'You don't look like you speak Spanish,' like Hispanic only means dark-skinned. Whatever." I sighed, and relaxed a little. "I think that you can kind of absorb the best of all places, and to do that it doesn't really matter where you're technically from, if you're technically from anywhere at all."

"Ooo, Isabel, be careful."

"Why?" I felt my brows furrow.

"You're starting to sound a little like an optimist." His smile was broad.

I scoffed. "Oh, please."

Our waiter brought our salads. He also asked us if we wanted anything else to drink. We ordered wine. I ordered a Cabernet.

"Feeling bitter?" Tarek asked me jokingly.

I chuckled. "I always feel bitter."

Then he was serious. "I told you before, I don't believe you're really like that."

"Well, you haven't known me for that long."

He didn't respond to that. I had the feeling he was choosing his words carefully. I had the feeling that he always chose his words carefully. I wanted to see him ruffled. I thought back to the first few days of this semester, when we kept running into each other, but hadn't really talked yet. A couple of times he had been a little uneasy, when I had caught him looking at me. Now, however, he was much more collected. I wondered if I would see him a little "ruffled" tonight.

The waiter brought our drinks. I took a sip of wine. It was tasty. I had to pace myself since I was a cheap drunk. I usually didn't drink that much.

"Speaking of where you're from, did you learn English in France? I'm guessing that you took English in school but weren't really fluent until after you moved there."

"That's right." He was looking at me in a way that I didn't fully register. It was like he was a bit impressed, but also, interested somehow. I was spending a lot of energy on trying to read him. "But the English classes you take in France aren't really that great," he continued. "I mean, besides, to be really fluent you have to maintain the language outside the classroom."

"It's similar in Spain. People who speak English well are the exception, usually."

"I wish I could lose my accent," Tarek said then.

"Oh, God no," I said. The thought was horrifying.

Tarek smiled. "Why, you like it?"

"Very much." I regained my composure a little. "But more important than whether I like it or not, it's part of who you are. Like I can't lose my Castilian accent when I speak Spanish. I can try an Argentine accent but it sounds forced."

"For the record," Tarek leaned forward, "I *love* your Spanish accent." He emphasized the word 'love' in a way that made my pulse race a little bit.

I was speechless for a few moments. I picked at my salad and took another sip of wine. Then I thought of something to say.

"So in Miami you hang around with a lot of Spanish-speaking people?" I was remembering his earlier comment about Latin women. He must have had a basis for saying that. I wanted to ask him how many Latin women he had dated in the past, but I didn't have the guts.

"Yes, a fair amount," Tarek answered.

"So how much Spanish do you really know?" I had the feeling he had been holding out on me.

"I can get by," he said. Then he added, "I know enough to have recognized your accent as being from Spain." He smiled.

He likes Latin women. And there's something he's not telling me. I didn't really *look* Latin, though, except for the dark hair and eyes. But I was assuming that he liked me. Did he like me?

Our entrees arrived. I had ordered pasta. I figured the carbs would give me the energy to dance later, and it was fairly innocuous to eat.

I was thinking. I looked down at my hands for a minute, gathering courage. There was something I was dying to know. But I knew he wouldn't answer it if I asked him directly. I considered that perhaps the question could wait. But wait until when? Once we were in the club, Josh and Eric would be there. It would also be way too noisy. I didn't know when I would have the opportunity to ask it again.

I would start with a seemingly unrelated question. My tactic was not to address it head on, but to find a way around it. Maybe this would work.

"So how were your grades at the school where you went in Miami?" I asked.

He looked at me, his interest piqued.

"They were good."

"Like, top ten percent good?"

"Why?"

I shrugged. "*You* asked *me* what my grades were." I was bluffing.

But he called it. "And you didn't answer, or you said something evasive."

I was about to put him on the spot. "As of now, I'm in the top ten percent of the class. What about you?" I reached for my wine glass and looked at him.

Checkmate. You have to answer now, and I already know what the answer is.

"I am too." He was looking at me a bit suspiciously. He hadn't seen this coming. I felt kind of bad blindsiding him, but not bad enough to stop. After all, he had hardly played any of his cards. In fact, I didn't think he had actually played any, if indeed he had any cards to play.

His look was questioning. I decided to get to the point. There was no time like the present. I put my utensils down and leaned forward across the table, folding my hands.

"Tarek," I began, a little nervously, "I'm a little curious. Your grades are excellent. So—why did you insist on studying with me?"

He was definitely surprised. He also looked like I had just beaten him at some competition. It was the look my sisters gave me whenever I crushed them in chess, which had been often when we were younger. Neither of them had had any patience for it.

He didn't say anything at first. I was looking right into his eyes and I could see him thinking about what to say. I immediately felt like I shouldn't have asked the question. He was new to the city, new to the school. I should be nicer to him. He had been so nice to me.

That last thought echoed in my head. There was something about the way he treated me. I felt like I didn't always deserve how he treated me.

Without thinking about it, I reached my hand across the table but then I came out of my reverie just in time and I started to control myself. I ended up touching the back of his hand with my index finger. I left it there for a second. At the contact with his skin, I felt electric. His skin was so smooth. He still hadn't said anything.

"Tarek, I'm sorry, I didn't mean to make you feel uncomfortable. I shouldn't have asked."

"It's OK. I—you know, I didn't know anyone here." He seemed hesitant, so I continued.

"The truth is—I don't care what the reason was." Wait, what? "I—I'm really enjoying spending time with you." The words had tumbled through my lips. The worst part was, it was the truth. Then I felt embarrassed, like I had played a major card I hadn't intended on playing.

I took my hand back as he was turning his over. Wait, was he going to touch mine? I couldn't tell.

I smiled nervously and could feel myself blushing. I looked down.

"Isabel."

I looked up again. I couldn't believe that I had played that card. The way things were going, I was going to be left standing with an empty deck by the end of the night.

"Why do *you* think I wanted to study with you?" A Socratic-type question. But he wasn't trying to trick me, I could tell, not like I had tried to trick him. He looked—a little *anxious*.

I shook my head and my brows furrowed. "I don't know, Tarek." That was a true statement.

He smiled hesitantly, and his eyes were charged, full of emotion. "Yes, you do."

He had finally played one card.

We lingered over coffee and tea because I knew that Josh was usually late, and I didn't want to wait for him on the street. He could wait for us.

Well, I had wanted to see Tarek a little ruffled, and I had. It was only a glimpse, though. But it was enough.

After our exchange we had sat in silence for a couple of moments. Then I had spoken.

"Tarek?"

"Tell me."

"I'm sorry I was such a jerk to you."

"What do you mean?"

"When we first met, when we first talked, I wasn't the nicest person."

He had smiled in a way that told me that that was an understatement.

"It's OK."

"It's easier that way. If I'm a jackass all the time then people don't talk to me."

"And you don't want to talk to people?"

"Not usually. People in this town usually disappoint me. And I always think the worst of people."

"So that you're not disappointed?" How did he know that?

"Right."

"Are you frequently disappointed?"

"Yes," I said, nodding.

"Were you disappointed with me?"

His question surprised me. I looked at his eyes. It was an honest question.

I answered immediately, without thinking about it. "No." It was almost a whisper. "*Au contraire.*"

His smile was genuine.

Now, while having our coffee and tea, we were talking about law school and classes and the students.

"Why don't you like Alyssa?" Tarek asked me then.

"Tarek, I don't like anyone," I said, somewhat resignedly. Then I qualified the statement. "I mean, the number of people that I actually like, I could count on one hand. My sisters, you, Josh, Melanie, Dinesh and Eric." I paused. "OK, so I guess that's more than five, but I don't like Josh and Eric all the time." I smiled.

"You don't like her because she's intellectually beneath you." He raised one eyebrow.

"Not exactly. I don't necessarily care about that. It's—she doesn't take anything seriously. She's a typical Millennial. For her, and people like her, it's all about planning nights out and shit."

"And you think everyone should take everything seriously all the time?"

"Don't *you*?" Now I raised one eyebrow.

"You didn't answer my question."

"Yes." Then I qualified again. "Well, I think that everyone should take most things seriously all the time."

"*You* take everything seriously, down to the clothes you wear." I ignored the reference to my clothes, or to the fact that his statement meant that he paid attention to what I wore.

My voice got quiet. "Life is too short not to take things seriously." I was thinking about my father. "Your life could change in a second. You know that."

Tarek's expression softened. "I can't argue with that."

My mood was getting too dark. I would try to lighten it a little. "Even having fun, that should also be taken seriously. I mean, that's why I schedule it in my calendar." I smiled.

He grinned broadly.

I looked at my watch. "We can get going whenever you want. It'll take about fifteen minutes to walk over to the club."

His grin was playful. What was he going to say? I suddenly got nervous. "What if I don't want to get going?"

"Then we'll stay. I'm easy." Wait, what? "I mean, I'm—I'm not easy—" My face felt flush. I started rambling. "I'm easygoing, as in, I don't care either way. Easygoing, that's what I meant. I swear to God."

Tarek appeared amused by my discombobulation. "I knew what you meant." His eyes were bright and smiling.

I exhaled.

Our waiter appeared then. "I'll take this when you're ready." He placed our check on the edge of the small table, so that it was equidistant from both of us. It made me smile inwardly.

As soon as the waiter turned his back, I firmly put my hand on the bill. Tarek did the same but I had planned ahead and was faster.

His hand ended up on top of mine, but mine didn't move. I was determined.

We were looking at each other. I could tell that he was a little exasperated with me.

"Isabel, I'm paying." He had a serious look on his face.

"Tarek, please let me pay." I was thinking again about the fact that he wasn't working.

"Look, I know you're a feminist—" he started to say.

"It has nothing to do with that." That was a true statement. In my mind, a woman should never assume that a man would pay for her. But I also thought, and Melanie agreed with me, that if the man asked the woman out, that the man should pay. Tarek had asked me to dinner so, following that logic, he should pay. But he had paid for me on other occasions, when the rules didn't require him to, and besides, this wasn't a date, like he said.

Oh wait, that was it.

"You told me that this wasn't a date," I told him. *Toma.*

Then I saw it. A flash of disappointment on his face. Was he disappointed that he had said that it wasn't a date, or disappointed that I had brought it up?

But he quickly regained his composure, like he always did. I still hadn't moved my hand. I was very much aware of his hand over mine, and was starting to become a little jittery.

"I did say that," he began, a bit grudgingly, "but nevertheless I invited you, so—"

I was on the fence. If I insisted and grabbed the check, would he be seriously pissed off? I wasn't sure, but I was certain that he wouldn't like it at all.

"Isabel, please," he said calmly. He blinked. It made me notice his eyes. They were absolutely gorgeous. I wasn't sure if he had blinked on purpose then.

I sighed a long sigh. "OK, since you said please."

I left my hand there for one or two seconds longer, and then slid it out from underneath his.

"Thank you," he smiled.

I felt a bit defeated, but I would survive. He had begun to show me another card. *Quid pro quo.*

When we were outside I called Josh to see where he was, since I refused to wait for him on the street outside the club for however long it would take for him to get there.

As luck would have it, he and Eric were almost there. I hung up.

I turned toward Tarek as we walked. "We're good. He and Eric are almost there. They'll wait for us outside."

Tarek nodded. "So how often do you guys go dancing?" he asked then.

"Um—our first year Josh and I went dancing pretty often, about once every couple of weeks. Then the—" I was going to say the shit hit the fan and we had to buckle down and really study, but I changed my mind. "Then we decided that we should probably study more, soooo, we went out less." I shrugged. "Josh goes out more often than I do. This is like a real treat for me."

As usual, downtown DC, especially the area where we were, was popping on a Saturday night. Groups of people flooded the streets. Someone almost ran into me.

Tarek put his hand on my back to steer me out of the way. I stepped closer to him.

I looked at him, wondering about something. Our faces were close together. "So do you dance? I mean, talking about Latin dance specifically."

He looked at me and his eyes were twinkling. "I'm from Miami," he said, as if that explained everything.

"That doesn't answer my question." I smiled a bit flirtatiously.

"I've been known to." He seemed to be deliberately exercising restraint with his answers. I guessed I would have to wait and see.

We took our time walking, mostly because I knew that Josh was a slow walker and I didn't want to get there before he did.

When we got there we met Josh and Eric outside. They had just arrived.

Josh leaned in and gave me two kisses; then Eric did the same. They were both impeccably dressed.

"Hey," Tarek said to me.

"What?" I shrugged.

"You didn't kiss *me* hello," he protested. Josh and Eric were looking at him too.

"You're not Latin," I retorted, trying to suppress a smile, as if that were a sufficient explanation.

"*You* lived in France," he said then. "Don't you remember how French people greet each other?"

He had me. In southern France, it was with three kisses. But in northern France, including Paris, where he and I had both lived, friends and family greeted each other with no less than four kisses.

What the hell. I would call his bluff. Before anyone could say anything, I grabbed his upper arm and leaned in. One, two, three, four kisses, alternating cheeks. His goatee tickled my face. Every time my cheek touched his, I felt like I didn't want to let him go.

Finally I leaned away and dropped my hand from his arm. I looked at the three of them. Tarek was smiling. Josh was trying not to chuckle.

"Is everyone happy now?" I said then, throwing my hands up in the air, Argentine-style. "Has everyone been sufficiently kissed?"

"No," Eric said, smiling. "If he gets four, then I want four too."

"No," I said. "Originally, you only had one, so consider yourself lucky." Then *I* couldn't help smiling.

We got in line. The problem with waiting outside for a while was that Josh and I couldn't keep our mouths shut about politics and, in a matter of minutes, we were arguing again.

This time the topic was welfare. It was a subject over which Josh and I frequently sparred.

"Throwing money at people is not 'helping' them, Josh," I said, using my air quotes for 'helping.' "It makes them dependent, so that they keep voting for the politicians that give them handouts. It's a political ploy. It's not about helping people."

This was a very sensitive topic for me, but I was trying to maintain my calm for the moment.

We were slowly moving forward in the line.

"But some people need help because they can't work," Josh said then.

"Yes, but there are very few people who can do absolutely no work."

"Yes, maybe people who are bedridden, or who have severe disorders," Tarek said then.

Eric looked exasperated.

"The bottom line is," I told Josh, "the more free stuff you give people, free housing, medical care, food, etc., the less motivation they have to work and contribute to the economy and to society. So at some point you will have more people receiving government handouts than people working and paying taxes to enable those handouts."

"A lot of people don't realize that the government generates no income," Tarek added. "The government's income, so to speak, comes from taxpayers, and sooner or later, people get tired of being taxed too much."

"Oh, right," Josh said sarcastically, "People like Bill Gates don't have enough money to pay taxes."

"For 'normal' people like us," I retorted, using air quotes, "there comes a time when you realize that you are working harder and making more money for what? To have the government take more of it from you. So you are less motivated to work and more motivated to get handouts. Why should someone work at a job making about $2,000 a month with health insurance, when he can get $1,000 or more a month in disability payments, food stamps, Section 8 housing, whatever, and not have to work?"

I continued. "My point is simply that at some point, people will weigh the costs and benefits of working versus living on the government dole, and will be less motivated to work. Everyone could reach that point. And for people with less skills, that point is reached much more quickly when they're working a minimum-wage job."

"If you make it easier for people not to work, they won't work," Tarek punctuated. "Not only that—" he was about to rant, I could tell.

Eric broke in then. "Guys, if you want to argue about this shit, fine. But as soon as we step into that club, shut it down!"

"Fine!" Josh and I said at the same time.

"I'm serious!" Eric insisted.

"All right!" I said, annoyed at his interruptions.

"I'm just saying," Josh continued, "that rich people should pay their fair share."

"Fair share?!" Tarek exclaimed. "And what is that? Seventy-five percent like they were talking about in some other countries? Why would you work then? And do you know all the good that rich people do? Like donate and invest in pharmaceutical drugs that wouldn't otherwise get invented, drugs that help people and manage diseases?"

"Maybe building schools?" I added.

Josh wasn't winning this line of argument, so he changed his tactic a little.

"So you're against giving people any kind of help?"

"No, but it should come more from the private sector," Tarek answered. "Don't overtax people and they will decide how to use and donate their money. Rich people already donate to various causes. I would prefer to spend my money how I want instead of the government taking it and spending it how the government wants."

I briefly looked around. The music from the club was thumping. We were almost there. I could feel the music in my chest. My adrenaline was starting to kick in a little. I couldn't wait to dance.

Then I noticed that people were looking at us like we were crazy. I didn't mind. I was used to getting that look in this city. It was a place full of vapid, superficial twenty-somethings, pumped up and feeling self-important because they had what they considered to be prestigious jobs. God forbid someone actually engaged them in a meaningful conversation about something significant like economics or private sector growth.

Their look said that they couldn't believe that there were people arguing about politics at midnight while waiting to get into a dance club. There were a couple of people who looked like they were about to protest our discussion. But I shot them a venomous look that dared them to do just that, and they quickly shut their mouths.

I turned my attention back to Josh. "Also, the more you tax rich people, the less they will donate, and money and investment may even leave the country," I added. I was thinking of Argentina again. The Argentine government made it difficult for foreign investment, so, consequently, foreign investors were reluctant to put money into the country, especially when it could be expropriated at any time.

"We're almost there!" Eric said. "Wrap it up!"

I looked. He was right. Without realizing it, we had been moving all along. There were only about eight people in front of us now.

Again, Josh wasn't addressing our argument, but riding on the outskirts of it.

"You know," he said then, "The author of the Harry Potters books was on government welfare, and she did OK."

"If she hadn't written those books and become a millionaire, would she still be on welfare?" I countered quickly.

Josh didn't answer.

I answered for him. "Probably, so working was the key to independence, right?"

"Even so, that's the exception," Tarek added. "For every exception, there are thousands of people who stay dependent on government assistance."

"All right, a few more steps and that's it!" Eric raised his voice then.

"All right!" I told him. Then I whirled on Josh.

"You know, Josh, if you're so concerned about giving people help, then please make your non-tax-deductible, voluntary contribution to the IRS at your convenience, or should I say, at your inconvenience."

Tarek laughed. "Yes, feel free to donate—"

"And that's it!" It was Eric.

I looked. We had just stepped into the club. I looked at Tarek and we smiled at each other.

Josh, Tarek and I had all stopped talking at once.

"Gentlemen," I said to both of them, "I'm afraid that's all for tonight. Let's dance."

It was late enough that the club was packed. Eric walked straight to the bar and the rest of us followed. I struggled to follow the guys through the crowd. We walked down a short staircase and I started to lose them. I was trying to get around people without hurting them. I wanted to elbow them out of the way.

Then Tarek turned around and saw me. He was a little further down the stairs than I was. He reached out his arm and offered me his hand. I hesitated for a second and then took it.

Rule Two was broken. Well, it was a technical violation of Rule Two but it was necessary and the hand-holding wasn't romantic.

Doesn't matter, the logical part of my brain said then. It's still a violation. Oh well.

We made it to the bar and Eric had already ordered the first round. He handed me my Cuba Libre. Eric and I always drank to a Cuba *libre*.

Josh was already talking to some girl.

I leaned toward Tarek to say something in his ear. It was so loud here. I figured I had already broken my no-whispering-in-his-ear rule, so what the hell.

"Josh is always talking to some girl," I told him.

"I've noticed," he said, smiling.

"Wait until he starts dancing. He'll have a swarm of girls around him."

The music was currently reggaeton, but a little later they would play more salsa and merengue-type music, which is what Josh really wanted to dance to.

"Come on, Isabel!" Eric shouted to me then, motioning for me to drink faster, "Let's go dance!"

"One minute!" I yelled back. If I drank too quickly, it would go to my head. I looked around briefly, but didn't see anyone else that I knew, not that I cared.

Eric knocked back his drink and then took my drink, which was only halfway done, and handed it to Josh. Then he took my hand. I made a motion for him to wait.

I took off my jacket and handed it to Josh. Then I turned to Tarek. "Are you coming?" I asked him, my mouth so close to his ear that it was a bit unnerving.

"In a minute."

"OK." Then I followed Eric to the dance floor. The music was great and we soon started to sweat. Eric held me really close and I had my arms loosely around his neck. I tried not to think about the fact that I was almost ten years older than he was. With the lighting in here, people couldn't really tell my age anyway.

Eric was a very fluid dancer. Typical Brazilian, I had thought the first time I saw him dance. If I was tired, sometimes I had trouble keeping up with him.

But he and I were both in top form tonight. He moved his hips constantly, swinging me around and then holding me close, his right hand on my waist, with my torso almost touching his. After a little while, we were both breathing hard. Our faces were close together and I noticed the sweat on his face.

"Let's get something to drink," I said into his ear.

"OK," he answered, then squeezed me once against his chest before dropping his arms. I let out a little shriek and laughed.

We walked back to the bar, and Josh and Tarek were chatting. They also had fresh drinks.

"What are you drinking?" I asked Tarek.

He told me. "Do you want to try it?" he said in my ear, then held it out to me.

I smiled and tried it. It was tasty. I only took a sip; I didn't want to get lightly toasted with Tarek here. Who knew what would happen then?

Salsa music started playing. Josh asked me to dance and we danced for a while. Then we rejoined Tarek at the bar and and I ordered another drink. I had to pace myself.

Eric was in and out, chatting with various people. He was always chatty. He seemed to know several people there.

When we were back at the bar, Josh started to regale Tarek with stories of how he and I had met. We had met at one of the initial receptions that the school gave for admitted students, before we had even formally accepted admittance. My take on how we met had always been that Josh had tried to pick me up.

"Yeah, whatever," was Josh's response to that.

"Then he found out where I was on the political spectrum, and he totally wrote me off," I told Tarek.

"Oh, so he's intolerant?" Tarek said, but it was obvious that he was joking. Josh laughed "That's not true!"

"Oh, so you haven't written me off?"

"Are you saying there's still a chance we could go out?" Josh looked right at me.

I stared for a second, then he and I both started laughing at the same time.

"Noooo," we both said through laughter.

It was true. Josh was like a brother to me. And siblings who were close usually argued, but they still loved each other.

Time went by quickly. I didn't want to know the hour because I was having too good a time, and I didn't want to leave.

After a while Josh left to dance with the girl he had been talking to before. Then Eric showed up and wanted me to dance with him again. I turned to Tarek and made a motion with my hand toward the center of the dance floor.

"I'm going to finish my drink," he told me.

I rolled my eyes at him. Maybe he didn't dance. Well, I wouldn't press him. I went with Eric.

But as soon as we started to dance a girl started talking to Eric. I recognized her from school. I guess Eric knew her but I didn't know her well. Eric told me to hold on one second as he chatted with her.

How rude, Eric! Don't leave me standing here! I can't dance salsa by myself.

But it turned out I didn't have to. Someone took my right hand and I turned around and it was Tarek.

"Come here," he said, smiling.

I slid my left hand over his shoulder and and we started dancing.

"Thanks for saving me," I said into his ear.

"Well, Eric's missed his chance so he's not getting you back for a while now."

I could feel myself blushing, but was sure that he couldn't tell in here.

We danced salsa and then merengue. The truth about Tarek's dancing was that he danced very well. I told him so.

"You've been holding out on me, with the Spanish, and with the dancing. It's a little ironic, a Lebanese-Frenchman who does Latin dance so well." My mouth was so close to his ear that his curls tickled my nose.

"Well, I used to date a Dominican girl, so—" he left the sentence hanging, as if that explained everything.

"For a while?" I asked.

"For about two and a half years."

"Recently?" I was curious. How much would he tell me?

"We broke up about—" he seemed to be thinking, "almost three years ago."

OK, so he *did* like Latin women. Dominican, huh? She must have been hot. That also explained why he danced well.

"When you were in Miami?" I asked.

"Yes."

I wanted to know more about this girl, but was afraid to ask.

"I'm sorry, Tarek. I didn't mean to be nosy."

"It's OK."

A rumba played then. I loved rumba.

I got even closer to his ear. I was feeling a little giddy at being so close to him. We had never been this close.

"Tarek, if you can rumba this may be love." God knows what possessed me to say that.

He did rumba. Oh God. Then he was chuckling.

The two of us danced very fluidly.

Then I was starting to feel like all the cells in my body were awake. Everything seemed to be more intense. My fingertips brushed his shirt and I could feel the warmth from his body and his hand on my back. With my left hand I hesitantly touched one of his curls.

We didn't talk for a while. We just danced. Salsa, merengue, rumba, bachata. I didn't bother asking him if he danced bachata. I figured if he liked to dance and had dated a Dominican girl, then he would know bachata. And he did.

"Eric was right," he said at one point.

"About what?" I asked, curious.

"This is the happiest I've ever seen you," Tarek said into my ear.

"It's because of the music," I started, "and because in the dark I can be totally anonymous."

Hmm, that was kind of deep for a Saturday night out.

Tarek chuckled and then we didn't talk again for a while.

I was enjoying dancing with him, and totally lost track of time. I kind of guessed how much time had passed because the music started to slow down. It must be getting late. Maybe 2 a.m., 3 a.m.? I wasn't sure.

Then one of my favorite songs started playing, a slower song that required significant hip action.

Oh *God*.

I hadn't seen Josh or Eric but then, I hadn't really been looking for them. I wondered if they could see us. Then I wondered why I cared. Then I decided that I didn't care.

This time, when we danced, Tarek held me closer. This particular song was deeply sensual, and I loved that and hated it at the same time, because it made my body respond in ways that I almost couldn't control. I was starting to get turned on, yes, but aside from that, I wanted to hold him closer to me. I moved as close as I dared, and moved my left hand from his shoulder to the back of his neck, where I could feel his curly hair, so that my left elbow ended up resting on his right shoulder. He responded by drawing me even closer to him, his arm curling around my waist, and suddenly there was no space between us, and I noted the feel of my breasts against his chest when I breathed.

This is the part that I loved about dancing. He and I were like one unit, moving with the music, and it was easy to move with him. When I danced with Josh, we danced well, but Josh and I really didn't have much chemistry. We were just good friends. When I danced with Eric, I had an incredible time, and our dance styles meshed really well. He had an energy that was completely unmatched. But as I was dancing with Tarek, there *was* chemistry. There was so much chemistry that I felt like we were combustible. There was electricity where my right hand touched his left and where I rested my left hand on his neck.

Then I began to get a bit carried away. I let go of Tarek's left hand and slid my right hand onto his other shoulder. I hugged him to me, as if we could get any closer.

Then he put his left hand around my waist.

Oh my God. If he asked me to go home with him right now, I would.

Our cheeks were barely touching, and I felt a thrill knowing that if I turned my head a little to the right I could kiss him, right by his ear. I used all my reserves to resist doing that. I didn't know if he wanted me to kiss him. When you were dancing with someone like this, it was easy to think they wanted you to kiss them. In fact, as I started to remember, this was how Santi and I had gotten together . . . dancing. But it could also just be that—dancing, and nothing else. At that moment, I realized that I hadn't thought about Santi for a long time. It surprised me.

Then Tarek started to get a bit carried away. His hands were on my back, at my waist. My shirt wasn't tucked into my pants, but loose.

Tarek's hand was finding its way under my shirt, at my waist and on my back. Now two of his fingers were touching the skin of my back. In response, I leaned into him and touched his cheek with mine. Then I was running my fingers through his curls, at his neck. My breasts felt tender all of a sudden. Oh my God, my nipples are probably hard. Would he notice? Could a guy notice that without seeing them? I wasn't sure.

All my senses were on fire all at once. I noticed then how hard his chest was. And I noticed the smell of his aftershave. And I felt how smooth the skin of his face was, right above his goatee.

I automatically inclined my head a little. The move was so slight that I hoped he probably hadn't noticed. His goatee was tickling my cheek. I wanted to kiss him, badly.

It was taking everything I had not to kiss him right then. I still wasn't sure if he wanted me to. But if he did want it, I had the feeling that it would be incredible between us. I was too scared to try right now. But if *he* tried to kiss me now, I had no doubt that I would cave. I wouldn't be able to resist him.

Then the song ended. That soon? Oh my God, what would I say to him? We stopped dancing but didn't let go of each other. I was afraid to because then I would have to look him in the face.

But I would have to eventually. I extricated my right hand from his hair and reluctantly slid both my hands from his neck to his shoulders and then down his arms. But I still didn't look at him.

He released my waist. At that point I thought of something to say.

"Do you want to get a drink?" I said into his ear.

"Sure," he said. Was he a bit breathless? Maybe it was my imagination. My pulse was racing.

I took his arm and we walked toward the bar. I didn't see Josh or Eric. Great. Now I would have to be alone with Tarek. My mind was spinning. What do I do now? Should I pretend that that didn't just happen?

When we got to the bar, he asked me what I wanted to drink.

"Actually," I paused, "I'm OK." Then I pointed to my wrist, asking him if he had the time. It was about 2:30 a.m.

He leaned toward my ear. "If you want—we can leave."

We, he had said. Was that code for, do you want to come to my apartment to have sex? I started thinking, which usually led me to overanalyze, which usually led to me driving myself crazy.

When I hooked up with guys, usually they were more direct than that, and I was more direct with them. I was in way over my head here. I was going to have to figure this out as I went along.

"Isabel?" Tarek was still at my ear. I needed to say something.

"Sure," I told him. "Wait one second." I looked around for Josh and Eric. I would text them that I had left. They were big boys, and they could take care of themselves.

Then I turned back to Tarek. "Let's go. I'll text them that we left." I still hadn't looked at him in the face.

We left then, me holding onto Tarek's arm on the way out. It was much more crowded than when we had arrived.

When we got outside I inhaled a deep breath. The city night air was fresh compared with the stuffiness inside the club.

"Are you OK?"

I turned and looked at Tarek finally. "Yeah," I nodded.

We started walking away from the club very slowly. I wasn't sure where we were going. I was still a bit giddy, and was trying to suppress a giggle.

"I had no idea you could dance like that," Tarek said. I sneaked a look at him. He was looking at me admiringly.

I laughed. "What, you thought I only danced tango and *paso doble* because I'm half-Argentine, half-Spanish?" Then I added, "Besides, there's a lot you don't know about me."

Tarek stopped and I ended up two steps in front of him. I turned around. He was looking at me. His look was a serious one. "I'd like to get to know you more, though."

I stared at him. He seemed surprised that he had said that. Had he said it without thinking? Did he mean it?

"What do you mean?" We were facing each other. As always, he looked amazing, tousled curls and bright eyes.

"I mean—" he was looking for the right words. He looked lost for a second, but quickly tried to regain his composure. I decided then that he hadn't intended to say that; the words had just left his mouth. I could tell by how discombobulated he was. So it was the truth, then. "I mean—it means—" he was shaking his head a little now, as if he were trying to clear it and think straight. "It means whatever you want it to mean," he finally said.

That was no answer. But I didn't dwell on it. I was too shocked that he had said it in the first place. "I—," I suddenly felt the need to be honest. "I'm not sure what I want it to mean."

He smiled, but was still unsure. "That's OK. You don't have to know right now."

Wait, what? Was he telling me that he was interested in me, but that he would wait for me to make up my mind if I wanted to date him or not? Or was he only interested in me for a 'short-term benefit,' I thought glibly, like Ariel had mentioned? Or did he mean that I had time to decide if we could be friends? But weren't we friends? Hadn't I told him the first day we studied together that it would be just that—studying and nothing more? Was he intent on changing my mind? He seemed so serious. I couldn't help but think that he had played another card.

"OK," I said, a little relieved but still confused. "So I don't have to decide now."

"No." He shook his head, but there was longing in his eyes.

"OK," I said again.

We continued walking. I still wasn't sure what had just happened.

It was colder than I had anticipated. My light jacket wasn't doing the job. I shivered, this time from the cold and not because of him.

"Here," he said, offering me his arm.

I took his arm, slipping my right arm through his left. He had his left hand in his coat pocket.

"Do you want my coat?" he asked. His coat was thicker than my jacket. He had been more prepared than me.

"No, thank you," I smiled. "I'll be all right." I looked around. I hadn't been walking anywhere in particular but now that I looked up I got my bearings.

"Umm—," I started, "we can cross at this intersection to get to the metro."

He nodded.

As we approached the metro I felt another gust of wind. Well, what did I expect? October was like two days away. I shivered again, but this time wasn't sure whether it was because of the cold or because of him.

"You're cold," Tarek said. It was a statement this time, not a question.

"Thanks for letting me know, because I would not have figured that out for myself," I told him, but couldn't help smiling.

He laughed. Then he spoke. "Isabel," he began.

I looked at him. "Yes?"

He looked a little nervous.

"Why don't you come over for tea, and then I can drive you home?"

I took a step back from him, but still held onto his arm. His invitation excited me but I also felt conflicted. He must have noticed, because suddenly he was very serious.

"Isabel, it's just tea. I promise." Our eyes met. "I don't expect anything of you."

That was enough for me. I believed him.

"OK, sure," I smiled.

Once we were in his apartment, Tarek made us tea and I sat on his couch. It was so comfortable. I leaned back and sunk my head into the pillows. I also slipped my heels off.

"Oh my God, this couch is so comfortable."

"My sister picked it out," he was smiling.

"Well, tell her that she has good taste." Then I thought of something. "Hey, is she still going out with that guy?" It had only been like a week or so.

"I think so. I haven't talked to her since then."

"That reminds me," I said, "I need to call my Mom. I haven't talked to her in like—" I was thinking, "a couple of weeks, I think."

I sighed a long sigh.

Tarek noticed. I was quickly figuring out that he was really good at reading my moods. "You don't want to talk to her?" He handed me my tea and I thanked him. Then he sat next to me on the sofa, but not right next to me. There was a comfortable distance.

"I love her, but it's always the same old story. 'Why are you working so hard?' 'Are you dating anyone?'" I sighed again. "The poor woman has been trying to find me a boyfriend since I was like sixteen years old. I mean—my sisters are attached. I don't see why she can't leave me alone."

Tarek laughed softly.

"I mean, how old am I?" I asked rhetorically.

"It's funny, all mothers share some things in common."

Was his mother giving him the same song-and-dance? But I didn't have time to ask, since he changed the subject slightly.

"I'm surprised that you and Eric haven't gone out."

I looked at him curiously. "What do you mean?" *I* wasn't surprised about that.

"You get along really well, I mean—" he was smiling, "as well as you can get along with anyone."

"Oh, thanks," I said sarcastically.

"I'm kidding," he said quickly.

"Tarek, he's nine years younger than I am." I emphasized the word "nine."

"So?"

"He's way too young for me."

He was looking at me intently. "So how young is too young?"

I knew what this was about, or at least I thought I did. Eric was nine years younger than me but Tarek was five years younger than me.

I decided to answer the question truthfully. "There is no real age limit. At least, I don't have one. But Eric is too young for me. It's not that he's immature for his age, although—" I paused, "arguably he may be. But he's too immature for me."

"Is he someone you would be interested in if he were older and—more mature?"

"No," I said automatically.

"Why not?"

Then I was thinking. I looked at Tarek and smiled. "Thanks, but I don't need your matchmaking services."

"I wasn't offering them." He paused, appearing to consider his next words. "And I didn't say that you needed them, even if I were offering them, which I'm not."

I didn't say anything; I just looked at him. I decided I was going to wait to see how long it took him to say something to avoid the silence. Or maybe he liked silence. I didn't. It always made me nervous. But when I started to get tangled up in my thoughts, I didn't mind it so much. Maybe if the silence went on long enough, with us looking at each other, he would kiss me. Wait, hadn't he hinted that he wouldn't do anything unless I did? Is that what he had meant earlier? Then maybe *I* would kiss *him*. Did I want to? Yes! Should I kiss him now? I don't know—

At last he spoke. "What are you thinking about?"

"Nothing," I lied.

He smiled in a way that told me he knew I was lying. But he didn't press me on it.

He put his mug of tea on the coffee table. "You didn't answer my question, Counselor."

"I'm sorry, *was* there a question?" I remembered, but I was stalling.

"There was. I asked you why Eric isn't someone you would be interested in, if he were older and more mature. That's the question."

I considered it. "Maybe I would be, if he were more mature. But—he doesn't really feel strongly about anything." I thought out loud. "Maybe it's because he hasn't lived enough yet. In any case—"

"He feels strongly about *you*."

I was confused. "Sorry?"

Tarek shook his head incredulously. "He likes you, Isabel."

"I guess he does, if he hangs around me and Josh all the time."

"No, I mean—he's crazy about you."

Now I was incredulous. "That's not true."

"Oh, it's true." Tarek was so sure of himself. "Pay attention to how he acts around you, how he dances with you."

I was getting worked up. I picked my head up from the back of the sofa and sat up straight. "Tarek, *all* Brazilians dance like that. It doesn't mean anything."

"To him it does."

I was suspicious. "Assuming it's true, which I highly doubt, how would you know that?" Was Eric talking to Tarek about me behind my back, like Josh had?

"He hasn't said anything, not to me at least, but it's obvious if you pay attention."

There was something else. He wasn't telling me something. I could see it in his eyes.

"What?" I asked.

"What do you mean, 'what?' "

I decided to press him this time. It was late and I was getting tired of innuendos. "Tarek, there is something about Eric that you're not telling me and I want to know what it is. Tell me—please." Maybe the please would be enough.

He sighed. "He doesn't like me."

"Why would you think that? Did he say something? If he did, tell me and I'll kick his ass."

Tarek laughed. "No, there's no need." He paused. "He hasn't said anything. But I don't think he liked me dancing with you. At least, that's the impression I have." He looked at me.

"Well he can like it or not, but he's not the boss of me. I'll dance with whoever I want to." But I was thinking back to the day that I had closed Eric's laptop on his hand after he had sneaked a peek at what Josh and I were conversing about online.

"Oh, I know," Tarek was smiling again. "No one is the boss of you."

"Huh," I said, still thinking. I drank my tea.

"What?"

"Nothing, just—it's interesting. That's all."

"What's interesting?"

I proceeded to tell Tarek about that night in class, after Sorority Girl had told him that I "slept around," that I had been chatting with Josh online, that Eric had snooped and read my messages to Josh, and that afterward Eric had confronted me.

"He asked me—" I was thinking over everything, thinking about whether there could be any truth to Tarek's theory that Eric was interested in me. Then I began thinking out loud, and before long I ended up playing another card.

I cocked my head to one side, deep in thought. "He asked me why I cared about what you thought. And I—" I felt my brows furrowing, "I told him I didn't know whether or not I cared about what you thought of me. But that's not true." Then I reached the logical conclusion that in my heart I had known all along. "But the truth is, I *do* care what you think about me, because otherwise why would I care about what SG said to you? Why would I care enough to bring it up to you later, to explain what she meant?"

I was suddenly shaken out of my reverie. I looked at Tarek. Oh my God, I *did* care what he thought about me. Why the hell had I stopped cursing around him? When the hell did I start caring about what people thought about what I said or did? I hadn't cared about hooking up with Saul when I had been out with Josh and Eric, and I didn't care about them knowing about it. But I cared about Tarek knowing about it, and I didn't want him to find out, especially since he apparently knew Saul.

I was like a deer in the headlights. I froze instantly, in shock. When was the last time that I had been over at a guy's place talking, not hooking up, this late at night? The answer was: never. I had never even been over at Eric's or Josh's this late.

"Isabel, are you OK?"

I looked at Tarek. His eyes were full of emotion, but what type I couldn't tell. Oh God, don't pity me, I thought.

"Did I say all that out loud?" That was a stupid question, I realized. You know you did.

He reached a hand toward my hair, brushing it away from my cheek. The feel of his hand against my face was enough to make my pulse speed up. I looked into his eyes and saw a question there. My face moved toward his. Then I freaked.

"I should go," I said automatically. I was so confused.

"I'll drive you home," he said, smiling, a bit wistfully.

The drive to my apartment building was pretty uneventful. During the entire car trip, I couldn't look at Tarek. He looked at me a couple of times, but I couldn't look back.

I couldn't believe I had let my guard down like that. It was late, my inhibitions had started to fall away, and I had started to bare my soul like a freaking idiot. Hadn't he said that this was *not* a date?

Then he startled me.

"What are you thinking about?"

"That I talk too much." That was the truth, at least partially.

He laughed. "I don't think you talk enough."

"Oh, ha ha," I mimicked.

"Isabel, I'm serious. I like hearing about you."

"Well, you know almost everything about me." I was looking out the window now. I still wouldn't look at him.

"I highly doubt that." His tone was serious.

I realized that I had been holding my breath. I exhaled slowly. I was starting to feel tired. I leaned my head back against the seat.

"Can I ask you something?" he said then. We were about to exit the highway near where I lived.

"I guess," I said. My tone was resigned.

"It's nothing bad," he said. I could hear the smile in his voice.

"What, then?"

"Will you take me to the shooting range some time?"

My head whipped around. "What?"

"You heard me."

"Have you ever shot before?"

"Yes, a long time ago."

"I usually don't teach people to shoot."

"Is that a 'no?'"

"It's a—" I looked at him. "It's a maybe, if you promise to listen to everything I tell you."

"Isabel, when have I not listened to you?"

"When I told you I studied alone. You didn't listen to me, then."

"Oh my God, you're going to bring that up for the rest of our lives?"

"Yes, I will!" I was glad that he hadn't listened to me, though.

"OK," he said slowly, "I promise that I will listen to everything that you say."

"And that you'll follow instructions?"

"Yes, I promise."

"It's a liability nightmare for me, you do realize that, don't you?"

"Then you can have me sign a waiver."

"You'll have to sign one at the range, but maybe I'll create one for purposes of you holding me harmless against any and all liability." I couldn't help smiling then.

Tarek smiled too, in a way that suggested that he was happy that I was smiling.

He pulled into the parking lot of my building and parked the car.

"Thanks for driving me home," I told him without looking at him.

"I'll walk you to your apartment. It's really late and this parking lot is not well-lit."

He was right about that. In fact, I had myself complained to management about the lack of lighting here. Even so, I wondered if walking me to my door was some kind of pretext. He didn't seem like the kind of guy to do that, though, so I quickly put it out of my mind.

When we got to the main door, I opened it and we walked upstairs. The lighting inside was much better. However, I still managed to trip on the stairs when my heel caught on the step.

Tarek grabbed my upper arm as I stumbled. I corrected myself.

"Are you OK?" he said.

"Yes, I—my heel caught. I'm just tired."

"Tired or a little drunk?" Tarek smiled.

"I didn't drink that much," I countered. "But it doesn't take much," I added ruefully.

"Oh really?" his eyes were playful.

"No, actually—I'm a cheap drunk."

"Well, I'll have to remember that next time."

"You wish," I grinned a bit.

He released my arm and we continued walking.

When we got to my apartment door, I fumbled with my keys. I realized that I was nervous.

"How many keys do you have?" Tarek asked me jokingly. He was leaning against the wall next to my door, close enough to make my pulse race.

"Let's see, one . . . two . . . three," I started to count them. I had a ton.

Tarek laughed. "Oh my God."

"Oh, it was a rhetorical question?" I asked with fake surprise. "You mean you didn't really want to know? Well, dude, you should make that clear next time."

Then I heard my neighbor's dog bark. It was a quick succession of ruf, ruf, ruf, ruf, ruf!

As I was opening my door John came out of his.

"Oh hey," he said to me. He was fully dressed. He must have been watching TV or something. That made me feel better because it meant that we hadn't woken him up with our chatter.

"Sorry for the noise, John," I told him.

"Sorry for the barking. He barks at anything." Of course he does. He's a Beagle.

John was looking at Tarek, so I introduced them.

"Is this your boyfriend?" John asked me.

"No, um—" I struggled nervously for a second, "he's a friend of mine from school."

A 'friend' who I happened to be bringing home at around 4 a.m. on a Saturday night.

"Oh, sorry," John said then, "I've never seen you with anyone before."

"It's because I'm antisocial," I said. "Or so I've been told."

Tarek chuckled and I hit him playfully on the shoulder with the back of my right hand.

"See you later, John," I told him.

"Have a good night." John smiled.

We entered my apartment and I closed the door. I was chuckling to myself.

"What?" Tarek asked me.

"'Have a good night,' he said." Then the words tumbled out of my mouth as I threw my keys on the counter. "It's obvious what he thinks we're going to do in here."

"Of course it is. What else would two law students do at 4 a.m. on a Saturday night?"

I looked at him, open-mouthed. He looked back at me, shaking his head.

"I meant studying, or arguing about the law, since law students like to hear themselves talk."

"Well, that's true," I conceded. Then we were looking at each other.

"Can I get you anything before you head out?" I asked him. "Coffee or anything?"

"You know I don't drink coffee."

"I know, but I still harbor the illusion that I can convert you one day."

He smiled. Then there was silence for a second. "No, thank you, I don't need anything," he said.

I suddenly felt the air heavy with the weight of the decision I needed to make, like this was the moment that I needed to decide what, if anything, to do about him, or with him. What had been my rules again? No arm-touching. Fail. No ear-whispering. Fail. No hand-holding. Fail again.

But I had told myself that I was open to kissing him tonight. Oh, who the hell was I kidding? If I kissed him, that would lead to sex because I would not be able to control myself.

I could feel my pulse and my breathing quicken. I concentrated on taking deep breaths to calm down. I needed to say something, but I also needed him out of here because the longer he stayed, the less resistance I would have.

"Tarek," I began, "Thank you for dinner. I had a really good time tonight." But he knew that, right? Hadn't I told him earlier that I really enjoyed spending time with him?

He took one, two steps toward me. I froze. We ended up less than a foot away from each other.

"Thank you for inviting me out tonight," he told me.

"Of course," I looked down.

"I had a good time tonight too," he said.

He didn't say anything else so I looked up.

"Isabel, I'm going to go but I want to tell you something."

Oh my God, what?!

He paused for what was probably a second, but to me felt like an eternity.

"I saw you the other day, you know?"

Holy shit, what was he talking about?!

"When?" I asked, confused.

"In the beginning, I saw you on the metro."

I was still confused. "You've seen me on the metro lots of times." I shook my head, my brows furrowing.

He looked into my eyes, smiling. "The day you were listening to your music, dancing."

Why did he feel the need to embarrass me now?

I crossed my arms, huffed and looked away.

"No, I mean—" he said quickly, placing both his hands on my upper arms, as if he wanted to prevent me from running away. "Before that, I saw you give your seat to that lady with a little child."

"And?" What was his point with bringing this up?

"And the first day of International Law class," he continued, "I saw you help Zara with the door."

"So? A lot of people do that."

"No, they don't," he said firmly. "But *you* do. And that's why—"

I could tell that he was struggling with what to say. With his hands on my arms, he was also drawing me closer to him. Oh no, I thought anxiously. Tarek, don't kiss me, I pleaded mentally. If you kiss me, I'll drag you into my bed and I don't want that. I mean, I *do* want that but I don't know if I want it right now. I was confusing myself again.

"Isabel, you asked me earlier why I was so insistent on studying with you." He said the next part quickly, like he was afraid that if he paused to think about it he wouldn't say it. "It's because I saw you and I knew that you were someone that I wanted to get to know."

I was shocked. He had actually said it. He had practically admitted that studying was a pretext to get to know me. This was all starting to be more than I had bargained for.

We were so close now that I could reach out my hand a little and touch his hair. And that's what I did. I couldn't help it.

With my eyes still on his face, I uncrossed my arms and touched his curls with my left hand, twirling one around my finger. Before I knew what I was doing, I was pulling on his hair, pulling him toward me. It wasn't difficult; he leaned in quite willingly. I could feel my breath coming more quickly. Every fiber in my body was suddenly on fire.

Then I had the thought, If I did this what would I feel like tomorrow? I would be happy, wouldn't I? But what would *he* feel like? I didn't know and the uncertainty totally freaked me out. I could not handle it if he woke up tomorrow and regretted this. I could *not*.

So as I drew him to me I tilted my head to the right and put my arms around him and lay my head on his shoulder, with my mouth away from his neck so that I wouldn't be tempted to kiss him there. I wasn't sure that this was a great idea either, since I could feel his body against mine with my breasts against his chest. He wrapped his arms around me and drew me to him.

I didn't want to let him go. I wanted him in bed with me right now. I felt his hands on my back and his head against mine. I closed my eyes.

I imagined holding him like this with no clothes on. That was a mistake. I shuddered.

"Are you cold?" Tarek asked me.

I pulled away all at once, dropping my hands. "A little," I lied. I smiled shyly and looked down. "It's late," I said softly.

"I'll go," he said, just as softly.

"I'll see you in class Monday."

"OK," then he added, "we're on for next weekend, right?"

I looked at him curiously. Next weekend?

"I meant studying," he said a little shyly.

I smiled. "Of course."

He turned and opened the door. I went after him, standing in the doorway with him just outside.

"Tarek, I—" I started, then lost the courage to continue, partly because I had no idea what to say exactly or how to say it.

He looked at me, and I must have had a pained expression of some sort on my face because he took a step toward me and touched my arm.

"Isabel, remember what I told you."

I was confused. It was a feeling I was quickly learning to live with. "About what?"

He sighed. "You don't have to decide right now."

Decide what? I wanted to ask. How long did I have?

Instead, I smiled faintly. I don't deserve someone like you.

"Good night, Tarek," I said.

"Good night." He smiled and left. I closed the door.

I started to wilt like a flower. I was tired and the last thirty to forty-five minutes had been so emotionally charged for me.

I was thinking back over everything that had happened that night. I had shown a lot of my cards. I hadn't intended to do that. Oh, well. I still have plenty left.

But that was a lie that I was telling myself. For some reason, that lie was easier than accepting the truth.

I was thinking about how incredible Tarek had looked tonight, and how nice he was, and how great a dancer he was, and how it had seemed like with only one sign from me, he was ready to kiss me.

But this hadn't been a date, right?

Then I realized something with a bit of dread. In an uncommon moment of sheer veracity, I admitted the truth to myself. For some reason, I needed to tell someone right away. I felt something tonight that I hadn't felt in a long time. I didn't recognize the feeling at first. I had thought that it was lust. But it wasn't. I wanted Tarek, but not for the reasons that I had originally thought. The realization made me feel *alive*.

I took my phone out. Lara would be sleeping by now, but I would send her a text message anyway.

OMG you were totally right. I like him. I mean, I want to date him.

Date someone. Whatever the hell that meant.

I was totally screwed. Admitting that meant admitting that he had some hold over me. Not that he necessarily meant to do that.

I was elated but I was also freaked out of my mind.

And I couldn't believe that he had said those things. He was interested in me as something more than a friend. He had admitted as much, hadn't he?

I went to stand in front of the window behind my dining table, and stared at the metro tracks, the lamps on the platforms lighting the way into Washington, without really seeing them.

I didn't know what to do. I gazed outside my window for what seemed like an inordinate amount of time.

In the end I knew I wouldn't do anything, even if I felt more alive. That is, I wouldn't do anything differently. I was too scared.

But, as I would soon find out, it didn't matter what I planned to do, or not to do. Things were going to turn out a certain way, and I could either accept them or not.

What would be surprising to me was how quickly I would acquiesce to my fate.